TO PAMELA:

HAVE FUN

READING MY

NOVEL!

A Question of Murder

©2022, J. M. Warren

ISBN: 978-1-66784-343-8

ISBN eBook: 978-1-66784-344-5

A

QUESTION

OF

MURDER

J. M. WARREN

PROLOGUE

Late evening, Thursday, June 18, 2009

J. ROBERT SIMPSON stood in front of the waist-high, mahogany liquor cabinet in his corner office. He sipped eighteen-year-old single malt Scotch while gazing at the lights of Manhattan through a floor-to-ceiling window. The past two weeks had been miserable with one rainy day after another, but a fortunate break in the weather had occurred hours earlier, and that evening, the city seemed more alive.

Simpson examined his reflection in the window and confirmed no strand of his medium brown hair with gray streaks was out of place. He turned his head to examine the right side of his large, square jaw and noticed a shaving nick had almost healed. After placing his Scotch tumbler on top of the liquor cabinet, he adjusted his striped silk tie. He then chuckled to himself for completing an unnecessary task, as he would soon remove the tie along with other articles of clothing.

Simpson again grasped the tumbler, took another sip, and grew impatient. He lowered his glass and glanced at his Cartier watch. His date had said she needed to make a brief phone call before coming upstairs, and too much time had passed. About one minute later, Simpson heard his office door swing open and smiled. He again placed his drink on top of the liquor cabinet and turned to his left. Instead of his statuesque date, he saw a much shorter person wearing a gray wig. His smile turned into a scowl, and his short temper flared.

"What the hell? Get out of my office!"

"No," the intruder coldly replied.

Simpson was about to engage in an expletive-filled tirade when he noticed the intruder point a .38-caliber revolver at his chest. His left hand trembled, and fear overwhelmed him.

"Over there," the intruder said and waved the gun towards a black leather couch and back to his chest.

He remained frozen in place except for the trembling in his hand.

"Sit down on the couch, now!"

Simpson started to perspire and was unable to obey the order. "What do you want?"

"Just do as I say, and no one gets hurt. Sit down!"

He took three tentative steps forward and sat in the middle of the couch.

The intruder pointed the revolver toward one of two navy-blue throw pillows lying on the couch. "Pick it up."

Simpson turned his head, saw the pillow, and nodded several times due to a nervous reflex. "Okay, okay," he said in a hushed voice. He grabbed the pillow and held it with both hands in his lap.

"Hold it higher."

"Huh?"

"I *said* higher! I don't want to see your face."

Simpson raised the pillow until he saw nothing but deep blue. The tremble in his left hand and the sweating continued.

The intruder moved toward him. "By the way, when I said no one would get hurt, I lied."

CHAPTER 1

Wednesday, September 16, 2009

THE PHONE RANG, and David was asleep in his comfortable queen-size bed. Following the second ring, he opened his eyes, rolled to his right, and glanced at the alarm clock on his dresser: 6:50 in the morning. He let the call go to his answering machine and rolled back onto his stomach. After two more rings, the answering machine activated.

"This is David Lee. I'm sorry I can't answer the phone right now. Please leave a message."

After the beep, he heard, "David, are you in? It's Irene. I've been trying to reach you since yesterday afternoon. You have a hearing in court this morning!"

David groaned and again rolled over. With his right hand, he reached for the landline phone on the end table.

"Are you there? Did you hear what I just said?"

David brought himself to a sitting position while his feet dangled inches above the hardwood floor. He then picked up the phone. "What are you talking about?"

"We've got a new client, and it's a murder case. She has an initial appearance at ten."

He snapped from groggy to fully alert, and his eyes popped wide. "We have a what! Why didn't you tell me beforehand?"

"Her parents came to the office late yesterday afternoon. I tried calling you."

"Well, I had a date and turned off my cell phone. I wanted to give her my undivided attention." David ran his left hand through his hair. He guessed he had never turned his cell phone back on and had not checked his answering machine last night.

"So, you were with her all night?" Irene asked in a judgmental tone.

David clenched his jaw and wanted to reply, "None of your business and you're fired." He instead controlled his anger and responded in a more matter-of-fact tone. "No, we got together early because she had a flight before dawn out of JFK. I then worked in the office until 11:30 or so. Did you send me something to my work and home emails?"

He waited for the apology he knew he would not receive.

"Uh … No," she replied with less attitude.

"You said it's a murder case?"

"Yeah. The hearing's at ten. Can you make it? I know Marc can't, and I haven't called Bev, at least not yet."

David closed his eyes and groaned again. "Don't call Bev. I'll make the hearing."

"Okay. I'll send the intake sheet to your home email right now. The client's name is Amanda Morelli, and her parents are Paul and Lorraine. I told them to meet you at the usual place inside the courthouse at 9:30."

"Fine. What do they look like?"

"The Odd Couple."

"What? You mean Felix and Oscar from the TV show?"

"Uh-uh," Irene said. "Two different sizes. Paul's big with broad shoulders and a barrel chest. He has thick, kinda wavy, salt and pepper hair and an apple pie face."

"An apple pie what?" David asked as he shook his head.

"An apple pie face. You'll see. Lorraine's much shorter, you know, petite. She looks much younger than she is, like Dick Clark. Just a few faint wrinkles. She also has short, dark hair, which looks natural but isn't."

"Whatever. I'll get over to the courthouse after I get ready and eat breakfast."

"Fruit Loops again?"

"Goodbye, Irene." David ended the call, stood, and shuffled towards his large bedroom window. He opened the thick burgundy curtains, revealing gloomy skies casting a pall over the city. "That's just perfect!"

Most mornings, David had eaten breakfast after he got out of bed, but this time he first needed a hot shower to relax and collect himself. While showering and shaving, he grumbled about Irene and asked himself why she was the receptionist/office manager at the Law Offices of D'Angelo & Lee. Of course, he knew the answer. Irene's full name was Irene Popova D'Angelo, and everyone related to his law partner, Marc, was part of one big, happy family, even if she married into it. He acknowledged Irene performed her job well most of the time and treated the clients with respect. However, sometimes she had been a royal pain to him.

While he remained annoyed at Irene, thoughts about a murder case intrigued him. It was his first one since he and Marc opened their own law firm. The gravity of the case would present a challenge, but David knew he could manage it. He also considered the massive number of hours required to defend the case and possibly take it to trial. David and Marc's hourly rates were not excessive, but they needed to make a living. He hoped Amanda and her family had the financial resources to cover his bills. Irene should have made at least a cursory review of his new client's assets and income before signing her up. He also wondered what would happen if Amanda could no longer pay them. Perhaps a judge would declare her indigent, and the court would cover their bills, just as when he had represented poor defendants.

After David finished in the bathroom, he put on a terrycloth robe and plodded toward his laptop sitting on his small dining room table. He turned it on and shuffled to his tiny kitchen. He studied three cereal boxes on the counter and grabbed one.

"Fruit Loops? I think not, Irene. Lucky Charms today."

As he poured cereal and milk into a bowl, David did not believe Irene should criticize anyone's eating habits given the awful snacks she brought to the office. While he did not have the best diet, he was slim and healthy. He also ran and worked out at the gym whenever he had the time.

David set the bowl on the dining room table, accessed his email, and opened Irene's attachment. While he ate, he read the intake sheet, which said Amanda Morelli was thirty-five, divorced, and had no children. She lived in an apartment in Murray Hill. She was currently unemployed and had been an attorney with Thorton, Saxer & Caldwell. Amanda's parents were retired and lived in Bensonhurst. Paul had been a union representative, and Lorraine had owned a travel agency.

The victim was J. Robert Simpson, a partner at Thorton, who had been shot to death in his own office. Irene had provided news articles and press releases about Simpson. David skimmed through them and discovered the deceased had been a high-powered civil litigator. However, he had never heard of Simpson as he paid little attention to the news.

Upon reading the next item, David almost choked on his breakfast. The Morellis had paid $30,000 in cash! At least this revelation gave some indication they could afford him. He also pondered whether Paul and Lorraine had ever heard of muggers.

David opened a link about the Thorton firm, which told him it was in East Midtown, about three blocks from his law office. Thorton handled mergers and acquisitions, business litigation, and appellate law. He checked the courthouse website and discovered Judge Conrad Graber had been assigned to the case. David knew his reputation, which was both favorable and unfavorable for him and his new client. The judge was lenient on bail and unfortunately possessed an inflated ego and a tendency to be a pain in the behind.

After finishing breakfast and changing into a business suit, David left his East Village apartment and hailed a taxi. During the drive through rush hour traffic, he blocked out the surrounding noise and ignored a mild stench of body odor inside the cab. He instead read the intake sheet again and smiled. While most people, even some attorneys, found courtrooms intimidating, David believed he was a born litigator and had no fears since his first court appearance. Then again, he had stepped inside a courtroom many times before he passed the bar exam.

WHEN DAVID WALKED through the main entrance to the courthouse in lower Manhattan, he checked his watch: 9:15. He spotted Paul and Lorraine near the end of a long hallway, sitting on a bench and holding hands. Irene's description of the couple was mostly accurate, including their different sizes, but David did not believe Paul's face resembled an apple pie. He only observed an older man with a round face and a scattering of wrinkles around the eyes.

As David approached them, Paul twice tugged the collar of his white dress shirt in quick succession. In addition, his blue tie was crooked, indicating he normally wore casual clothes. Lorraine had donned a light blue sweater and had a serene appearance. Both Paul and Lorraine stood and greeted him with warm smiles.

"Good morning. I'm David Lee," he said pleasantly. "You must be Paul and Lorraine."

Paul nodded. "That's right." He gave David a firm handshake.

Lorraine then shook his outstretched hand, and he noticed the scent of lavender perfume.

"Hey, don't mean to give you the bum's rush, but Amanda's hearing will start soon," Paul said. "So, if you don't mind, let's get down to business, okay?"

"Fine, fine," David replied.

The big man retrieved a white folder laying on the bench. "Your assistant told us to bring this stuff." He opened the folder. "Here's the paperwork for our home, where we've lived over forty years. We paid off the mortgage a long time ago." Paul flipped to another document. "Here's what we have in the bank." He pointed to a line in the middle of the page. "See, right here: 163,000 and change." He turned to another page. "We co-own a ten-unit apartment building in Flatbush with a good buddy of mine and his wife."

"What about the other stuff, Honey?" Lorraine asked.

Paul smiled. "Yes, Dear. It's in here. It says the mortgage on the building was paid off. Here you go." He handed over the folder.

"Thanks," David said.

Paul looked over David's shoulder. "Hopefully, Daniel can make it."

"Daniel?"

"He's our son, and he lives in Westchester County." The big man refocused on David. "By the way and no offense, we figured your law partner would help our daughter. He's a nephew of another good buddy of mine. Your assistant said he wasn't available, but she didn't tell us why."

David believed Paul's comment was odd because they supposedly knew Marc but were unaware of his health. "Sorry, Irene should've said something. Marc contracted leukemia, and he's been off work for some time. He's improving and will be back in the office by the end of the year."

Paul nodded.

"I'm sorry to hear that," Lorraine said. "So, you're a defense attorney too?"

"Yes. Our firm handles mostly criminal defense and some civil rights cases."

"Civil rights, huh. Anything we might know about?" Paul asked.

"Possibly. Just before Marc got sick, we settled an excessive force case against the NYPD. We also sued a school district in Nassau County on behalf of the parents. Campus security for the high school did some really stupid things. We also settled that one."

Paul and Lorraine looked at each other, and their facial expressions indicated they were impressed.

Paul waggled his right index finger in the air. "Yeah, yeah, that's right. I think I heard about the school district thing on the news." He turned back to David. "Have you had many criminal cases? What about a murder case? You know, my Amanda didn't do it."

David held up his right hand momentarily. "One thing at a time. I've been an attorney for eight years, and I've had many criminal cases, including murder."

Lorraine tilted her head. "How old are you?"

"Thirty-three. I know I'm younger than some lawyers, but I know what I'm doing. If you'd like, I'll put you in touch with some of my past clients. Perhaps they'd give you some peace of mind."

Lorraine seemed oblivious to his last comment. "Are you Chinese?"

"Yes, I am."

"How tall are you? Six feet?"

"Almost, five-eleven." David wondered what was happening inside Lorraine's head.

With a wide-eyed expression, she turned toward her husband. "Oh, Honey, that's why he reminds me of that neighbor who lived down the street. What was his name?"

Paul patted his spouse on the shoulder and grinned. "You're thinking of Tony Wilkins, and he wasn't Chinese."

"I still see the resemblance, just look at his –"

"Look, we need to focus on your daughter's case," David said politely. "This morning, Amanda will enter a plea of not guilty, and we'll get to bail. I'll see if CJA finished their write-up and we'll –"

"What's CJA?" Paul asked.

"It's the Criminal Justice Agency. They interview defendants before arraignment and make recommendations whether they should be released on bail. Now as I was saying –"

David stopped talking as he noticed Paul's attention being diverted elsewhere. Both parents' lack of focus amazed him.

"Hang on for a second, Counselor," Paul said. "Our good friends Pete and Debra are here."

David glanced over his shoulder and saw another Italian couple in their sixties approaching. He paid little attention while Paul, Lorraine, and their friends chatted about an inconsequential dinner party. While most parents would have been anxious before an initial hearing, Paul and Lorraine behaved as if it were a sunny day with no worries.

After chatting with the newcomers for about a minute, Paul asked, "You were about to say something about bail? How much will it be?"

David raised an eyebrow. "That might be a tough one. Let's go inside the courtroom, and I'll see what I can do."

David waited while the two couples discussed another trivial matter. He shook his head in disbelief and entered the courtroom alone, where the usual gaggle of attorneys, clients, and family members milled around among the rows of benches in the gallery.

David spotted Jacqueline Marshall, one of the District Attorney's most experienced prosecutors. Her reputation proceeded her, which could be summed up in one word: formidable. Jacqueline appeared deep in thought as she leaned over her podium and reviewed paperwork. David noticed she had changed her hairstyle from a short afro to a slicked-back look.

"Hey, Jacqueline. So, we finally crossing swords again. It's been a while."

She remained stone-faced and did not take her eyes off her paperwork. "That's right. The CJA report is over there." She pointed her thumb toward the small table at the far end of the courtroom.

David ignored Jacqueline's attitude, strolled to the table, and took a copy. He skimmed through it and found no surprises. The report listed the usual biographical information for a criminal defendant and revealed Amanda had no prior arrests or convictions. It also contained a list of available financial resources and sources of collateral for bail, including her brother's house.

David glanced toward the back of the courtroom, where Paul, Lorraine, and their friends were taking their seats along with another couple in their late thirties. He had brown hair, and she was a blonde.

Paul mouthed, "That's Daniel, Amanda's brother, and" something else David could not make out, probably the name of Daniel's wife.

David ambled toward Jacqueline. "Can we talk about bail?"

She stepped away from the podium, faced David, and stared upward into his eyes. Without a hint of levity, she said, "Bail? You're kidding, right? We indicted your client for murder."

David forced a smile. "I know, but she has no priors and many ties to the community. How strong is the evidence against her? Do you have a confession?"

Jacqueline did not verbally respond or gesture in any way.

Thus, he assumed Amanda had not confessed. "What about the murder weapon? Do you have it? How about any eyewitnesses?"

Jacqueline put her right hand on her hip and continued to stare at him. "We've got plenty of evidence, such as your client sending a fascinating email to her little friend in the office. It said, 'Let's kill him.' Three days later,

Simpson was shot twice in the head. I highly doubt it was just an interesting coincidence."

David was startled and tried not to show it. "Well, let's talk about discovery. I'll send a demand letter to you by Friday."

She gave a dismissive wave. "Don't bother. I'll send it by Tuesday next week, Wednesday at the latest. I hope you have plenty of storage space."

"Sure. Now getting back to bail. You know we have Judge Graber today. He's about to retire and in a giving mood." He tilted his head and bent at the waist. "If I make a reasonable bail request and you stand firm, what happens? Another thing, is my client young and attractive? How will that factor in?"

Jacqueline exhaled through her nose, and David guessed she was swearing in her thoughts.

"Do you have anything else besides what's in the CJA report?" she asked.

David gave her the folder Paul had provided. He heard Jacqueline flip through the pages while he scanned the courtroom.

Without taking her eyes off the documents, she said, "They're not here. You're looking for reporters, right?"

The answer was yes, but he did not reply.

Once Jacqueline finished reading, she returned Paul's folder and glared at David. "What'd you have in mind?"

"Well, half a million sounds like a decent number, because my client doesn't have significant financial resources."

Jacqueline scoffed. "I know, and I can guess why. I was at her apartment when the search warrant was executed. She really knows how to spend money on clothes and shoes. You should like that." She pointed to his jacket. "You're wearing Brooks Brothers, right? As for half a million … no. Her family can assist and pay a bail bondsman. One million cash or bond, no less."

"Give me a moment, please."

David spun around and walked confidently towards Paul. Once he reached the rail between the attorney's tables and the gallery, he leaned forward and whispered, "One million, all cash or bond. Think you can handle it?"

Paul pouted his lower lip and gave a thumbs-up sign.

David gave a brief wave of his right hand in acknowledgement and then looked over his left shoulder. He did not have to relay the message to Jacqueline as she was watching from a distance.

CLOSE TO TEN o'clock, David took a seat in the gallery's front row. He hoped Judge Graber would not arrive late, but his reputation indicated he was never on time. By 10:15, David tired of waiting and reflected on many stories he had heard about Judge Graber, such as his constant talking about himself and his alleged connections to celebrities. David believed no one had time for that, especially in court. He imagined the judge was on the phone, bragging about himself without paying attention to the time.

Finally, David heard, "All rise!" as Judge Graber entered the court-room. His black robe somehow covered his enormous girth. He had a short and well-groomed beard, and his balding, gray hair touched his collar. David glanced again at his watch, which told him it was 10:40. He wanted to blurt out, "Thanks for showing up," but knew better.

Judge Graber sat down and in a booming voice said, "Good morning, everyone. Please call the first case."

The court clerk bellowed, "Calling case number 09-36472, People versus Amanda Morelli."

David moved forward and took his proper place. From his left, he saw Amanda shuffle into the courtroom with hunched shoulders and a hung head. David guessed she was a petite five-four, about an inch taller than her mother, and her thick auburn hair flowed about three inches past her shoulders. Once Amanda lifted her head, David noted her high cheekbones and large brown eyes, which were bloodshot and surrounded by dark circles. He imagined she had almost no sleep during her night in jail. Even in her less-than-ideal condition, Amanda appeared twenty-five, not thirty-five, which meant the Dick Clark genes had to run in the family. David also noticed the judge taking a long, leering look at Amanda, and he thought, one way or another, this pervert would grant bail.

"Jacqueline Marshall for the People, Your Honor."

"David Lee for the defendant. One moment, please?"

"Of course," Judge Graber said as he waved his right hand.

David leaned toward Amanda and whispered, "Your parents just hired me. It'll be all right. You'll get released from custody in no time."

She showed a wan expression and remained silent.

David turned his attention to the judge. "Thank you, Your Honor."

"Ms. Morelli," Judge Graber boomed. "The People have charged you with one count of murder in the first degree. How do you plead?"

"Not guilty," she said in a low and cracking voice.

His Honor's eyes narrowed, and he leaned forward. "I'm sorry. I didn't hear you."

"Not guilty, Your Honor," she said louder.

"Parties on bail?" Judge Graber asked as he leaned back in his chair and shifted his eyes toward Jacqueline.

She stood with an air of confidence and replied, "Your Honor, the parties have agreed to one million dollars, cash or bond."

"Standard terms and conditions?"

"Yes, Your Honor."

"Excellent!" Judge Graber flashed a smile. "So ordered, and the Court thanks both of you. Let's call the next case."

David leaned over and whispered to his client, "We'll talk really soon, okay?"

Amanda stared at him for a moment, and then a court officer whisked her away.

David peered into the gallery and saw Paul giving another thumbs-up. David left the courtroom, and all six members of Amanda's party followed him like lemmings. Paul provided a brief introduction to his son and daughter-in-law, but David did not catch her name, perhaps Trudy. Daniel, Trudy, Pete, and Debra said a few words to Paul and Lorraine and then proceeded to the courthouse's entrance.

David then addressed Amanda's parents. "So, here's what you need to do to get your daughter released –"

"Don't worry about it," Paul said as he held up his hand with the palm facing out. "We brought a bail bondsman and can take care of it." He scanned the hallway. "Now, where is he?" His expression changed to a knowing recognition. "He's right over there, talking to that guy who looks like another attorney. The bail bondsman's a friend of a good buddy of mine."

David had difficulty understanding Paul and Lorraine's behavior. They had brought plenty of paperwork and a bail bondsman to court but had not hired a defense attorney until after the police took their daughter into custody. They should have known she had been under investigation.

"I guess you'll take care of it," David said. "On another note, I'd like to talk to someone at Amanda's old firm. Any ideas?"

Paul looked in the air. "Try Valerie, Valerie Fernandez." His eyes refocused on David. "She was Amanda's paralegal, and they're friends. I think she's still working at Amanda's old firm. Nice girl. Right, Honey?"

Lorraine smiled. "Oh yes. She and her kids came over for dinner a couple of times. We also saw her at the office Christmas party two years ago. It's too bad they didn't have one last year. Right, Paul?"

"Okay," David said as he interrupted. He did not need them spinning off onto another tangent. "Could you tell Amanda to come to my office on Friday at 11:30? Beverly should have returned from court by then, and I'd like Amanda to meet her."

"Whose Beverly?" Paul asked.

"Beverly Cohen. She's of counsel to the firm."

Paul and Lorraine gave puzzled looks.

David released a faint smile and said, "Beverly was a partner with my old law firm, and she retired a couple of years ago. She heard about Marc contracting leukemia and offered to help out for a while. She's an excellent criminal defense attorney."

"Okay," Paul said. "We'd love to meet her, and thanks for getting my daughter released on bail. We'll be seeing you." He shook David's hand.

Lorraine did the same and said, "It was nice to meet you. I hope you can come to the house for dinner sometime."

"That'd be nice," David replied.

Paul and Lorraine walked down the corridor, hand in hand, and engaged in idle banter.

David again noted their carefree mood sharply contrasted with their daughter's indictment for first-degree murder, which carried a sentence of twenty-five years to life imprisonment. He went outside, found a spot on the courthouse steps where he believed no one could overhear him, and made a call on his cell phone.

"Irene, it's me."

"Oh, the hearing's already over?"

David rolled his eyes because the hearing should have concluded much earlier. "Yeah, that's right. We're done, and Amanda got bail. Please send a copy of the intake sheet to Marc."

"Right now?"

"Yes, now. Thanks."

"Okay."

"Bye." David ended the call and said aloud to no one, "Gee, Irene. When would it be a good time to send the information, maybe sometime next year?" He then made another call and heard a groggy, "Hello."

"Hey Marc, can you talk for a few minutes?"

There was a brief pause. "Yeah … sure. Why don't you come on over and give me a great, big hug?"

David chuckled. "That's what your wife is for."

"I know but Steph's not home right now, and you're *the* best hugger."

"You wish. Look, I need to discuss a couple of matters, and the first one's Irene."

Marc let out a heavy sigh. "What'd she do now?"

"She got mad at me because she couldn't reach me while I was on a date."

"That undivided attention thing, right? By the way, who was the date?"

"Eileen."

"Oh yeah," Marc said, as if he had made an important scientific discovery. "She's a flight attendant with Air Canada."

"Yeah, that's her. Anyway, I need you to talk to Irene about her attitude *again*. Also, she signed up a client without speaking to me. Bev wouldn't sign anyone up, and she didn't speak to you about it, right?"

"Ah, crap. She did that? Who's the new client, another bozo arrested for DUI who'll refuse to pay his bills?"

David gave a wry smile. "Not exactly. Amanda's been indicted for murder, and she's accused of shooting another attorney in her own law firm."

"What? Wow! When's her first appearance?"

"Already happened this morning, and she was ordered released on bail."

Marc chuckled. "She got bail after being slapped with an 'A' felony? You're good but not that good. You had help."

"Well, yeah," David sheepishly said. "Judge Graber. Anyway, Irene's sending you the intake sheet on Amanda. On another note, there's something odd about her parents." He flicked his left arm in the air. "Well, a couple of odd things. Paul, that's her father, asked for you and said you're the nephew of one of his friends, but he didn't know you had leukemia. I think he handed me a line of bull. Can you check to see if anyone in your family knows him?"

"Sure. No problem."

"Thanks. Talk to you later."

CHAPTER 2

Later the same day

ARLY AFTERNOON, DAVID arrived at the drab, off-white building containing the Law Offices of Thorton, Saxer & Caldwell with his black leather briefcase in hand. He observed no interesting architectural features: only a large box with windows. A plaque to the right of the entrance stated, "The O'Connell Building."

As David entered the lobby, he noticed a tile floor, a marble counter-top for the security desk, and harsh overhead lighting straining his eyes. The directory on a wall told him to proceed to the tenth floor. Before leaving the lobby, he decided to check for any security measures on the ground and tenth floors, which were obviously inadequate during the evening of the murder.

Two turnstiles stood in front of four elevators. Two bored security guards stood behind them and watched individuals swipe key cards as they passed through the turnstiles. Since David did not have a card, he reported to a third guard at the front desk, where he showed his identification, signed his name in the register, and listed his intended location. Without a word, the third guard waved him away. David noticed two black half-globes with security cameras affixed to the ceiling, one on each side of the lobby.

After passing through a turnstile, David entered the first elevator on the right and detected a musty smell rising from below. He then noticed a stain on the floor. Perhaps it caused the smell, but he had no desire to get down on his hands and knees to conduct a closer examination. He also saw a camera in a back corner, just below the ceiling. The elevator had two columns of buttons for floors numbered B2 to 14. David pushed "10" and noticed a slot above the buttons. He had seen a similar slot in the elevators for the building containing his law office, where an individual needed to insert a key card in the slot to operate the elevators at night and on the weekends.

When David arrived at the tenth floor, the Thorton firm's entrance was across the hallway. Before going any further, he stopped himself. He suspected the killer did not use the main elevators to avoid the security guards, and there should be another way to access the floor.

David turned right and traversed a long hallway, which had the same awful overhead lighting but no security cameras. At the north end, he made another right turn and walked to the end of a shorter hallway. He opened a heavy metal door, which revealed access to a freight elevator. He realized the heavier door could not be opened from the other side without a key card. Thus, he placed his briefcase on the floor and wedged it against the door to prevent it from fully closing. He summoned the elevator, and seconds later, its doors opened.

Upon entering the freight elevator, David pushed a button for another floor, and nothing happened. He pushed two other buttons with the same result. He then spotted another key card slot above the buttons and concluded the freight elevator would not work without a card no matter the time of day. Once he glanced higher, he spotted another security camera in a back corner next to the ceiling.

David left the freight elevator and saw a door to a stairwell next to it, which probably led to an emergency exit on the ground floor. He retraced his steps and found doors leading to two interior staircases, one on each side of the elevator banks. From the hallway, anyone could open these doors, but the other side had no handles or knobs.

David approached a middle-aged receptionist for the Thorton law firm, who sat behind a sizeable dark-colored desk of unknown origin. Her lethargic movements and sad eyes surprised him as he expected a receptionist to project a more inviting and enthusiastic personality. A seven-foot, clear plexiglass wall stood behind her with the law firm's name etched near the top.

"May I help you?" she said with a flat affect.

"Yes, please. I'm David Lee, and I'm here to see Valerie Fernandez."

The receptionist's eyes drifted toward her phone. She grabbed it and put her right hand over her mouth, which prohibited David from understanding her brief message. Shortly thereafter, a woman in her early forties glided towards him with long, wavy coal-black hair flowing behind her.

"I'm Valerie," she said with a serious expression. "You're David?"

"Yes. Nice to meet you." Given her lack of warmth, David did not bother to extend his hand.

"Uh-huh. Let's talk inside."

Valerie escorted David to a large conference room boasting floor-to-ceiling glass walls and a glass door. He counted sixteen chairs around an oblong table and noted the lack of curtains or blinds to permit more private meetings. On the way, he saw almost the entire floor had an open concept filled with bright but soft lighting. The cubicles for the support staff filled much of the middle space. The attorneys' offices surrounded the cubicles and the conference room and also had glass walls and doors.

David saw one obvious exception to the floor's layout. An office in the northwest corner had solid walls and no apparent door. He speculated he could not observe the door from his vantage point and wondered about that office. It was in a prime location, which meant it probably belonged to one of the firm's partners, and perhaps someone placed a premium on privacy. He also noticed several empty cubicles and offices, and the firm's atmosphere seemed depressing. No one was in a good mood.

Once the conference room door closed, David sat down and retrieved a notepad and a pen from his briefcase.

Valerie took a seat next to him, leaned back, and crossed her arms.

David said, "As I explained on the phone, I'm a defense attorney, and I'm sorry to tell you Amanda's been indicted for murder. She made her first appearance in court this morning, and she's being released on bail."

Valerie made a frown, and her eyes dropped toward the beige carpet. "Oh, that's too bad."

"You don't seem shocked by the news."

She looked at him with resignation written all over her face. "No, not really. I knew the cops searched her place. An arrest wasn't a surprise, but I know she didn't kill anyone."

David's curiosity peaked, and he inched forward in his chair. "Why do you say that?"

"Earlier that day, Amanda went home sick, and she was asleep all night."

"Okay, how do you know that?" he asked as he scribbled on the notepad.

"She told me. Besides, I think I know her pretty good. She's not a violent person."

"Alright. If you don't mind, I'd like to ask you a few questions about yourself and the law firm."

With her arms still crossed, Valerie said, "Go ahead."

"So, how long have you worked here?"

"About twelve years. Since I started, I've been a paralegal, and this was a great place to work until recently."

"How so?"

Valerie paused and twisted her mouth. "As opposed to some other places, the senior partners cared about their employees. I found out the hard way. I'd only been with the firm about seven months when my husband Henry passed away one night. We were told he had an aortic aneurysm, and it ruptured."

David felt a punch to the stomach. "I'm really sorry."

Valerie briefly smiled. "Thanks. The people here provided me with lots of emotional support, and the Old Man insisted the firm would pay all the funeral costs. I never expected that."

"The Old Man?"

"Old Man Thorton," Valerie said as she relaxed her arms. "I mean Charles W. Thorton. He started this firm, and everyone loved him. Still do, I guess. He always asked how we were doing, and he was interested in our families. He couldn't have been a greater boss or a greater person. The Old Man had a big personality and a great laugh. When my kids were younger, they called him Uncle Charles."

David nodded and scribbled a few notes. "What about the others at the firm? How was the workload?"

"The other senior partners knew we had our own lives, and they tried not to overwork us most of the time. My job was kind of boring, but we all got along. The pay was good but not great."

"Uh-huh. What about Amanda?"

"I enjoyed working with her. After we met, we quickly became friends, and we went to lunch together, sometimes once a week, sometimes a little more."

David suspected Valerie was the "little friend" who received the "Let's kill him" email but did not mention it. He instead stated, "No one around here seems to be in a good mood. Why'd things change?"

Valerie scoffed and crossed her arms again. "Because Big Bastard arrived."

"Who?"

"Robert Simpson, the guy who was shot. He sometimes called himself Big Bobby, and he referred to a body part by that name. Guess which one?" Valerie's frown returned. "Some of us called him Big Bastard because it was more fitting. He was an a-hole and made lots of sexual comments and innuendos. Sometimes comments were followed by touching, but he never touched me, which was fortunate … for him. You know what I mean?"

Valerie's colorful language and candid responses surprised David. In addition, Simpson's behavior appalled him, and he tried not to show it.

"Simpson was that bad, huh?"

"Oh yeah," Valerie said angrily. "He was a total pig and didn't care who he offended. I know I'm not supposed to speak ill of the dead, but hey, there's nothing good to say about him."

David grimaced and scribbled again. "Did he treat all the women the same way?"

"Of course! He treated Walter really badly too."

"Walter?"

"Walter, Walter Bennett. He was a paralegal who worked on the ninth floor. Nice guy, really quiet. He tried very hard to keep his private life, you know, private. Somehow, Big Bastard found out Walter was gay, and after that," Valerie briefly raised her arms, "whenever he saw Walter, the taunting was out of control. Most of the time, Walter avoided him by staying downstairs. The rest of us weren't so lucky."

David stopped scribbling and focused on Valerie. "Where was Simpson killed?"

"Back there." She pointed over her left shoulder toward the back corner with the solid walls.

"Did Simpson want an office where he could work in private?"

Valerie's head lurched back, and her eyes got wide. "You're kidding, right? It was the exact opposite. His office looked like all the others. That a-hole loved it because he always wanted to be seen. How'd he put it? Something like we'd see him work his magic." She shook her head.

"Why does it look different now?" David asked.

"After Big Bastard was killed, some crew arrived. They cleaned up the blood, replaced the couch, stuff like that. Still, no one wanted to look over there. The firm hired another crew, and they put up the walls, which helped some, I guess."

"Valerie, can you let me see the inside of that office?"

"Not possible. Now it's solid walls and no door. Come back with a sledgehammer."

David tried to process what he had just heard. He did not understand why a law firm that cared about its people welcomed aboard such an obnoxious jerk and why the office was so depressing. If everyone had hated Simpson, they could not be mourning him months after his death. David surmised Valerie had answers, but he also wanted to speak with a partner to obtain another perspective. He was about to ask another question when a slim, white male with an oval-shaped face and deep frown lines opened the conference room door.

"Who the hell are you and what are you doing here?"

"I'm David Lee, Amanda Morelli's defense attorney, and you are?" David stood and offered his hand.

The other man did not reciprocate. "Richard Caldwell," he said. Turning to Valerie, he barked, "Get back to work and speak to this guy on your own time." He then stormed away.

Setting aside his poor first impression, David went after Caldwell and had to speed walk to catch him. "Can I speak with you for a few moments?"

Caldwell stopped and spun around. "You can't be serious," he said with a sneer. "I have more important matters on my plate, such as trying to save what's left of this damn firm."

"But I just need a –"

"I spoke with the police enough times, and you can read about it in their reports. I'm sure you'll get copies of them soon enough."

Caldwell's attitude did not discourage David, and he pressed on. "If you don't have the time, can I speak with another partner?"

"I suppose that'll be the only way to get rid of you. Try Saxer. You can waste his time. After you speak with him, let me know what the hell that idiot is doing! He's practically abandoned the firm, and I *really* need to rip him a new one. Follow me."

David trailed Caldwell at a brisk pace towards the southwest corner of the floor until they reached the cubicle of a female paralegal, who appeared as worn out and depressed as everyone else.

"Remember Morelli? This is her defense attorney," Caldwell barked. "Give him Saxer's phone numbers." He then abruptly left before receiving any acknowledgement of his order.

Without saying a word, the paralegal typed on her keyboard, examined her computer screen, and wrote three phone numbers on a sheet of paper. She tore the sheet from the notepad and handed it to David.

"Thanks," he said. "Could I speak with you for a few minutes?"

The paralegal sighed. "No, I don't have any time to spare."

"Well, I only need a list of those employed by the firm. I'm not asking for anything else, such as home addresses, phone numbers, and email addresses, just the names."

The paralegal frowned and did not otherwise react.

"Please. That's all I need."

"For what month and year?"

David paused in thought for a moment. "How about January 1, 2009?"

The paralegal typed again, printed a list, and gave it to him.

"Thanks again."

With a frown still on her face, the paralegal rose from her chair and motioned for David to proceed toward the receptionist.

"Hold on a minute," he said as he raised his right index finger. "I left my briefcase in the conference room." While he strode toward it, he scanned the floor, searching for Valerie. He wanted to say goodbye to her but failed to spot her. David packed up his briefcase and then glanced toward the reception area. The same paralegal stood next to it with her arms folded. Her attitude bothered him, but nonetheless, he made a quick exit from the floor.

Once he arrived in the lobby, David approached the nearest security guard, who stood next to a turnstile.

"Excuse me," David said.

"Yes?" the guard replied while focusing ahead.

"Do you know there's a musty smell in one of the elevators?"

"We're aware. Someone will take care of it."

"Could I ask you some questions about building security?"

"No."

David felt discouraged but did not need to badger the guard. He hoped Frederick Ferguson, his favorite private detective, would be available. Freddie could investigate the building's security and take care of other matters.

CHAPTER 3

Thursday, September 17

D AVID SAT AT his office desk, glanced at his watch, and realized William Saxer was late for their two o'clock meeting. He gazed to the left and spotted Irene, a stocky, middle-aged woman with shoulder-length gray hair. She wore her awful pale pink sweater with a small stain at the waist. At least three times, David had asked her to take it to the dry cleaners to get the stain removed. She had apparently ignored him and did not care enough about her personal appearance. He found her attitude disappointing, as to a large extent, she was the law firm's public face.

David decided to pass the time by talking to someone else. He declined to call Marc again and possibly interrupt well-needed rest. So, he instead went to Beverly Cohen's office. While David, Marc, and Irene affectionately called her "Bev" amongst themselves, they never used the nickname in front of her because she was too serious and formal.

Bev was reading legal documents through her stylish glasses and was dressed professionally, as always. David and Marc had established proper attire for the firm included business casual, which Bev ignored. David was uncertain as to her age and believed it would be impolite to inquire. There were a few clues, including her marriage to Stanley for nearly forty years, her short white hair, and some wrinkles, the most prominent hidden underneath bangs. David could not find any faults with her, except that her smile almost never revealed itself.

"Hi, Beverly," he said. "Got a couple of minutes? Saxer said he'd be here at two, and he's late."

Bev looked at David without revealing her current mood. "You have many good traits, but patience isn't one of them."

"Only good traits, not great?" he asked while flashing a devious grin.

"Cute," she replied with a slight frown. "I heard about your new client, Amanda Morelli. Who's the ADA?"

"Jacqueline Marshall."

"Interesting." Bev removed her glasses and stared into the distance. "I know her but never litigated against her. She's a heavy hitter, which means the DA's office isn't fooling around." She returned her focus to David. "Did you know our old firm tried to hire her?"

"No kidding?"

"We brought her into the office and gave her the nickel tour. We offered her a partnership and a generous signing bonus, but she declined."

David pretended to be hurt. "No one offered me a partnership."

Bev frowned again. "You weren't with the firm long enough to be considered." She returned her glasses to their proper place.

"Yeah, I know. Did you hear about Amanda's parents showing up with thirty grand in cash?"

"Yes. Irene told me about it. Any thoughts?"

David shook his head. "Besides believing they're naive about muggers and crime, not really. I haven't asked where it came from. They have money in the bank, but perhaps they don't fully trust them. If so, I can't blame them after the mortgage meltdown and the stock market coming close to a complete panic not too long ago. Maybe they stashed some of their life savings in their mattress."

"Could be, but remember, don't jump to conclusions."

David held up his hands with the palms out. "I know, I know. Gather the facts first. You've told me that quite a few times." He glanced again at his watch and wondered where in the world Saxer was.

"Anything else?"

"Yeah. Jacqueline mentioned Amanda sent out an email to her so-called little friend in the office with the message, 'Let's kill him.'"

"That's certainly not good," Bev said stoically.

"Yeah, I know. She didn't say if Amanda sent the email from work or from home. I can't imagine any law firm allowing the police to rummage through their emails and violate attorney-client privilege. No way Marc and I'd allow it."

"Agreed. Our old firm would've vigorously litigated any attempt to seize emails. Most likely, Morelli sent it from her home computer." Bev pursed her lips. "However, there's another possibility. If she emailed from a work computer, the police might've arranged for an attorney to review them and not reveal sensitive communications. Then again, we shouldn't speculate. It'll become clear once you review the discovery."

"Sure," David said even though he was unconvinced.

He knew Jacqueline Marshall was a straight shooter but had doubts about the NYPD. During his civil rights case against the police, their attorneys had failed to turn over copies of two personnel files, which had forced David to file a motion to compel with the court. The attorneys claimed someone had misfiled the documents, and it had taken time to track them down.

Such a mistake could have happened, but David suspected they tried to hide what turned out to be damaging information.

"This murder case will chew up a lot of my time," David said. "Could you take care of some extra matters for me?"

Bev leaned back in her chair. "That's why I'm here. What'd you have in mind? Another rich kid with a drug problem?"

David gave a wry smile. "Yeah. Another rich kid, but it's not exactly routine. Remember the college kid who came to the office with her parents last Friday afternoon?"

"Vaguely."

"Well, it doesn't matter. Susan has a nasty little cocaine habit. A few weeks ago, she and two sorority sisters went to visit the Statue of Liberty after it reopened last Fourth of July."

"Yes, I remember. Go on."

David could not contain his enthusiasm. "Alright. Before climbing the stairs to the crown, Susan wanted to snort a line of coke in the bathroom, and her friends tried to talk her out of it. They made too much noise and attracted an older woman's attention. First, she saw the argument and then the cocaine. The woman got a park ranger, who arrested Susan for possession." David laughed for a moment.

Bev remained stone-faced.

"Susan gave the park ranger a lot of attitude and refused to go with him. Apparently, she didn't realize park rangers are law enforcement officers, and she almost got charged with resisting arrest. The National Park Service wanted to make an example of her, and since the Statue of Liberty is a national monument, that means federal jurisdiction. I guess the U.S. Attorney's Office agreed to prosecute for the press release and some deterrent effect. They even charged Susan with a felony."

Bev raised her left eyebrow. "A felony for first time possession? That's not consistent with federal law. What am I missing?"

"It's her third arrest. The first time she was a juvie, and the second occurred three weeks after she turned eighteen. Susan's parents want to get her into rehab, but I got the impression she has other plans, such as continuing to be a spoiled brat and a recreational drug user. Maybe she'll listen to you, and you can help her get her life on the right track."

"I'll see what I can do. Anything else you have for me?"

"Maybe, I was thinking about –"

David heard an unfamiliar male voice. He turned around and saw a slender man in his late fifties, about his height, with light brown wavy hair. He was talking to Irene, and his drab brown suit matched his boring yellow tie. David glanced back at Bev and said, "Sorry. I'll get back to you." He strolled to the stranger at the front desk.

"William Saxer, but you can call me Bill," he said as he put out his hand.

David shook it.

"Sorry I'm late."

He kept his thoughts about tardiness to himself. "That's okay. Would you like some coffee?"

"No thanks. Never drink the stuff."

"Okay. Let's talk in my office."

Once they sat down, David grabbed a fresh notepad from a desk drawer. "Mind if we start with some background information about your law firm?"

"Sure," Saxer said with a weak smile. "Let see … Charles Thorton founded the firm in 1974, and Caldwell and I joined several years later. For many years, our firm was prosperous and stable. The Old Man was proud that we never laid off anyone, at least no one before 2009." Saxer's cheerful outlook momentarily disappeared. "Anyway, our firm's organization was a little different from other law firms. Just before Simpson came on board, there were thirty-one attorneys in total, five senior partners, nine junior partners, and seventeen associate attorneys. Only the senior attorneys voted on strategic decisions. The junior partners were well paid and usually remained with the firm for years. Many associate attorneys departed after they did not make partner, which was fairly typical."

"Yes, of course," David said while taking notes. "Please continue."

Saxer nodded. "Right. We had the usual number of paralegals and support staff. The other senior partners and I tried to create a positive work environment, and the turnover rate for the staff was significantly lower than other firms." He smacked his lips. "My mouth's a little dry. Do you have any water?"

"Sure. Not a problem." David reached into another desk drawer and retrieved a bottle of water. "I hope you don't mind it's not cold."

Saxer smiled. "No, that's fine."

David held out the bottle.

Saxer tried to grasp it, and it slipped from his hand.

"Sorry. I'm a bit of a klutz," he said.

After picking up the bottle and taking a large sip of water, Saxer continued with his story.

"Once the economy went south, the firm's financial situation dramatically changed for the worse. Our biggest client went bankrupt almost overnight and left a mountain of unpaid legal bills. Unfortunately, new clients weren't coming through the door. Due to the economic downturn, many of our clients wanted quick settlements to limit their legal fees and the damage to their bottom lines."

"What happened next?" David asked without lifting his head as he continued taking notes.

Saxer sighed. "Nothing good. The firm rapidly ran through most of its cash reserves, and we faced the prospect of laying off a sizeable portion of our attorneys and staff. The Old Man injected a considerable sum of his personal fortune to right the financial ship, but it provided only a short-term fix. Meanwhile, everyone tried to work with a business-as-usual attitude, but we were fooling ourselves."

"So, that's when Simpson came on board?" David asked.

Saxer nodded. "Right. We needed a miracle and thought we'd found it in J. Robert Simpson. To convince him to join us, we offered to make him our newest senior partner. We knew he had a falling out with his prior firm but didn't investigate what happened and didn't care."

Saxer paused, which caused David to look up from his notes.

"That wasn't very smart, was it?" Saxer asked. "We only knew Simpson had a reputation as a ferocious litigator and brought with him a client with deep pockets. He had a long-term relationship with Bennington, a pharmaceutical company fighting off a massive class action suit. Joining the firm made sense for him. He needed litigation support, both lawyers and paralegals, to properly mount a defense, and payments from Bennington made a significant difference. We became a little bit more stable, though things were still precarious. I thought the firm's financial situation would improve once the economy did." Saxer took another sip of water.

"How'd you describe Simpson's personality?"

Saxer's mood darkened. "His presence was incredibly toxic, and he had a massive ego," he said as he held out his arms. "He berated everyone around him. It didn't take too long to notice he treated the women horribly and constantly bragged about his sexual conquests. He sometimes called himself Big Bobby, but among themselves, others called him Big Bastard. While I wanted everyone to maintain a level of professionalism, I ignored the negative comments about him."

David thought so far, his story made sense. "It was really that awful?"

Saxer scoffed. "Absolutely. About two weeks before the murder, Simpson, a few others, and I were having a meeting about the Bennington case in the tenth-floor conference room. Big Bobby noticed a tall blonde messenger talking to our receptionist and skipped out to meet her. He spent so much time with this woman that the rest of us gave up waiting and returned to our offices." He scoffed again. "Can you believe it? Needless to say, it was really frustrating and exasperating." Saxer took a swig of water.

"Did you or anyone else talk to Simpson about his behavior?"

"Of course. The senior partners tried to convince him to stop it, and he could've cared less. He knew what we knew. Without him and his deep pocket client, the firm wouldn't survive. Old Man Thorton wanted to part ways with Simpson anyway, but the other senior partners and I prevailed. I really didn't want to oppose the Old Man, but I thought I had no choice. I stupidly believed we could tolerate Simpson until the economy got back on track, and I also knew we risked a lawsuit from the women at the firm."

Saxer paused and hung his head, looking sadder than a hound dog who had received a scolding after destroying his owner's flowerbed.

"We really screwed up, didn't we?"

David agreed and did not want to make him feel any worse. He instead asked, "What happened after Simpson's murder?"

Saxer sighed and lifted his head. "Even though I couldn't stand him, I was in shock. The police asked if he had any enemies, and I told them, 'Take your pick.' After being exposed to him for a few months, I thought anyone who had ever encountered Big Bobby hated him."

David stopped taking notes. "Yesterday, I saw empty cubicles and offices, and I met Caldwell. He was in a rotten mood."

Saxer swallowed and appeared as if he needed a moment to compose himself. "Yeah … Richard wasn't always like that. I can't blame him … The firm's dying." He became teary-eyed and took another sip of water.

"What happened?"

"After Simpson's murder, the firm tried to hang onto Bennington. Upper management liked us on a personal level but believed we didn't have the necessary experience to handle the class action suit. As a result, the firm lost its biggest client in mid-July. The Old Man wanted to inject some more capital into the firm. He put two of his three houses on the market, but they never sold, and no new clients came through the door. Thanks to the murder, the firm was famous for the wrong reason."

Saxer shook his head, and his lower lip trembled.

"Immediately after the losing Bennington, we told the staff about the firm's financial situation. It was a difficult meeting, and … many tears were shed." His lower lip quivered again.

David said nothing and thought it was best to wait until Saxer was ready to continue.

"The senior partners offered to write letters of recommendation, and anyone could look for another job during normal working hours. About a third of the attorneys and staff found other jobs or have been let go. The latter received the equivalent of four weeks' salary, and I don't know where the Old Man found the funds for the severance checks. The firm will need to release another third very soon. Caldwell has been talking to a couple of law firms about absorbing the last third."

Saxer hung his head for about thirty seconds and then raised it long enough to gulp the remaining water in his bottle.

"I'm really sorry about what happened," David said. "I'm not trying to give you a tough time, but I need to ask you about something else. Caldwell said you had abandoned the firm."

With his head still hung, Saxer rubbed the light gray carpet with his right foot. "That's not true. I tried to think of solutions to our financial problems, and I didn't come up with any decent ideas. No one else did either. I was constantly talking to Bennington's executives. They didn't leave us due to a lack of effort on my part."

"Are you leaving the firm?"

Saxer looked at David and gave a weak smile. "As a matter of fact, yes. For the past few years, I've been an adjunct law professor at CUNY in Long Island City. I really enjoy teaching, and one professor is retiring. I'll be taking her place and teaching full time starting spring semester. I would've left even if the firm was financially sound. I liked being a lawyer, but I was getting burned out. It's time for a new chapter in my life."

"What about the other senior partners? What's going on with them?"

Saxer sighed again. "The Old Man was devastated. He was already semi-retired, and lately, he hardly ever comes to the office. Tim Zhang is also getting up in years and quit." Saxer snapped his fingers. "Just like that, without any notice. Michaelson's still there, and I think he'll follow Caldwell to another firm."

"So that's why Caldwell feels he's left holding the bag?"

"I guess so."

"What about Amanda Morelli? Was she a capable attorney?"

"Amanda …" Saxer stared into space. "I suppose I need to be honest about her. She was competent but never seemed happy with her career. Before the economic downturn, she applied to be a junior partner, and the vote was five to zero against. We didn't believe as a partner Amanda would actively solicit or attract new clients. I know she hated Simpson just as much as the rest of us, but I never imagined she'd shoot him."

"Who said she did? Maybe the police and the DA's office made a mistake."

Saxer shrugged. "Yeah, maybe. I hope so."

"Hey, one last thing, and I hope you don't mind me asking. How are you going to talk in class when your mouth constantly gets dry?"

Saxer gave a half-smile, held up his empty water bottle, and waggled it.

David chuckled. "Oh yeah, right. Well, Bill, that's it for now. I really appreciate you coming to the office."

"Sure. Call me if you need anything else."

CHAPTER 4

Friday, September 18

WHILE DAVID HAD asked to meet only with Amanda, she arrived with her parents. He first heard and then saw Paul and Lorraine having a pleasant chat with Irene. Amanda appeared sullen and did not take part in the conversation. Her hair was pulled into a ponytail, and she did not wear any make-up. Nevertheless, David thought she was attractive.

David greeted the Morellis and brought them to the conference room, which was much smaller than the one at Amanda's old firm. It only had eight chairs and a rectangular table with a glass top. A television and a combination VHS/DVD player rested on a stand along the back wall. While Paul and Lorraine appeared ready to engage in conversation, Amanda slumped in her chair.

Lorraine asked, "How's your partner doing?"

David appreciated her interest. "He's slowly getting better. Thanks for asking."

"Is he hurting for money?" Paul asked. "We brought another twenty thousand."

Without hesitation, Lorraine opened her purse and retrieved a bundle of cash.

David was alarmed and tried not to visibly overreact. "Please put it away. Both Marc and our firm are doing fine. Marc was wise enough to buy long-term disability insurance shortly after he got married. So, he's been collecting from the insurance company. On top of that, once Marc started improving, his wife Stephanie returned to work."

"That's nice," Lorraine said as she closed her purse. "What does she do?"

David gave a wry smile. "Steph was a flight attendant. After they got married, she transferred to another job with the airline so she could be home more often. She now works on the ground at JFK. Getting back to the money, I'm not trying to lecture anyone, but it's not a good idea to walk around this city with a large wad of cash."

Paul waved his right hand. "Don't worry about it. I have a question. How long is it going to take before this case is over? Amanda needs to get past this and get on with her life."

Lorraine nodded in agreement, while Amanda had an expression David interpreted as "You've got to be kidding me."

David nodded and tried to be diplomatic as he explained the situation. "Well, I understand where you're coming from, but there are certain realities to consider. The first one is the Speedy Trial Act. Under this law, the DA's office has six months to prepare for any felony trial, and this case started with the indictment earlier this week. So, the DA doesn't have to be ready until mid-March next year."

"That's nuts!" Paul said while raising both his hands and eyebrows. "The Speedy Trial Act doesn't sound speedy at all."

David's eyes tilted upward momentarily. "I know. Many times, the law doesn't make sense, and we're stuck with it. Besides, I'm going to need time to prepare a proper defense if this case goes to trial. The DA's office is sending over discovery next week, and Jacqueline Marshall told me there'll be a lot. We'll also need to conduct our own investigation and see if we can punch any holes in their evidence." Given Jacqueline's past performance, he doubted he would find a flaw in her armor. "There's one other thing to remember. While this is my biggest case, I have a few others, and I have to give my other clients the proper amount of attention."

Paul exhaled and flicked his right hand across the conference room table. "Do you think there's a chance the case won't go to trial?"

David paused and considered how to phrase his answer as he wanted to be honest yet subtle. "There's always the possibility we'll find an issue with the prosecution's case. After all, nobody's perfect. If we find a flaw, perhaps the judge will grant a motion to dismiss. Unfortunately … this scenario seems unlikely. The district attorney's office tries to get all its ducks in a row before charging someone with murder."

With a despondent expression, Amanda dropped her right elbow on the table and pressed her forehead into her palm.

"Uh-huh," Paul said as he apparently took the news better. "But Amanda didn't do it, and that's the big flaw. One day, they'll figure it out. If there's anything you need from us, please let me know."

"I'm sure we'll be in touch quite often." David knew he would be in constant communication with Amanda but was uncertain whether any interaction with her parents would be productive or worthwhile.

Paul and Lorraine asked David questions about his family. He politely answered them while giving as few details as possible, because he avoided telling his clients, or their parents, about his personal life. After a few more minutes of innocuous conversation, David told Paul and Lorraine he needed to speak to Amanda alone. They were about to leave when Lorraine excused herself to use the restroom. Paul and David made small talk until she returned, while Amanda slumped in her chair and said nothing.

After Lorraine returned and sat down, she said, "I think you said Marc's married. Does his wife work?"

Paul patted her hand. "Honey, David told us already. She works for an airline at JFK."

Lorraine laughed a little. "Oh yeah. Just old age creeping up on me."

"Don't worry about it. It happens to all of us sooner or later. David, we'll be seeing you."

AFTER PAUL AND Lorraine departed, David attempted to boost Amanda's spirits, even though he figured it would be a futile gesture. He told her, "Since it's a nice day outside, why don't we walk to a restaurant for lunch? One of my favorites isn't too far away, and you might love the food and the atmosphere. Okay?"

Amanda shrugged, which was close enough to an agreement.

WHILE WALKING TWO blocks to reach the restaurant, David and Amanda did not engage in conversation due to the noise from the traffic. When they arrived at their destination, the sign outside included the word "Café," but the interior was consistent with a diner as it contained red leather booths and chairs, neon lighting, and images from the 1950s on the walls. Other customers had taken most of the tables and the seats at the counter. Between the clanking of silverware on the plates and the various ongoing conversations, the noise level was almost uncomfortable for any person with normal hearing.

A young host with short red hair, a big smile, and slightly crooked teeth approached David and Amanda. "Back again, huh?" she said to him. "Give me a few, and I'll be right back." She then hustled to a far corner of the restaurant.

After a few moments of silence, David asked Amanda, "How are you feeling? You look better today, not as tired."

"I'm fine. You looked a bit tired too."

David gave a little grin. "Yes, well, not a big deal. We got through the hearing, didn't we?"

The host returned and led them to a small booth in another corner. Once they sat down, she supplied their menus and left to attend to other customers.

David was grateful the booth somehow dampened the noise level. He leaned toward his client. "You know, the food here is really good. I've never had a bad meal."

Amanda scanned the menu with little interest. She had not yet finished when a young African American woman with chin-length braids came to their table.

With a smile, she asked, "Are we ready to order?"

"Not quite," Amanda said. "Start with him."

"I'll have a burger and fries, please."

Amanda skimmed the menu one more time and twisted her mouth. She then closed her menu and handed it to their server. "I don't know. The same for me."

After the server departed, she finally engaged with David. "My parents told me you've been doing criminal defense for seven years."

"Eight years, actually. At my old firm, I mostly represented white-collar defendants. Marc's a former prosecutor, and we met in law school. About four years ago, we formed our own firm. We've had some white-collar defendants, and we're assigned to federal and state defendants who are indigent. In

43

multi-defendant cases, the public defender can't represent everyone. We've also represented many rich kids with drug problems."

"You also told my parents you've handled other murder cases."

David gave a half-smile and nodded. "That's right. This is my fourth one, and Marc was second chair for a murder trial when he was with the DA's office. They're not much different from other criminal cases, except the stakes are much higher, obviously."

Amanda grimaced and put her head in her hands. "Geez, you didn't have to remind me. I know what I'm facing."

David felt a little embarrassed. "Sorry. Do you want to hear about the other murder cases?"

She picked up her head and slumped on her side of the booth. "Sure, whatever."

"Okay. While at my old firm, I handled the first two *pro bono*, and other attorneys pitched in, especially Beverly Cohen. The first one concerned an adult son who committed a mercy killing. His mother was dying of cancer and really suffering from an incredible amount of pain. We pled it down to second degree manslaughter, and the judge was rather lenient in sentencing."

David noticed Amanda was listening but did not react.

"The second murder case was quite different. We represented the second of two defendants, and both stupidly insisted on going to trial. Big mistake. The evidence against them was overwhelming, and they got hammered at sentencing. I filed an extensive appellate brief for both defendants, but it doesn't look good."

Amanda frowned and looked at the table. "That's not too comforting."

"Well, sometimes people are guilty."

The gloom on her face became even more apparent.

David leaned forward and said, "Look, I didn't mean to imply anything about you, okay. That's just what happened."

"Yeah, I get it. It's probably not a good idea to hear about the third murder case, but fire away."

"Are you sure?"

"Yeah, whatever."

"Alright. It was a three-defendant case, and I represented the third one, Benny Chang. Benny and his two friends were accused of robbing a liquor store at gunpoint, and things went sour. Thus, the murder charge. The DA alleged his friends were inside the store, while Benny was the lookout. The case went to trial, which resulted in a hung jury, eight to four to convict for the others and nine to three to acquit for Benny. Nine to three was surprising because the evidence against him was very weak. Anyway, the DA's office is retrying the case against the other two and dismissed the charges against Benny."

Amanda appeared perplexed and asked, "Why'd that happen?"

"Best guess ... The DA believes they have a better chance the second time by focusing on the other two. Good for my client, I guess, but he'll get himself arrested again. He's pretty young and already has a long rap sheet. Before the end of the year, he'll be back in jail."

"Are you going to represent him again?"

David scoffed. "Fat chance. The public defender can deal with him." At that moment, his cell phone rang. He checked the caller ID and let it go to voicemail. "Mind if I ask some questions about you and your family?"

Amanda shrugged.

"Your parents told Irene you're not working. When did you leave Thorton and why?"

She made a sour face and said, "Terrific. More great table conversation. I thought Valerie told you about it. I was fired after they discovered the police searched my apartment and my parents' place. I didn't tell anyone at the firm except Valerie, and I know she didn't say anything. Somehow the senior partners still found out. The firm was already in rotten shape and letting people go. Others got a severance package but not me." She leaned forward, and her eyebrows drew closer together. "Just to be clear, I *didn't* kill Simpson."

David smiled in an effort to dissipate the tension. "I never said you did. I'm only asking questions to get to know you and to better understand the case. Okay?"

Amanda's face relaxed, reflecting her mood changing from open hostility to resignation. "Yeah, okay."

"Getting back to the search warrant, did the police seize anything?"

"No, nothing from either place."

"What were they looking for?"

Amanda looked to her right and stared into space. "Let's see ... a .38-caliber handgun, some clothes ... a purse, a gray wig, a cane, and something else ..." She tapped her right index finger on the table several times and then said, "Two cell phones."

David suspected the killer wore a disguise but was uncertain why the police searched for two cell phones. At first blush, searching for only one made more sense.

"Did you ever talk to the police?"

"Yeah, a few times. They wanted to interview everyone at the firm. Saxer and Caldwell said it was each person's choice, and they encouraged cooperation."

Good grief, David said to himself. The partners told potential suspects to cooperate with law enforcement. Any competent defense attorney would have encouraged them to take a more cautious approach.

"I'm fairly certain your partners didn't give good advice."

"Maybe, but I didn't see the harm. I had nothing to hide."

David received a text message from Marc.

Remember when you told me Pauley said
I was a nephew of one of his friends?
He lied. None of my uncles knows him.

As David read the message, his eyes popped, and then he hoped Amanda did not see his reaction. He glanced in her direction and noticed she was staring at her lap, which meant he avoided an awkward conversation. On the other hand, Paul's misstatement raised a concern. David could not imagine a reasonable explanation why he had fabricated an indirect association with Marc. It was a trivial matter, and David did not care why Amanda's parents had chosen his firm. He also concluded he could not trust Paul and hoped his daughter did not have a similar character flaw.

David asked, "So, do your parents always walk around town with a stack of hundreds?"

Amanda rolled her eyes. "Stupid, right? I don't know much about their finances except they never worry about money ... or practically anything else. After I lost my job, Dad offered to pay the rent on my apartment, because he knew how much I loved the neighborhood. I didn't want to be a burden but moving back home was less appealing. As for my rent, he said, 'Don't worry about it,' which I've heard far too many times."

"I guess your parents are always positive people. Most family members look really stressed out in court."

"Yeah, I know," she said as she held out her hands. "I'm certainly not like that. Sometimes I'd tell people I was adopted, just as a joke. There's one good thing about their attitudes. I've never heard them argue with each other." She sighed. "I don't know how they do it, but Mom and Dad always look at life as the glass being half-full. For me, it's hard to see it that way."

"Well, believe it or not, there's a positive side. You were released on bail. Do you get along with them?"

Amanda tilted her head. "I guess so. Growing up, I was closer to Dad than Mom, but they didn't play favorites. Dad took me to hockey games, both the Rangers and the Islanders." She released a half-smile. "Those were really good times. We also saw the Mets, and Dad had a good buddy who sometimes gave him free tickets."

"It seems your father has many good buddies."

Amanda smirked. "Yeah, I know. Dad could walk down the street anywhere in the city – Harlem, Staten Island, Tribeca, wherever – and someone might say, 'Hi, Paul' or 'Hey Pauley, how's it going?' Everyone likes Dad because he's a people person."

"Your father was a union rep. What exactly did he do?"

Amanda held up her hands with the palms up. "No clue. I asked once or twice, and he didn't provide me with any details, just some vague comments. When I was a kid, Dad took me to construction sites a couple of times. He shook hands with the workers and introduced me, like he went there to socialize. One time, he took me to an unfinished floor of a high-rise. We stood close to the edge as he talked to some construction workers and plumbers. It was really high, and we were exposed to … you know. It was terrifying!"

The food arrived, and both Amanda and David were well-mannered enough to not eat and talk at the same time. David enjoyed every juicy bite of his medium rare burger and found the fries to be fresh and crispy. Meanwhile, Amanda took three bites of her burger and left most of her fries on the plate. When they finished eating, the crowd had thinned out, and no one waited for a table. Thus, David believed there was nothing wrong with continuing their conversation at the restaurant instead of heading back to the office.

"Amanda, tell me a little bit about your mom. She owned a travel agency, right?"

"That's right. She sold it for a 'tidy sum,'" she said with air quotes. "No idea what that means. After Mom bought the business, she hired some of her friends from the neighborhood, including Debra. My folks have known Pete and Debra so long that when Daniel and I were growing up, we called them aunt and uncle. Still do I suppose."

"So, your mom was a good businessperson?"

Amanda raised her eyebrows. "Seems hard to believe, doesn't it? She's always been scatterbrained."

"When you were growing up, did you do any mother and daughter activities?"

"Yeah, sometimes. After I joined Thorton, Mom came to the office about once a month, and we went to lunch, which was nice. In the weeks before the … you know, Mom and I had lunch about once a week. Sometimes she came with Debra. Maybe she came more often because she was bored after she sold the travel agency. Mom stopped coming to the office after the … incident. Kind of hard to blame her. We still had lunch, but we met at a restaurant."

Amanda looked at the table and swirled the straw in her water glass. "There's something else bothering me. I don't know. Maybe I shouldn't tell you. It's not that important."

"No, it's fine," David said. "Go ahead."

"There's something about Pete and Debra, but I don't know what it is. Sometimes I get the feeling they're talking in code in front of me, like they don't want me to know something. Maybe it's my imagination, or maybe they still see me as a little kid."

"I don't know. Sometimes the older generation is like that. What about your brother? Is Daniel older than you?"

She frowned at the mention of his name. "Yeah, by four years."

"I got the impression you and Daniel were close. Did you know he allowed his house to be used as collateral for bail?"

Amanda's eyes got wide. "Really? That's surprising. We're not close."

"Does he have a family?"

"Yeah. A wife and three kids. He's an architect and lives in Westchester County. When the economy slowed down, it didn't hurt him. Daniel and some of his college friends had invested in another friend's business, and that friend invented a cheaper, stronger, and lighter version of bulletproof glass. The economy went down, but the glass money started rolling in." Amanda scoffed. "That's typical for Daniel. *Everything* goes his way."

"So, there's a lot of money in bulletproof glass?"

"Are you kidding me? They put that stuff in police cars, armored cars, limos, maybe even in military vehicles. Then there's the worldwide market, including embassies in certain countries."

"Sorry, I didn't know, but I guess you do." David detected more than a hint of jealousy.

"No choice. I heard about it many times during family get-togethers. The company's now working on a better version of storm windows. They want them to withstand a Category 5 hurricane. I'm sure another ton of cash is coming Daniel's way."

"I think I saw his wife at the initial hearing."

She twisted her mouth and nodded. "Yeah ... Trudy was there. Yes, that's her real name, but her blonde hair is fake. She's a little too perky, *and* she's a kindergarten teacher. Guess what she did in high school?"

"Cheerleader?"

"Bingo," Amanda said as she pointed at him. "She still is, sort of. Most of the time she's happy peppy, and then she has other moments. I once told Daniel that Trudy was bipolar, which led to a really uncomfortable Thanksgiving dinner with the family."

David received another call on his cell phone, checked the number, and again let it go to voicemail. "How have you been spending your time lately?"

"Besides hanging out in jail? Not doing much. I've been sleeping in, and I'm in the middle of Geoffrey Ward's book on FDR. I was a history major in college and still enjoy it. On the weekends, I get together with Valerie or other friends. Sometimes I go shopping with Mom."

"It might be a good idea to exercise. I run when I have the chance."

"Yeah, I've been thinking about that. I ran the mile in high school."

David smiled. "Really? So did I."

"What was your best time?"

He paused for a moment and tried to remember his personal record. "Not sure. It was 4:40 or 4:41, something like that. And you?"

"Not that fast. I could run, but you can't do it all day. Maybe I could work again as a model, but I'm probably too old."

David was caught off guard. "You worked as a model?"

"Yeah. Only a couple of times while I was in college. Back then, I was in really decent shape, better than now." Amanda gazed at her glass and swirled the straw again. "The first time a student studying photography hired me for a project. It was no big deal."

"What about the other one?"

She frowned and waved her right hand. "It was ridiculous. Some company wanted to create a calendar called 'Country Girls,' and all twelve girls of the month lived in the city. The photo shoot was on a farm upstate, and we were supposed to be wholesome and a little sexy. They dressed me in a red plaid shirt, denim shorts, and cowboy boots. I had to sit on top of a hay bale and smile. It was hard to fake a good time since it was really cold outside. I mean, I was freezing! Besides, do you see me as a country girl?"

She pulled her hair out of her ponytail. She then made pigtails with her hands, tilted her head, and gave a fake smile.

David chuckled and noticed her facial expression called attention to her high cheekbones.

Amanda's smile disappeared, and she put her hair back into the ponytail. "Yeah, I know. Really lame, right? Modeling seemed so phony, and I had enough of that."

Even though Amanda was not in the best of moods, David still enjoyed their conversation, but more pressing matters awaited him.

"Sorry, I need to get back to the office. I almost forgot to give you this." He pulled a business card out of his shirt pocket and handed it to her.

"My cell number is on the back. One other thing and please don't take it the wrong way. I'm not trying to run your life, but you should find a job, any job, to keep you busy."

Amanda raised her eyebrows. "And what will they ask me during a job interview? 'Why did you leave your last job?' Oh, it was nothing much. They fired me after one of my bosses was shot to death, and I've been indicted for his murder."

"Try to leave that part out," he said with a wink. "I'll get the check on the way out."

WHEN DAVID RETURNED to his law firm, Irene was missing, which improved his morale. He also noticed Bev working in her office and wanted to chat with her before she left for the day. While it was barely the middle of the afternoon, she only worked part time.

David asked, "How was this morning's hearing?"

"Just as expected," she said without a hint of emotion. "My motion to suppress was granted, and I'll move to dismiss first thing Monday morning."

David nodded. "Sounds good. I'm sure the client will be pleased."

"Indeed. How was your working lunch or was it a date? You were gone for some time."

"It wasn't a date, and she's not my type."

Bev raised an eyebrow. "Oh, why is that?"

"Amanda's attractive … Okay, she's gorgeous, but it's nothing like that. She's not my type because she's a client. You told me never to cross that line with one, and I never have." He tilted his head. "Although I have to admit there haven't been too many female clients."

"Are you going to bill her for lunch?"

"Nope."

"Good man. Did you learn anything useful?"

David bobbed his head back and forth. "Perhaps a few things, and I received a text from Marc. Remember when I told you what Paul said about wanting to hire Marc? Well, take a look."

Bev viewed the relevant text message and frowned. "Morelli's father lied. Let's hope it's not a family trait."

"No kidding."

"What are your plans for the weekend?"

"Before leaving today, I'll try to call Marc and bring him up to speed."

"Don't you usually brief him in person?" Bev removed her glasses to clean them.

"Yes, but I'm busy this weekend. On Saturday, I'll be in the office to prepare for my DUI trial on Monday. On Sunday, I'm meeting with Morales at the federal jail in Brooklyn. Man, he is such a pain! After that, it's dinner with my family. Do you have any plans?"

Bev returned her glasses to their rightful place. "It'll be mostly a quiet weekend at home, but tonight, Stanley and I are having dinner at Le Cirque. We've been looking forward to it for a month." She turned off her computer, grabbed her satchel on the floor, and rose from her chair. "Now if you don't mind, it's time to pack up for the day."

"Alright. See you next week."

CHAPTER 5

Sunday, September 20

DAVID'S EXTENDED FAMILY gathered at his parents' Brownstone home in the Upper West Side of Manhattan to celebrate his younger sister, Courtney, obtaining her PhD in economics. While David and his sister were on good terms, they had little in common except for their tall, slender builds, complexions, and senses of humor. Nevertheless, David relished the opportunity to catch up with her.

Besides getting her degree, Courtney could also celebrate the reputation she had begun to build. While completing her dissertation, an investment group called Peabody Gleason had hired her as a consultant. In early 2007, she had provided Peabody with a detailed report explaining why a recession was on the horizon, but the report did not convince them. During a three-hour meeting, the investors peppered her with questions as she went through the current and future state of the economy in extensive detail. Once they finally understood, Peabody sold most of their stocks and real estate in more risky markets. After the economy tanked, they bought low, and two years later, Peabody had more than doubled in value.

After dinner, David guided Courtney to the small patio off the living room so they could talk without interruption.

"Congratulations again," he said while raising his second glass of champagne of the evening.

"Thanks." She clinked her glass with his.

"Now that you have your PhD, what's your game plan?"

Courtney cocked her head and gave a big smile. "I have some good options. Four out-of-state universities are considering hiring me as a professor, and Peabody wants me to come on board permanently."

"Sorry to hear about your suffering."

Courtney smirked. "Yeah, it's been terrible."

"As for a career choice, I suggest you take the one that makes the least amount of money, which will disappoint our parents the most."

"That's not a bad idea, if we're only considering your entertainment," she said while lightly slapping his chest. "I think I've decided what to do. While I'd love to be part of the academic world, Peabody offered me a generous salary and an obscene signing bonus. It's more like a big thank you for my past consulting work. Plus, there's one other important consideration."

"Which is?"

Courtney took a step closer and whispered, "I'm in a serious relationship, and Chris lives in Manhattan."

David's mouth dropped open. "What! Why didn't you tell me about him sooner?"

"Give me a break," she said with a grin and a gleam in her eye. "Do you tell me all the details of your social life? I don't think so. Besides, I wasn't ready to tell you or anyone else until the relationship became more serious.

It is now, and … I have a feeling he might propose. If I take another job out of state, I can't stay in the city, and his practice is here."

"He's a lawyer?"

"Oh no … much better. Chris is an orthopedic surgeon, and he just finished his residency."

David chuckled. "Geez. Thanks for the little shot. So, he has a great job, but does he look like a troll?"

"No, sorry about that. I tried to find an ugly white guy who's a disreputable used car salesman, and it didn't work out."

David held up his hands. "Okay, okay. When do you think Doctor Loverboy will pop the question?"

"I don't know. Maybe I should drop a hint or two."

"Well, you could do that, or you could ask him."

She momentarily froze. "What? You mean I propose?"

"Why not? I don't see a problem. Do you? It's not like we're stuck in the 1950s."

Courtney stared into the distance while engrossed in thought. "Hmm … I'll get back to you on that one."

CHAPTER 6

Monday, September 21

LATE MONDAY MORNING, David placed a call to his law partner. "Hey, Marc. Got any time for me today?"

"What do you think? Steph's at work, which means we can get into a lot of trouble. What'd you have in mind? Skydiving?"

David smirked. "Sure, why not?"

"Hey, wait a minute. I thought you had a DUI trial this morning."

"Yeah. I did, but it went away. As soon as the judge took the bench, the ADA dismissed the case."

Marc chuckled. "Are you serious?"

"Yup."

"Who was the ADA?"

"Andrew Johnson. He made a point of telling me he was named after a terrible president."

"Johnson … unruly hair, swears in ordinary conversation?"

"That's him."

"Why'd he move to dismiss?" Marc asked.

"No clue. I asked, and he didn't tell me. Afterwards, our truly wonderful client bragged, 'I told you we'd win.' I said if the DA refiles, he needs to plead out, or he'll face a stiffer sentence after a jury convicts him. Funny, he didn't take the news well, even though he'd heard something similar beforehand."

"Tough," Marc said. "If the DA refiles, are we going to represent him again?"

"Do we need the money that badly?"

"Good point."

"So, I have plenty of free time on a weekday, which probably won't happen again for months. Can I come over, or do you have plans?"

"My lunch date with the Queen of England isn't until tomorrow, which means I'm free. I planned to watch a movie with Steph tonight. We can instead watch it this afternoon."

"Sure. I'll leave the office in a bit, and I'll pick up lunch on the way to your place."

"Great! Can you get Chinese?"

David sighed. "You want the crummy soup again, right? Yeah, sure."

DAVID ARRIVED AT Marc and Stephanie's apartment in Lenox Hill, and the door was answered by "The Creature," a nickname Marc gave himself due to chemotherapy's side effects. While David and Steph never used the nickname, it was fitting, as Marc's hairless head sat on top of his unusually pale and thin frame. While he lacked energy, he maintained a positive outlook.

While they ate, David brought Marc up to speed on the events of the last few days, and they cracked jokes about their caseload.

After Marc finished his soup, he noted, "From what you told me, Simpson was a real piece of work."

David nodded as he swallowed the last bit of noodles, which he found subpar due to a lack of flavor and seasoning. "Yeah. He was a sexual harasser on steroids." He snapped his fingers. "There's something I forgot to tell you earlier. Simpson called himself Big Bobby, but the women in the office called him Big Bastard."

"Big Bastard? Did they get it from Fat Bastard?"

"From what?"

Marc rolled his eyes. "You know, Fat Bastard from the *Austin Powers* movies."

David smiled. "Oh yeah. What a horrible character." His smile then disappeared. "Oh, no. This isn't an excuse for you to do another Austin Powers impression. I'm so tired of it."

Marc chuckled. "But Steph still likes it."

"She's just used to you and had all her shots. We really need to change the subject. What movie are we watching?"

With his right hand, Marc retrieved a DVD hidden behind a sofa cushion. He held it at shoulder level and placed his left hand on his chest. "On tap for this afternoon is *The Silence of the Lambs*."

David's anticipation was quashed. "Really? Can't we watch something else? You know I'm not into horror movies."

Marc put down his hands. "Come on. It's a great movie, and I haven't seen it in forever. It's only one of three movies to win Best Picture, Director, Actor, Actress, and Adapted Screenplay."

"Didn't it come out in 1991, which was a weak year for movies?"

"I've heard some people argue that, but I don't agree. You don't think Jodie Foster and Anthony Hopkins are great actors? Besides, it's a psychological horror movie, not a cheap, slasher flick such as *Halloween* or *Friday the Thirteenth*."

"I get it, but can't we watch something else?"

Marc shook his head. "It's either Hannibal Lecter or the two of us cuddling on the sofa. Your choice."

David threw up his hands. "Hannibal Lecter it is!"

DESPITE HIS INITIAL reluctance, David found himself enjoying the film to an extent. Once it ended, Marc was asleep, and David had no idea how much he missed. It did not matter as he could watch it again with Steph.

David looked to his left and examined the rest of Marc's movie collection, which sat on three shelves bolted to the wall. Almost an entire row consisted of classic movies, including *Bonnie and Clyde, Some Like it Hot, Psycho,* and *The Great Escape*. Another row featured movies from the 1980s. When David saw *Back to the Future*, he said, "Sorry, Marc. I would've preferred to watch it again."

CHAPTER 7

Thursday, September 24

T HURSDAY MORNING BROUGHT a sentencing hearing for
another rich kid with a drug problem. As soon as it concluded, David
returned to the office.

As he passed by Irene, she said, "David, we got –"

"Sorry, not right now. Have to pee." While dashing off, he thought
out of the corner of his eye, he saw Irene scowl and put her hands on her
hips. He did not understand why she was upset but acknowledged he could
be mistaken. After finishing in the restroom, he returned to Irene's desk.
"What's up?"

"The DA's office sent over the discovery for Morelli. It's in the conference room."

"Okay, thanks."

David walked over there, where he counted twelve large boxes covering most of the glass-top table. He also noticed numbers one through twelve written in black marker on the lids of each box and on each side. While the sense of organization pleased him, Irene's decision to place the boxes on the table was a different matter. She had previously scratched the glass by doing the same thing. Afterwards, David had instructed her to place future deliveries on the floor, and once again, she had not listened to him.

Moments later, Bev arrived at the office and joined David in the conference room.

"Hi, Beverly. How was your appointment with the doctor?"

"I just had my annual physical and can't complain. Neither could my doctor. Mind if I look with you?"

"Of course not."

They took the tops off the boxes, and its contents impressed David. For many "discovery dumps," the prosecution had thrown the documents together with the apparent attitude of "let them figure it out." This time, the boxes were well organized. Someone had placed each item in a separate folder with a label, except for the subject matters with voluminous paperwork. A large, sealed envelope contained videos on disks, and phone and bank records for the deceased filled two boxes. Jacqueline Marshall had also provided documents concerning cell tower data from the night of the murder. David also found a table of contents in the box marked "1."

"Beverly, have you ever seen discovery delivered in such an organized fashion?"

"Not very often. I suspect this is an exact duplicate of Marshall's files. Perhaps she believes she has nothing to hide. The police must've thrown considerable resources into the case to create all of this in only three months."

David nodded as he examined the first box's contents. He removed a magazine with a middle-aged attorney on the cover.

"Oh look, an alumni magazine from a second-rate law school in the Midwest. That must be Simpson on the cover. Look at his pose. What an arrogant jackass." David tossed the magazine back into the box. "Do you think we can argue justifiable homicide?"

Bev frowned and glanced upward at him through her stylish glasses. David also noticed her white bangs almost touched the top of the frame. Based upon past experiences, he expected she would visit a hairdresser in two weeks.

Irene stood at the door frame and leaned into the conference room. "David, Judge Chavez's clerk is on the phone."

"Which Judge Chavez, state or federal?"

"Federal. Remember the hearing scheduled for 1:30 this Thursday? The judge wants to move it up to eight. Can you make it?"

He gave a dismissive wave. "Not a problem."

"Are you sure? Can you get up early enough?" Irene asked sarcastically.

"Just tell her I'll be there at eight."

As Irene left, David clenched his jaw and closed the conference room door while preventing himself from slamming it in a fit of anger.

"Did you hear that? Ever since Marc had to take a leave of absence, I've had to put up with her crap, and I'm getting sick of it."

Bev raised an eyebrow. "Will you do anything about it?"

"I don't know yet," he said as he crossed his arms. "Ordinarily, I'd fire her in a heartbeat, but I can't make a unilateral decision, and she's part of Marc's extended family. Marc has talked to her multiple times, and it's made no difference. Maybe her behavior will improve once he starts working again, but I doubt it. Any suggestions?" His cell phone rang. "Hold that thought, please."

Bev nodded.

"This is David," he said as he put the phone to his ear.

"It's Jacqueline."

"Oh, hello. I'm here with Beverly Cohen. Can I put you on speaker?" He switched over and placed the phone on the table before receiving a reply.

"That's fine. I'm calling to make certain you received some of the discovery we sent over this morning."

"I'm looking at it right now. Did you say 'some'?"

"Yes. We sent over twelve boxes, and you'll get another four tomorrow, which have phone records for Morelli and her parents, plus some miscellaneous items. Once you've reviewed everything, get back to me. I might allow your client to plead guilty to murder two. Frankly, if I'd worked for Simpson, I might've blown him away."

David tilted his head and looked down at Bev, who raised an eyebrow.

"Okay, thanks," he said. "We'll get back to you."

"Not a problem. Goodbye."

David kept his focus on Bev. "Jacqueline's a hard charger, and I've never known her to offer a deal right after an indictment. Something's up. What do you make of it?"

Bev removed her glasses and tapped an earpiece on her right cheek three times. "Perhaps there's a weakness in her case. Only time will tell."

"Care to be my trial partner, if it gets that far?" he asked.

She donned her glasses and gave a subtle shake of her head. "I'm not as young as I used to be, and I can't work many long-hour days needed before and during a trial."

David was disappointed and about to drop the matter when he had another thought. "How about carrying about twenty percent of the load? Maybe a little more or a little less? By the time we get to trial, Marc should be back, and he can also work on the case."

Bev stared at the wall for a couple of moments. "A smaller percentage of the load? Fair enough. You have a trial partner."

"Excellent!" he said as he pumped his fist. In some ways, it would be like old times except for their reversal of roles. This time, he would take first chair for the defense.

"Just remember, if we go to trial, it'll be my last one. When the Morelli case is over, Stanley should be ready to retire, and we can start on our bucket list."

"Sounds good."

They continued to examine the boxes' contents for several minutes. David found the crime scene photos and the coroner's report, which he decided to review first.

He again addressed Bev. "We'll need Freddie to look into a few things if he's available. We'll also need someone to examine Simpson's financial records. Any ideas?"

Bev stared at him. "You don't have a clue? What name just popped into my head?"

"Stanley?" he asked with his eyebrows raised. "I didn't think he does this kind of work, which would include potentially testifying as an expert witness."

"I believe he will this time. He seems interested in the case."

"Alright, great! So, I'll finally get to meet your husband. I imagine his services won't come cheap. I'll have to run it past the Morelli family, and I'm sure they'll approve. We'll also need someone to review the phone records. If I have to do it, I'll get a massive headache."

David's cell phone rang again, and it was Paul Morelli.

"Hey, David. Lorraine, Amanda, and I are in Murray Hill and just finished brunch. We want to stop by your office and see how things are going."

David was not certain whether all three had the same desire. Nevertheless, he believed Paul should see all the boxes so he would realize Amanda's problems would not vanish in the near future.

"Not a problem," he said. "Come anytime. I don't have any appointments or court appearances for the rest of the day."

WHEN THE MORELLIS arrived, Bev was on a call in her office and waved to them. David guided them to the conference room and asked them to remain standing so they could better observe what was in the boxes. He surmised Amanda was in a somewhat better mood, because she cracked a smile when she saw him. David referred to the table of contents and explained how each portion of the discovery could relate to the overall case. He also mentioned the boxes scheduled to arrive the following day. Paul and Lorraine remained attentive during David's ad hoc presentation, while Amanda appeared bored and leaned against a wall.

"Paul, look at box number six," Lorraine uttered. "There's a file with your name at the top, and the one next to it has mine."

David said, "The police spoke with both of you, right? Every time they interview someone, they create a report, and the ADA has to provide copies of them to defense counsel." He noticed Paul's file was much thicker than Lorraine's. "In addition to reviewing the discovery, we'll need to conduct our own investigation and look for any holes in the prosecution's case. In the past, I've hired Frederick Ferguson, who's an excellent private investigator and a retired NYPD detective. We'll also need an accountant to look through Simpson's finances, and Beverly's husband might make himself available. I strongly recommend hiring both, but this will increase the costs."

"Don't worry about it," Paul said. "Just give our daughter the best defense you can."

Amanda took her shoulder off the wall and stood straight. "What about a jury consultant? The lawyers at Thorton used them all the time."

David held up his right hand. "Let's not get ahead of ourselves. Any possible trial is way off in the distance. Besides, jury consultants are a waste of money. Beverly wrote the book on how to pick a jury, literally, and there's a copy in my office. You can borrow it if you like."

"Sure, why not?" Amanda said.

Irene returned to the conference room again. "David, the Morelli case has been assigned to Judge Perkins, and a status conference has been scheduled for this coming Monday at 11:30."

Paul looked in the air as if he were viewing a calendar on the ceiling. "11:30, huh? We might not be able to make it."

David shook his head in disbelief. "With this judge, checking your schedule is irrelevant. Unless you have a hearing in federal court, you're in the hospital, in jail, or dead, you better appear in his courtroom. Sometimes, even jail isn't a good enough excuse. Irene, tell the judge's clerk Amanda and I'll be there. Paul, I don't want to be too blunt, but if you and Lorraine can't attend, there's not much I can do about it."

CHAPTER 8

Monday, September 28

DAVID, AMANDA, AND her parents arrived early for the hearing with Judge Sherman Perkins, who had presided over David's civil rights case against the NYPD. Judge Perkins had been a federal prosecutor, but on the bench, he did not favor the District Attorney's Office and had no tolerance for police misconduct.

Judge Perkins set exacting standards for himself and could quote chapter and verse of any aspect of the law. He was always prepared and expected the same from the attorneys. When a lawyer made a frivolous argument or was clueless, Judge Perkins did not yell, but no one doubted he was upset. The fact that he never raised his voice made him more intimidating than other judges.

David had heard about one occasion in which a defense attorney had irritated Judge Perkins. The defendant in question had been incarcerated in a Connecticut jail, and the judge had known he had no authority to transfer him to Manhattan without going through an extradition process. Nevertheless, he suggested a transfer, and it happened. During the next hearing, the defense attorney gave Judge Perkins a fistful of attitude, which resulted in a $500 fine. The attorney refused to calm down and continued his rant. Judge Perkins responded by glancing at his bailiff and giving an imaginary slap of his hand. Before the attorney realized what had happened, he was spending the night in jail.

David had recently seen a ten-year-old picture of Sherman Perkins taken at an NAACP dinner to honor his elevation to the bench. He was surprised the judge looked the same, except for faint wrinkles and bags developing under his eyes. Over the years, Judge Perkins had kept the same short afro and thick mustache. Given the judge sat higher than others in the courtroom and his reputation, he had appeared taller than his actual height. Once David and His Honor arrived at the courthouse at the same time, and David discovered the judge was five inches shorter than him.

When David and the Morellis entered the courtroom, three elderly men sat in the gallery's fourth of six rows. The man in the middle held his index finger to his mouth and said, "Shh."

David whispered, "Thanks. I already know." He motioned for Paul and Lorraine to sit in the first row, while he and Amanda went to the defense table.

Jacqueline then entered and took her seat at the opposite table. An African American woman in her thirties typed at the clerk's station and nodded to acknowledge both attorneys. The bailiff, a middle-aged and overweight Caucasian man, sat in a corner. His eyelids kept closing and reopening as if he were trying not to fall asleep.

As David waited for Judge Perkins, he thought the "quiet rule" was ridiculous. No one else demanded almost complete silence before a hearing started. David glanced above and to the left of the bench, where the judge's portrait hung from the wall. In the painting, he rested his chin on his right hand and gave an eternal downward gaze upon all those who entered his realm. David had met many judges and attorneys with large egos, but the painting reflected the judge's inflated view of himself, which fell into another category.

Promptly at 11:30, David heard a side door open, which caused the sleepy bailiff to jump to his feet and announce, "All rise! The Supreme Court of the State of New York is now in session, the Honorable Sherman Matthias Perkins presiding!"

Judge Perkins stomped into the courtroom, and in a raspy voice, he said, "Good morning," without the slightest hint of warmth.

David never failed to notice his droopy eyelids, which gave him a look of permanent disappointment. The judge's demeanor intimidated most attorneys, but not David, who instead took it as a personal challenge to never have him become upset. If it did not occur, it would be his own little victory.

After all parties took their seats, Judge Perkins asked, "Ms. Marshall, what's the current status?"

Jacqueline rose to her feet. "Your Honor, the People turned over sixteen boxes of discovery, and no more is forthcoming. If the People conduct any additional investigation, which produces more evidence, they will notify the defense immediately."

Judge Perkins paused and gave a slight wave of his right hand, which indicated some level of disapproval. "Do you mean to tell the Court you indicted before finishing the investigation?"

Jacqueline did not flinch. "Not at all, Your Honor. The People are simply not foreclosing the possibility of additional discovery should anything arise prior to trial."

The judge put down his hand, and his expression did not change. "Anything else?"

"No, Your Honor." Jacqueline then took her seat.

"Mr. Lee, should I expect any motions in the near future?"

David stood and said, "No, Your Honor."

"Anything else?"

"No, Your Honor." He then sat down.

"Very well. We'll have another status conference on Monday, November 16, 2009, at 11:30. Both parties shall follow the rules of this Court to the letter and without exception. Any motions shall be filed at least one week prior to the next hearing. We're adjourned."

After the judge departed, Paul asked with a confused expression, "That's it?"

David took him aside and further away from the microphones at defense counsel's table. He whispered, "Yes, for now, and careful what you say. Those microphones could still be on. If so, the judge can hear you from chambers."

In a hushed voice, Paul said, "Got it. Why'd we have to show up?"

"Judge Perkins requires it, which is reason enough. If both sides have nothing to discuss, he's fine with it. Besides, I wouldn't ask why we have short hearings. The judge can do just about whatever he wants. Other hearings will take longer."

Paul's distaste for court disappeared as he clapped his hands together. In a louder voice, he asked, "Now that we're done, care to join us for lunch?"

"Sure," David said with a smile. "There's a great Chinese restaurant only three blocks away. It's called the Red Chili House. Sound good?"

"Let's go."

WHEN DAVID ARRIVED with the Morellis at the restaurant, he saw an establishment with its walls painted yellow and a dragon sculpture hanging on the back wall. The right wall held a more unusual sight: photographs and signatures of well-known people, including the current and two past mayors. Nearly all the tables were taken, and the conversations throughout the room created a racket.

Mr. Chen, a diminutive Chinese man with wire-frame glasses and a bad comb-over, spotted David. He rushed over, vigorously shook his hand, and greeted him as if he were an old friend. Mr. Chen seated David's party at the first available table, even though others had arrived before them. After he left, David explained the special treatment.

"That was the owner. I come here frequently, and his son was a client."

"For a criminal case?" asked Amanda.

"Yes. Fortunately, the DA agreed to reduce the charge to a misdemeanor, and his son was sentenced to probation. Obviously, Mr. Chen's still grateful." David held up his hands. "What can I say?"

After the waiter provided the menus and later took their orders, the conversation continued.

Lorraine asked, "David, why'd you become a lawyer?"

He paused for a moment and considered whether he should answer. He preferred not to discuss his personal life but surmised there was no harm in telling the story.

"Well, during my freshman year in college, I was home during Spring Break. Early in the week, I wandered around the city and ended up in front of the federal courthouse. I went inside and found a criminal trial in progress. It was a white-collar crime case with three defendants."

Paul and Lorraine inched forward while Amanda slumped in her chair and seemed disinterested.

"I didn't fully understand what was happening, but it was interesting. During a recess, I tried to speak with one of the defense attorneys. Two of them did their best to ignore me. However, the one representing the third defendant gave me a few minutes of her time. She said she'd answer more questions if I joined her for lunch at the courthouse cafeteria, which I did. During lunch, the lawyer brought me up to speed."

"That was sweet of her," Lorraine said.

David grinned. "Yes, it was. I watched the afternoon session, came back the next day, and we again had lunch. I was back for a third day, and during the morning session, the defense rested. There was no rebuttal case. I made a comment about the case during lunch, and the attorney used it in her closing argument. I never expected it."

Paul nodded while pouting his lower lip.

"While waiting for the jury verdict, the attorney invited me to her office and introduced me to some of her colleagues. Little did I know I was on a job interview. A few days later, the attorney called and told me the jury convicted the two other defendants and acquitted her client. She also offered me a summer job, and I accepted. I worked at the law firm every summer until I graduated from law school. During that time, I attended about ten hearings and a couple of trials. I guess after all that, it was inevitable I'd become a litigator."

"That's really nice," Lorraine said. "Did you stay in touch with the lawyer?"

"Oh yes. She's Beverly Cohen."

"How about that!" Paul exclaimed. "Is she going to help you out with Amanda's case?"

"Absolutely."

CHAPTER 9

Tuesday, September 29

D AVID SET ASIDE a large block of time to study the crime scene investigation for the Morelli case. He reviewed the materials in the conference room, where he had more room to spread out the documents, and the boxes now sat on the floor. Among other items, one box contained the crime scene photos and the schematics for the tenth floor of the O'Connell building.

The schematics held no surprises as it listed each paralegal's cubicle and each attorney's office by name. Amanda's former office was on the right side, and Valerie Fernandez's cubicle sat directly in front of it. Old Man Thorton and the other senior partners had offices on the tenth floor across the back row. As expected, Simpson had the largest office, in the northwest corner, which formed a Tetris shape, three blocks across and one block protruding down from the right. The conference room was in the center, and other attorney offices fell in a row along the left side.

David turned to the crime scene photos, which were high-quality color copies. The first photograph showed the receptionist's desk and the space behind it, but Simpson's office was not visible. The next several photos depicted the area behind the receptionist, including the conference room, various cubicles, and attorney's offices. He did not understand why so many photos showed areas with no connection to the murder.

David then found images of the crime scene. First, he saw Simpson's office from a distance. The glass wall would have allowed for a clear line of sight to the inside if not for two black leather chairs blocking the view of the deceased, a rather large man in a business suit slumped over a black leather couch. However, David could still see a dark red stain on the wall behind Simpson's head. For some unknown reason, the next few photos showed the floor outside of his office, which only revealed short, thick beige carpet, typical for office buildings.

The next several photos supplied a closer view of the office's interior. The far left contained Simpson's black leather chair and oversized mahogany desk, both of which appeared more expensive than the rest of the law firm's furniture. A computer screen and keyboard sat on one corner of the desk, and two small stacks of papers laid on another. Other than these items, the desk's surface was bare. David saw no pens, notepads, or any other items indicating Simpson had regularly worked at his desk. Perhaps he had kept any necessary materials inside a drawer.

To the right of the desk sat the black leather couch and matching chairs. A small navy-blue pillow was propped up on the side of the couch closer to the desk. To the right, Simpson was slumped over. Since his head had fallen forward, David could not clearly observe his face. He instead viewed the top of his head, which was covered in blood. He tried to hold back his nausea and feared he would see more graphic images.

Simpson's right hand rested on his right thigh, and his left arm hung down. Another photo showed a closer view of the dried blood splatter on the solid off-white wall behind him. In addition to its repulsive appearance, the splatter's location caught David's attention in another way. Most of Simpson's office had floor-to-ceiling windows, but the section behind the couch did not, indicating part of the building's superstructure ran through it. He also wondered whether the killer picked this location to shoot Simpson so that a bullet would not shatter a window and rain down bits of glass, calling attention to the grisly scene above.

David rifled through another box to find the autopsy report, which said Simpson was fifty-three years old, six feet two inches tall, and 216 pounds. Upon viewing the corpse again, he concluded Simpson carried an extra three to four inches around his waist.

The next few photographs depicted Simpson's clothing. Thanks to a close-up image of his watch, David read the manufacturer's name: Cartier. He also determined Simpson had worn a dark gray Armani suit, a silk striped tie, a silk dress shirt, and Prada shoes.

David noticed the artwork hanging above the couch, a quasi-impressionist painting of two sailboats racing. With a magnifying glass, he made a closer examination of the bottom right-hand corner, and as he suspected, the painter was Leroy Neiman. David checked the painting for any blood splatter and only found two small spots at the bottom.

The next two photos depicted the area to the right of the couch, which included a mahogany liquor cabinet with glass doors and a floor-to-ceiling window behind it. A glass tumbler etched with Simpson's initials had a small amount of liquid and rested on top of the cabinet. The inside had various bottles of scotch, bourbon, and other hard liquor.

The corner was solid, and David surmised it was part of the building's superstructure. To the right was the rest of Simpson's office, which had another giant window and a solid wall to the far right. A small mahogany conference table and four matching chairs with black leather seats sat in front of the liquor cabinet.

David also saw a large photograph hanging on the wall behind the table. It featured Simpson holding high a champagne glass in his right hand while he stood on the stern of a small yacht called *The Apex*. David scoffed at the entire scene and wondered if there had been no limit to Big Bobby's ego.

The next few photographs showed much closer views of Simpson's body and the area surrounding it. At first, David thought he noticed Simpson's left hand holding a second dark blue pillow and then questioned whether a dead hand could grasp anything. Perhaps the pillow stood upright on its own and leaned against the hand.

Closer views of the pillow revealed two bullet holes, one slightly higher and to the right of the other. One side had gun muzzle imprints and powder burns surrounding the two holes, and several specks of blood stained the other side. David tried to determine what had happened. Simpson could have tried to shield himself with the pillow, which did not make sense. Maybe the killer had used the pillow to muffle the sound of the shots, indicating an amateur's work. A professional hit man would have brought a silencer.

David studied a few more photographs and once again believed the crime scene photographer had taken too many unimportant pictures, including images of the floor in Simpson's office from multiple angles. He only saw beige carpet and the furniture legs, not even shoe prints. He then realized no shell casings had laid on the floor and imagined two possible explanations. The shooter had used a revolver, which did not eject shells, or he had used a semi-automatic pistol and retrieved them before making his escape.

David grimaced as he examined the next several images, which provided an even closer view of the dried blood splatter on the wall. One photo had two blue ink circles drawn amid two large, dark red patches, which highlighted the slugs' locations. He also gasped at the sight of scattered, tiny gray bits on the wall, which were probably pieces of Simpson's brain and skull.

Additional photographs had closer images of Big Bobby's face and head. His assassin shot him through the right eye and slightly above and to the left. The distance between the bullet holes appeared consistent with the distance between the holes in the throw pillow. David then recoiled upon viewing the back of Simpson's head, which had been blown apart.

The crime scene investigators had also taken photographs of the slugs after they had removed them from the wall. The corresponding forensic report said the bullets were fired from a .38-caliber weapon at a slight downward angle, approximately five degrees lower than horizontal. The report also concluded the gun was in contact with the pillow when fired, and the pillow was within inches of Simpson's face. A lab report said the only DNA on the pillow belonged to the deceased.

Another report stated the police had found several fingerprints in Big Bobby's office. However, both door handles had been wiped down, resulting in no identifiable prints. David thought the lack of shell casings and fingerprints showed a professional hit man committed the crime but knew those two facts were not conclusive.

David turned to the autopsy report and the corresponding photos. The first photo showing Simpson on the autopsy table was horrific, and the subsequent images were more graphic. While holding back nausea, David flipped through the images to make certain he did not miss any more crime scene images. He knew Judge Perkins would allow the jury to view some images of Simpson's body, but the autopsy photos were too shocking for the ordinary citizen.

The cleaning crew had found Simpson's body at about 3:30 in the morning. Soon thereafter, the police, the medical examiner, and the crime scene investigators had arrived. Based upon the body's lividity, the medical examiner concluded no one moved Simpson since the time of death, which occurred between 9:30 and 10:30 the prior evening. The examiner also established the estimated time of death based upon multiple factors, including the temperature of Simpson's body at the time of examination, the amount of rigor mortis, and the extent of his stomach contents' digestion.

Simpson's last credit card charge had occurred at a restaurant earlier during the same evening as the murder. Two detectives went to the restaurant, which was about five blocks away from the building housing the law firm. They obtained a copy of the receipt, which someone originally printed at 9:16, and the manager confirmed the credit card machine was in good working order.

The detectives had also spoken with the server who waited on Simpson's table. He said the deceased had been a difficult customer, and he also remembered the tall blonde woman who had accompanied him. According to the server, Simpson insisted they sit in a back corner so that he could face towards the rest of the restaurant, which meant the server mostly saw his date's back. He could not provide a detailed description of the woman and only recalled she was tall with long, straight blonde hair. He paid little attention to her because he preferred redheads.

David jumped upon hearing a knock on the conference room's door frame. He looked over his shoulder and saw Bev.

"I'm sorry. I didn't mean to startle you."

"It's okay," he said and spun in his chair to face her. "I'm fine. What's on your mind?"

"Remember Susan Thompson?"

"Who?"

"The college student caught with cocaine at the Statue of Liberty."

David chuckled. "Oh yeah, right. What about her?"

"I just got off the phone with her parents. Susan's hometown newspaper published a story about her arrest and has continued to report on the case. The university is certainly not pleased, and Susan's sorority is more upset. The National Council told her to straighten herself out, or they'd ask her to leave."

David laughed hard. "So, let me get this right. A sorority has no problem with binge drinking but snorting coke at a national treasure is another matter."

"Apparently so," Bev said with a straight face. "Susan's now open to enrolling in a rehabilitation program as part of a plea deal for a lesser sentence. I don't know if she agreed so she may remain in her sorority, or if she really intends to be drug free. Perhaps the AUSA will reduce the charge to a misdemeanor. Whether it's a felony or not, the sentencing exposure is about the same."

"Sounds good. I almost wish I had kept the case due to its entertainment value."

CHAPTER 10

Wednesday, September 30

D AVID HEARD A knock on his open office door. Before him stood a muscular, light-skinned African American whose shaved head almost touched the top of the door frame. Despite the lighting bouncing off his dome, David noticed the roots of his speckled gray and white hair.

Frederick Douglass Ferguson gave a wide, toothy smile. "Good afternoon," his baritone voice proclaimed. "Hope you don't mind I let myself in. Didn't see Irene."

David also smiled. "Of course not. Please have a seat." He gestured toward a chair. "I gave Irene the day off. Marc hasn't returned to work yet, and Bev's out too. So, it's just me." After Freddie sat down, he asked, "Hey, how's Helen doing?"

Freddie let loose another wide smile. "My Sweetie is *just* fine, thank you. Every day with her is a blessing. You should've seen Helen work her magic two weeks ago during the black-tie fundraiser for the children's hospital. No doubt her speech convinced a donor or two to give even a little more. Oh, let's not forget one other important thing. I looked good in a tux, you know, really good."

David chuckled. "I'm sure you did. I'd love to hear more about it, but we need to discuss Morelli."

"Right, right. In your email, you said she's charged with murder."

"Yeah. Amanda worked for a law firm in Manhattan, and the victim, J. Robert Simpson, was a real piece of work: a sexual harasser on steroids. He was a partner with the same firm, and he took two .38-caliber bullets to the head in his own office."

Freddie's eyebrows raised. "In his own office? Someone had a lot of nerve."

"No kidding. Could you start working on the case right away?"

"As a matter of fact, I can. Just turned in a final report about a cheating husband." Freddie exhaled. "That's going to be a *very* nasty divorce, sorry to say. Also finishing up another assignment and can make you my top priority real soon."

"Terrific." David slid four thin folders across his desk toward Freddie. "The top file contains a summary. You got a pen handy? I have a to-do list for you, including maybe some paralegal work."

"That's fine, but thought you had a paralegal. What was his name? Quincy? Don't believe I ever met him."

"You didn't, and he wasn't here very long."

"Oh, why not?"

"He discovered he didn't like legal work." In a mocking tone, he said, "'I need to find a less confrontational and a warmer, more supportive environment. I need a space where I'm surrounded by positive vibrations and healing crystals all the time.'"

"Oh, one of those people," Freddie said as he shook his head.

"Yeah, one of those people," David said in his normal voice. "By the way, who names their kid Quincy?"

Freddie's eyes got wide as he lurched back in his chair. "Maybe his parents named him after Quincy Jones, music producer extraordinaire."

David raised his right index finger. "Let me rephrase. What white parents would name their kid Quincy?"

Freddie held up his hands and laughed. "Okay, I got nothing."

David laughed as well. "Getting back to Morelli. First, look into Simpson's two ex-wives and see if NYPD missed anything. Their information is in one of the files I gave you. They probably weren't involved, but it doesn't hurt to check them out."

"Will do," Freddie said while taking notes on a small pad he had removed from a pants pocket.

"I also want you to look into Simpson's clients for the past two years and see if any of them had a motive to kill him. I doubt it, but you never know. Same goes for the opposing parties. Maybe someone had a shady background. Simpson represented a pharmaceutical company called Bennington when he was part of his last two law firms, and another file has the info on Bennington and the firms."

"Okay, what else?"

"Please talk to security for the O'Connell building. That's where the murder took place. No one saw the killer enter or leave the building. How come? I also need you to review security camera footage. The disks are in the conference room along with the rest of discovery."

Freddie nodded and continued writing. "Sounds like quite a bit to do, which is okay with me."

David leaned forward and put his elbows on the desk. "There's something else I want you to quietly investigate and bill separately. I won't charge my client for this part. For now, don't mention it to anyone, including Amanda, her parents, and especially Irene."

Freddie stopped taking notes and looked up.

"I need you to investigate Amanda's father, Paul Morelli. A copy of his file is on the bottom." David casually pointed to the ones on the desk. "NYPD took a good, hard look at him, and they contacted the FBI, who gave them no answers. Maybe the FBI has something on Paul, or maybe they have nothing. Who knows?"

Freddie inched forward in his chair. "What's the deal?"

"Well, Paul is a retired union rep, whatever that is, and the police suspect he has ties to the mafia. They questioned him about it, and he vehemently denied it. Paul told the police he knew some wise guys, and that was it. He also said the mob took its cut from the unions, construction companies, and so on. Nothing we don't already know, but I'm not convinced he was honest with the police. He's already lied to me once by claiming Marc was a nephew of a good friend. So ..." David raised his eyebrows and held out his right hand.

Freddie pointed to him. "Gotcha. Maybe Amanda was wrongfully charged, and this was a mafia hit."

David leaned back. "Well, I don't know, could be. It's worth considering that angle. Simpson was murdered in his own office, and there were no witnesses. The shooter wiped down door handles to his office and left no shell casings behind, both of which have the mark of a professional. On the other hand, it looks like the killer used a throw pillow as a silencer."

"What?" Freddie said as his forehead furrowed.

David raised his hands. "I swear. It was a throw pillow."

"Anything else?"

He mulled it over for a moment. "Do you have time to examine the crime scene photos? I might have a question or two for you."

"Am I on the clock right now?"

"Yeah."

Freddie chuckled. "Then I have the time."

David escorted him to the conference room and grabbed the folder containing the crime scene photos. He then spread them out on the glass-top table.

"Simpson was six-two, and the forensic report said the bullets were fired at a slight downward angle, about five degrees. In addition, the gun contacted the pillow, which was right in front of Simpson's face. From this information and these photos, can you make an educated guess regarding the shooter's height?"

"It's possible. Please point me to the report's section on the bullets' trajectory."

"Okay." David found the forensic report, turned to a specific page, and placed it on the table. "Would you like any coffee? I made a fresh pot a couple of hours ago."

"Please," Freddie said as he sat down.

David went to the breakroom and poured coffee into two plain white mugs. He then returned to the conference room and set down Freddie's cup on top of a coaster. "Here you go."

Freddie was so engrossed in the crime scene photos he failed to notice the coffee. For a few minutes, he studied the forensic report and the corresponding images while David patiently sat and waited.

While still staring at the photos, Freddie said, "Alright … Need to figure out if Simpson was sitting upright when he was shot. We could then figure out the shooter's height from the position of Simpson's head and the angle of the shots. Best guess, probably not slouching at all. I'd pay close attention and sit upright if someone pointed a gun at me. Hold on." Freddie turned his head towards David. "Did the autopsy report mention Simpson having any back issues?"

"Not that I recall."

"Okay, and the killer had his full attention." Freddie turned back to the photos and then closed his eyes. "Yeah … Upright and wasn't leaning towards the killer. Only a complete fool would get closer to someone pointing a gun at him … Assuming the killer took a proper shooting stance with the knees bent …" Freddie opened his eyes and again looked at David. "Just an educated guess, no promises, right?"

"Right."

"The shooter was short, probably five-three or five-four. Five-five, maybe. Definitely no taller than that. How tall is Amanda?"

David groaned. "Five-four. What if a taller person, say five-ten or so, held the gun lower? You know, with one arm or both bent at the elbow?"

Freddie gave a slight nod. "Get it and not likely. Simpson's head started to drop right after the shot, which meant the second one had to follow very quickly. If the shooter's arm was bent, it would've been difficult to manage the recoil and fire again accurately. Also, doesn't make much sense to shoot that way."

"What about a taller person sitting down in a chair?"

"Anything's possible, but it would've been awkward. The shooter would've needed to move the chair really close to Simpson so he could fire into the pillow. Who'd do that?"

"What about a taller person crouching down and holding his arms straight out?"

"Yeah. See where you're going," Freddie said. "Again, anything's possible, but why crouch? Would've been more difficult to fire the gun. Maybe someone would do it to disguise his height, yet who'd think of it? Doubt even a pro would. In all my years as a cop and a private investigator, never heard of that one. Based upon what I see, the killer was between five-three and five-five. Sorry, got to call them as I see them."

David sighed. "Yeah, I know. Even so, the murderer could've been a short contract killer."

"Could be. Didn't anyone at NYPD take a guess as the shooter's height?"

"Yeah," David said with a certain amount of disappointment. "Their expert said five-four, give or take."

"If you want to be sure, you could hire your own expert. Can the client afford it?"

"I thought about hiring one … I don't know. It might not be worthwhile. Amanda's parents are paying the legal bills. They act like money isn't a problem, but something's fishy."

"Oh?"

"They have money in the bank, but it's not an endless supply. Get this. They're paying me in cash, and like I said, the police questioned Paul about any mob ties. See why I want you to investigate him?"

Freddie casually pointed at him. "Got it. Anything else?"

David glanced at the boxes with the phone records. "Since you asked, there's one more thing. Someone needs to review the phone records for anything suspicious or unusual." He gestured toward those boxes. "They have the phone records for Simpson, Amanda, and her parents. I feel a little guilty dumping it on someone else, but I'd rather not do it. Do you know someone who likes to wade through a lot of numbers?"

Freddie grinned. "That would be me."

David was caught off guard. "Really?"

"Hey, why not? Know it's tedious, but have you ever been on a stakeout at night in the middle of winter? Shoot. Going through phone records is nothing."

"Sounds good. You're hired again."

AFTER FREDDIE DEPARTED, David needed a break from the Morelli case and turned his attention to other matters. About thirty minutes later, Beverly Cohen arrived at his office door. Her short white hair and glasses with white rims blended together. "New glasses?" he asked.

"No, these are my back-up pair," Bev said in her usual stoic manner. "I accidentally scratched a lens on my other one, and I should have a replacement lens in a few days."

"Okay. What's new? I didn't expect to see you today."

"I finished my errands and decided to work for a couple of hours. I also wanted to drop off Stanley's analysis of the victim's financial situation. Here's his report and his bill." She laid a manila folder on his desk.

"Stanley went through the records already?"

"Yes, he was here last weekend. As you know, we'll be out of town next week to visit old friends and attend a wedding. Stanley didn't want to wait until after we returned."

"You know, this means I missed another opportunity to meet your husband."

"Apparently so," Bev said with a flat affect. "I read Stanley's report, and here's the *Reader's Digest* version. Stanley found nothing terribly unusual. Simpson owned two homes, one in the city and one on Long Island, but not in the Hamptons. Financially speaking, he was doing fairly well. He had a mortgage on the Long Island house, and the other he owned free and clear. You already know about the yacht. Simpson made substantial alimony payments to his second ex-wife and had manageable credit card debt, at least manageable for his income."

"Okay. Any evidence of debts to a bookie or loan shark?"

"Stanley found no reason to suspect an unconventional loan, so to speak. Simpson had expensive tastes in clothes, shoes, and liquor. He owned two Mercedes with no outstanding loans and used his credit cards at the better restaurants. Bottom line, he could handle all his expenses without much difficulty. He didn't have a retirement account, which was rather foolish. Obviously, it doesn't matter anymore."

"Yeah, obviously. Stanley didn't have any concerns, nothing at all?"

"I'm sorry to disappoint you, but there was nothing out of the ordinary."

David sighed. "Alright. Please give your husband my thanks."

"He was happy to assist, and your prompt payment of his bill will be thanks enough."

CHAPTER 11

Thursday, October 1

F OLLOWING A HEARING in federal court, David once again buried himself in the discovery for the Morelli case. After about one hour, he read one document and shouted, "Shit!" while slamming his right hand onto the conference room table. He immediately regretted what he did and checked the glass top for any cracks. Upon finding none, he breathed a sigh of relief.

David then realized he had left the conference room door open. He peered towards the reception desk and saw Irene, Bev, Marc, and his wife, Stephanie, standing next to it and staring at him. Bev's frown lines were evident, while Irene had her hands on her hips and a scowl on her face. On the other hand, Steph and Marc were trying to contain their laughter. David ambled towards the front desk and could not avoid noticing Steph's long strawberry blonde hair and the Yankees baseball cap covering Marc's bald head.

"That was some greeting," Marc said. "It's nice to see you too."

"Sorry about that. I was reviewing discovery and reacted to something I just read. You're looking better. Gained a little weight?"

"Good news," Steph chimed in. "We just came from the doctor. He said Marc can start working part-time next week, maybe a few hours a day."

Marc gave a wink. "That's right, but we'll need to keep Nerf basketball on hold. So, what's with the profanity?"

"I'll show you."

Marc and Bev followed David to the conference room, and once they sat down, David supplied an explanation.

"Okay, Jacqueline told us about the 'Let's kill him' email, and there's more to it. Take a look." He turned a paper around for their benefit.

Morelli, Amanda

From: Valerie Fernandez
Sent: June 15, 2009 2:08:32 PM
To: Amanda Morelli
Subject: Re: Big Bastard

Sure

On Mon, 15 June 2009, at 14:08:05, Morelli, Amanda wrote:

Discuss over drinks and dinner?

From: Valerie Fernandez
Sent: June 15, 2009 2:07:21 PM
To: Amanda Morelli
Subject: Re: Big Bastard

Are you serious?

On Mon, 15 June 2009, at 14:06:49, Morelli, Amanda wrote:

Let's kill him.

Marc shrugged. "What's the big deal? We already knew about it."

David held up his right hand with a gesture indicating stop. "Wait, there's more. You need to read one of the detective's reports." He paused for a moment. "On second thought, I'll tell you what's in it. After work, Amanda and Valerie went to a restaurant a short distance from their law firm and sat at a table near the bar. The place wasn't busy, and the bartender overheard almost their entire conversation. According to him, Amanda and Valerie plotted how to kill Big Bastard, and they weren't joking, for the most part. They imagined many ways to kill him, such as throwing him off a roof, stabbing him, poisoning him, and so on. Take a guess at which method they finally chose."

"Shooting him," Bev said with an eyebrow raised.

"And …"

"Twice in the head."

"Exactly! Thus, the expletive."

Marc turned his head towards Bev. "Is this the part where you say *oy veh*?"

Bev did not react and instead addressed David. "Time to have a little chat with Amanda?"

"That's what I was thinking. I'll call her right now."

"Wait a minute," Bev said. "Wouldn't it be better to wait until you're a little less emotional?"

David waved his right hand. "No, I'm fine. I can keep it under control. Besides, I won't mention the email and what happened later. I'll only ask her to come to the office to discuss a few matters."

David called Amanda on his cell phone and put it on speaker. After three rings, she answered.

"Hello."

"Hey, Amanda. It's David. I've been going over the discovery, and we need to chat about a couple of things. Can you come to the office, say sometime tomorrow morning?"

"Um, not really … Mom, Dad, and I are in Charleston, South Carolina right now."

David's eyes bugged out as he mouthed, "What the hell?"

Marc raised his eyebrows and his hands, while Bev appeared unfazed.

Over the phone, David calmly said, "Charleston? What are you doing there?"

"Mom always wanted to visit Charleston and Savannah. We're going there next."

David frowned and shook his head. He also thought if he were an older man, this family would give him a heart attack. "As part of the terms of your release from jail, you're not supposed to leave the state or even the city."

"Oh … we didn't think it was a big deal. We're flying back on Monday. How about I come by Tuesday at three?"

David sighed. "Fine. See you then. Bye."

"I'm sorry. Bye."

Marc slumped in his chair. "It looks like we'll have to wait until Tuesday for some answers."

"I don't think so," David said. "Her little friend was also at the restaurant. Time to call her?"

Bev gave a slight wave, which indicated her approval.

David called Valerie Fernandez and again put it on speaker. "Hi, Valerie. It's David Lee. Can you talk right now?"

"Not really," she said politely but firmly. "I'm at work. You know how it is."

"Yeah, I do. Any time tomorrow good for you?"

"No. Friday's bad too. Working all day. Sorry."

"Okay. Can you come by my office this Sunday afternoon, maybe around two?"

"I … think I'm available. What are we going to talk about?"

David inhaled and glanced at Bev. "Well, we need to discuss what happened during the week of the murder, including the 'Let's kill him' email and what you and Amanda later discussed at the restaurant."

"Oh … yeah … that," Valerie uttered. "I'll be there."

"Okay, bye."

David shook his head. "Did you hear that? 'Oh yeah, that.' Hey, not a big deal, just an itty-bitty detail that helped get Amanda indicted."

"I know it's bad," Marc said as he leaned forward and put his hands on the conference room table. "But don't think about it too much. We'll get some answers on Sunday. The doc said I can start working next week, and Sunday's next week. We can even wear matching underwear as a sign of mutual support."

Marc's comment somewhat amused him. "I'll pass on the underwear thing. Beverly, I believe you'll be out of town?"

"Correct. We're leaving Sunday morning. Now, if you don't mind, there's another matter needing my attention."

AFTER MARC AND Steph left, David continued to review the discovery for the Morelli case until well into the evening. He specifically read about two dozen files concerning some of the attorneys and paralegals at the Thorton law firm. During their initial interviews, NYPD detectives had asked them to provide their locations at the time of the murder and state whether they had owned or used any firearms.

One report had a summary of Amanda's answers. She had disclosed when she was growing up and, on several occasions, her father had taken the family to "a good buddy's" two-story cabin in upstate New York. The cabin had been in a wooded area and had been stocked with rifles, shotguns, and handguns. Her father's friend taught her and her immediate family how to shoot them. While Amanda found firing a .22-caliber rifle to be tolerable, she hated the shotguns and more powerful rifles. She also learned how to use various types of handguns, including a .38 revolver, the same caliber as the murder weapon. She never enjoyed these family outings and believed she was too young to object.

Detectives had also asked Amanda whether her parents ever owned any firearms. She had acknowledged her father had owned a .38 revolver and had kept it in the house for protection. As an adult, Amanda disliked firearms even more than when she was a child, and as her parents grew older, she became more concerned about the revolver in their home. She feared one day there could be a tragic accident. About three to four years beforehand, she repeatedly asked her father to get rid of the gun, and he finally relented. Amanda did not remember what happened to the revolver and did not care. She was simply relieved it was out of the house.

During another interview, Amanda had told a detective she did not own any firearms, and two weeks later, the police had searched her apartment. In a back corner of her bedroom closet, the police had found a .22-caliber pistol inside a gun case. Since the pistol was clearly not the murder weapon, the police did not seize it and instead took photos of the closet, the case, and the pistol. The detectives never informed Amanda they found the pistol or asked follow-up questions about it.

David then discovered more damaging statements. Amanda told the police she had worked on the Bennington case and had interacted with Simpson regularly. According to one detective's report, she had said she never went into Simpson's office and tried to avoid him as much as possible. On the other hand, a forensic report said a fingerprint found on the lower right corner of Simpson's desk matched her right thumbprint. David compared the two fingerprints, which had been copied into the report, and they indeed appeared identical.

The police had questioned everyone at the Thorton firm about their opinions of Simpson. The women's responses had ranged from reluctant admissions of disapproval to outright disgust. Valerie's blunt answer came as no surprise. Amanda provided a much different point of view when she said, "He wasn't so bad." David imagined according to the police, Amanda had lied given she had been the author of the "Let's kill him" email. However, no one asked her to further explain her opinion.

David read another police report concerning an interview with Leslie Van Martin, who worked for the EEOC. Exactly two weeks before the murder, Amanda had visited the local EEOC office to file a complaint against Simpson for sexual harassment and creating a hostile work environment. Van Martin remembered Amanda calling him Big Bastard and saying he would be "better off dead." She explained the lengthy EEOC process, which frustrated Amanda. The next day, Van Martin started a two-week cruise. After she returned to the office, she caught up on the latest gossip, including the murder of an attorney, which the news had mentioned. She put "two and two together" and called NYPD.

Amanda's statements to the police irritated David because he did not believe any potential suspect should be so forthcoming without counsel. Even an innocent person's statement could create an unfavorable impression on a jury. Upon further reflection, David thought there could be a silver lining. He could turn her cooperation into an advantage at trial by arguing she had spoken freely with the police as she had nothing to hide.

Later in the evening, David realized he was tired and had read enough for one day. He considered calling Marc and Steph to determine if they were available for dinner. Before doing so, he glanced at his watch and discovered he had worked past eleven o'clock. He chuckled to himself and recalled it had been months since he had worked so diligently that he forgot to eat dinner.

CHAPTER 12

Sunday, October 4

DAVID WAS ASLEEP when his phone rang. After the third one, he answered.

"Hello?"

"Hi, it's me!" his sister Courtney said excitedly. "What time is it? 1:30, oops. Sorry about that. Were you asleep?"

David yawned. "Yeah, but it's okay. Why'd you call? Is something wrong?"

She gave a little laugh. "No, no, nothing like that. Earlier this evening, or I guess yesterday, I did it. I did it!"

"Did what?"

"I proposed to Chris, and he said yes!"

David became fully alert. "Wow! Congratulations! When's the wedding?"

"No date yet. You won't believe what else happened?"

"I don't know. You're going to appear on *Jeopardy*?"

Courtney laughed again. "That would be fun, but I've got better news. Last Friday, when was that? Oh yeah, two days ago, Peabody sweetened their offer. I can also teach so long as they come first. I won't be able to join a prestigious out-of-state university, well, out of most states, and I might be restricted to an adjunct professor position, but how can I pass up Peabody's offer? That gave me the push to propose to Chris. Now I can stay in the city, get married, and work for one, maybe two great employers! I can't tell you how happy I am right now!"

"That's great, really great!"

"Any ideas where to go on a honeymoon?"

David ran his fingers through his hair. "I don't know. How about Paris or the south of France?"

"Maybe, maybe. Both are excellent choices. When can we get together? I want you to meet Chris. Are you available for lunch tomorrow, I mean today?"

"Sorry, I can't make it because I have a date. We'll get together real soon. Promise."

"Okay. See you soon. Bye."

David was truly happy for his sister and wanted the best for her but also noted his *younger* sister would marry first, which did not sit well. He made a quick assessment of his own life. He was dating Eileen, the flight attendant from Air Canada, and their relationship was not serious. Over the past few weeks, he had a few first dates, which did not lead to second ones.

David flashed back to a recent afternoon when he had seen an elderly couple holding hands. Their body language spoke volumes about their devotion to each other, and they cared for each other in the same way as Amanda's parents. These long-lasting relationships contrasted with the lives some of his friends, who had been married and divorced within a few years. He wondered if he would ever get married, and if so, whether it would last until "death do us part."

ON SUNDAY AFTERNOON, David found Marc in the conference room, reviewing documents for the Morelli case. Marc had planted an elbow firmly on the table, and his chin rested in his hand. He again wore a Yankees cap to hide his bald head and missing eyebrows.

"So, what do you think?"

Marc let out an exaggerated exhale. "It's a lot to take in. I read your summary of Amanda's statements to the police. I've had better news. How was your lunch date with Eileen?"

"Terrific," David said with a half-frown. "She's quitting her job to become a wedding coordinator in Toronto."

Marc's eyes got wide. "Are you serious?"

"Yeah. She became a flight attendant to see the world and no longer wants to live her life out of a suitcase. She's going into business with her sister."

"Sorry about that. Are you disappointed?"

David glanced up and flicked his right hand. "To some extent, I guess. We were never that serious, but we had some fun."

"Yeah, I get it."

"Now, let's move onto another pleasant subject. Have you seen the crime scene photos?"

Marc chuckled. "That's pleasant? Sometimes you're worse than me. Sure, let's take a look."

While Marc examined the photos, David gave a running commentary. Just as they reached the autopsy photos, David heard the front door open.

Valerie Fernandez arrived in a Mets T-shirt and had pulled her long, wavy black hair into a loose ponytail. Marc put away the graphic images while David stepped out to greet her.

"Thanks for coming," he said. "We'll chat in the conference room."

"Fine with me."

A few steps later, David said, "Valerie, this is my law partner, Marc D'Angelo."

"Nice to meet you. Sorry for the way I look," Marc stated sheepishly.

"You should be," Valerie deadpanned. "Your Yankees cap is really offensive."

David unsuccessfully tried to hold his laughter.

Marc first dropped his jaw in disbelief and then chuckled. "Tough. The cap stays. I meant the way I look. I recently went through chemo."

"Amanda told me about it," Valerie said. "You don't look too bad. A friend of mine dealt with it a few years ago, which means I sort of know what you've been going through."

David held out his right arm with the palm facing up. "Please have a seat."

Valerie took the chair closest to her, while David and Marc sat on the opposite side of the glass-top table. David also grabbed a pen lying on top of a notepad.

Valerie said, "Before you called, I knew Amanda was out of town. I guess you couldn't wait for some answers."

David nodded. "Something like that. So, let's go back to the Monday before the murder. What happened that day and why did Amanda send the 'Let's kill him' email?"

Valerie exhaled and gazed at the blank television screen in the conference room, as if she could use it to view images in her memory. "Let's see. Monday was like every other day, which meant Simpson was being an a-hole.

Amanda and I were assigned to Bennington, which meant constant exposure to him. I can think of better things to do than dealing with him, like getting a cavity filled without Novocain. You know what I mean?"

"So, what happened?" David asked. "Please start with Monday morning."

"Nothing much, just the usual work. Amanda and I went to lunch at a coffee shop, and we complained about work, again. We wanted to find something else, but the job market stunk, and I couldn't quit. My son's a junior in college, and my daughter started this semester. They have scholarships, but there are other expenses."

"Okay," Marc said. "What happened after lunch?"

Valerie's mood darkened, and she folded her arms. "Big Bastard was in Amanda's office. I couldn't hear their conversation because the door was closed, but I could see them. Obviously, Amanda was not enjoying herself, and after he left, she made this face. At first, I thought maybe she was ticked off at another crude comment. I sort of said, 'What's going on?' without actually saying it." Valerie perked up. "Then Amanda sent me the email about killing him. It was really funny."

Neither the email nor Valerie's comment amused David. "What happened at dinner? Did the two of you really plot to kill him?"

"Yes and no," Valerie said with a smile that almost appeared as a grimace. "We were only blowing off steam. Come on, Amanda's not a violent person. I guess I've had my moments, but I never wanted to kill anyone, not even him."

"The bartender thought you were serious."

"We weren't laughing that much, but we weren't being serious. I guess he overheard us, and we didn't care. Maybe it was the alcohol, even though I only had a couple of glasses of wine. Same for Amanda."

David stopped taking notes and considered what he just heard. Valerie's version of events seemed plausible, and he wondered what a juror would believe. "What happened Tuesday and Wednesday at work?"

Valerie twisted her mouth for a moment and continued to cross her arms. "Same old stuff. Probably a crude comment or two from Big Bastard. I think Amanda's mother came by for lunch on Tuesday." She glanced sideways and pursed her lips. "Or was it Wednesday? Not sure. Nothing unusual about that."

David scribbled a few notes. "Anything unusual happen on Thursday, the day of the murder?"

"The morning was the same as always. Amanda and I brown-bagged it for lunch. Around two, Amanda said she wasn't feeling good, and she was holding her stomach. Maybe it was something she ate. She then left the office." Valerie shrugged. "I think that was about it."

"Where were you that afternoon and evening?" Marc asked.

"At work the rest of the afternoon. Later, I called Amanda to see how she was doing. She didn't pick up, and I left a voicemail message. I went out to dinner with my mom and kids. The police asked for the receipt, and I gave it to them."

David had already read Amanda's version of what transpired on Thursday. Amanda had told a detective she went home mid-afternoon and had gone to bed early. She did not call anyone that evening, and no one could confirm she was in her apartment all night.

David inched forward in his chair and said, "Valerie, the murder took place late in the evening. Did anyone ever work late at Thorton?"

She shook her head. "Not most of the time. We came in early if we needed to put in any extra hours. That way we could still have the evenings with our families. A few times, I got in around six, and some people were already there. Several attorneys sometimes worked in the office on a Saturday. Of course, the hours got longer when we were preparing for trial, but we didn't have one pending last June."

David nodded and stopped taking notes. "Okay. What happened the day after the murder?"

"I got to work around … 8:20, I guess, and I saw the cops. I asked the receptionist what was going on, and she didn't say anything. She was completely out of it, you know. A couple of attorneys were talking to the cops in the conference room. Betty told me Simpson had been killed in his office. I was shocked and not sure what to think." Valerie again stared at the television screen. "I don't know why I tried to get a look, but the cops wouldn't let me get too close. I still saw the blood on the wall but not his body. I guess it'd been taken away before I showed up."

"Probably," David said. "A police report said you called Amanda that morning and told her about Simpson's death."

"Yeah," Valerie replied as she nodded. "I stepped into an attorney's office, closed the door, and called Amanda. I was a little freaked out. At first Amanda thought I was joking, and she also freaked out once the news sunk in."

Marc asked, "How are things at Thorton right now?"

Valerie offered a sour frown. "Still going down the drain. It looks like a handful of us will join another law firm … Harrison Day, I think. It's only going to be Caldwell, six other attorneys, and a few paralegals, including me. I think we're moving at the end of the month. Three junior partners kept some of Thorton's clients, and they're forming their own firm. Two paralegals might join them. Anyone who's left must fend for themselves. It's really sad, you know."

"Of course," David said. "So, you'll still work for Caldwell and have to deal with his attitude."

"Probably, but he's not so bad. You caught him on a bad day."

"What about Charles Thorton?"

Valerie shook her head. "Don't know. I haven't seen the Old Man for a long time. I feel really bad for him because none of this was his fault."

David pulled out two lists from a folder in front of him. "I got the first list when I visited you at the law firm, and it shows who worked at Thorton as of January 1, 2009. The firm gave the second list to the police, which was current as of June 2009, when the murder occurred." He handed Valerie the older list. "I highlighted the names of two people who were no longer with the firm by June. Do you know what happened to them?"

"This first one," Valerie said as she studied the list. "Jason ..." She looked in the air and then smiled. "Yeah, I remember him. Nice kid. He's one of the Old Man's nephews, and he took a semester off from college. He worked in the mailroom for a little while and then went back to school."

"So, he was long gone by the time Simpson arrived?"

"Yeah, lucky him."

"What about the other one, Donna Conway?"

"Donna ... Donna ..." Valerie gazed at the ceiling for a couple of moments and then looked at David. "I kind of remember her. She wasn't with the firm for very long. I think she was Walter's friend from high school, maybe? Donna was a paralegal on the ninth floor, the one below me, and she was the last person hired before Big Bastard arrived. One day, she was just gone. I think something really bad happened. The senior partners were really quiet about it, and no one gave me the details."

David smiled. "Okay, that's it for me. Marc, do you have any questions?"

"Nope."

"Alright. Thanks a lot for stopping by."

"Not a problem," Valerie said. "If you need anything else, just let me know." She smiled as she rose from her chair.

David noticed her dimples and wondered why he had not previously seen them. Then he realized there was nothing to smile about when they first met.

AFTER VALERIE LEFT the office, David said, "Hey Marc. I don't think the police interviewed Jason and Donna. Maybe they never knew about them. I don't care about Jason, but Donna's another matter."

Marc smirked. "No kidding. I'd like to know why Donna left the firm. Maybe she was a malcontent or had a drug problem."

David checked the table of contents Jacqueline had provided with the discovery. "Just as I thought. There's no mention of the police interviewing Donna Conway." He then examined the tabs for the files concerning Thorton's paralegals. "No file on her either. Bill Saxer can probably tell us what happened to Donna. I'd also like to know how the police got copies of the firm's emails."

"So would I," Marc muttered.

David called Saxer and put it on speaker. "Bill, it's David. I'm in the office with my law partner, Marc, and we have a few more questions. Is this a good time?"

"Sure, go ahead," Saxer said in an agreeable tone. "I've got a few minutes."

"Okay. As part of discovery, we received a stack of Thorton's emails. How'd the police get them?"

"We made an arrangement. NYPD paid for an attorney to review the firm's emails from the month before the murder to the week afterwards. The attorney acted like a special master and never disclosed most emails. He only printed the ones that were non-privileged and non-work product. He also withheld emails concerning personal matters between family members. It took him some time to review all of it."

David shook his head, and Marc whispered, "What the hell?" David would have never allowed the police to go through his firm's emails without a court order.

He then asked, "Why did the firm agree to release any emails?"

"We already had financial difficulties, and we didn't want to lose any more clients. We wanted to show them we were fully cooperating with the police, within reason."

"Okay. Do you remember a paralegal by the name of Donna Conway?"

"Oh sure, she was Walter Bennett's friend. I think they grew up in the same neighborhood. Donna enlisted in the Air Force, and I heard something happened while she was serving overseas. I don't know any of the details. After she was discharged, Walter asked the Old Man to hire her."

"Why'd she leave?"

"Oh, that … she had to leave."

David's eyes got wide. "You mean she was fired?"

"Uh … yes."

"What happened?"

"The senior partners wanted to keep it quiet. To make her termination a little less harsh, the Old Man gave her a generous severance package."

Saxer's evasiveness began to irritate David, who pressed for a more direct answer. "Come on, Bill. What happened?"

Saxer gave a heavy sigh. "Okay, okay. According to Simpson, Donna threatened to slit his throat."

David's mouth dropped open, and he noticed Marc jumped back in his chair. "Was that true?"

"Probably. Donna was in Simpson's office, and from a distance, I could tell they were having a heated argument. Donna made some gesture, which I couldn't see clearly. Right after she stormed out, I walked into Simpson's office and asked him what happened. He was furious and cursed out Donna. He said she made a death threat with a slashing gesture across her throat. When I asked Donna about it, she didn't confirm it, but she didn't deny it either."

The wheels in David's head spun, and he realized the police missed a viable suspect. He thought this could be significant, in fact very significant, even a game changer.

"When did the death threat happen?" he asked.

"Mid-May, I believe."

"Did the police ever ask you about Donna?"

"Well ... I don't think so ... Oh, wow, do you think –"

"Maybe, but let's not jump to conclusions," David said. "By the way, how tall is Donna?"

"Five-four or five-five. Why do you ask?"

"Just curious."

"So, Donna could've done it? It never dawned on me."

David rolled his eyes. "Don't dwell on it, and don't get carried away. We'll look into it and notify the other side if necessary. That's it for now, and thanks for your time."

"You're welcome," Saxer replied in an awkward tone.

After David hung up, he and Marc stared at each other for a few moments.

"Holy crap!" Marc eventually said. "Donna Conway's about five-four, the same height as the killer, and she made a death threat! Wouldn't it be great to spring those nice little tidbits during trial?"

David cocked his head. "Or?"

"Yeah, yeah, I know," Marc said with his hands raised in the surrender position. "We investigate, and maybe Amanda doesn't have to go to trial. Time to call Freddie?"

"Yup. I'll ask him to make finding Donna his top priority. Do you want the pleasure of reviewing all the Thorton emails? I haven't gone through them yet."

"Sure. Let me have all the fun," Marc said sarcastically. "I'll get started tomorrow afternoon and flag any containing negative comments about Big Bobby. As compensation, you need to bring me Chinese takeout for lunch."

David scoffed. "Not that crummy soup again? I'm embarrassed to even order that dreck. Geez, can't I introduce you to some real Chinese food? You know, authentic Chinese that tastes great?"

Marc feigned being hurt. "Would you deny a poor man recovering from leukemia his favorite comfort food? You're cruel and heartless."

David chuckled. "And you're a pain in the ass. Fine. I'll get the crummy soup."

CHAPTER 13

Tuesday and Wednesday, October 6 and 7

D AVID ARRIVED AT the office just after 9:30 in the morning. "Look what the cat dragged in, finally," Irene said while sitting at her desk.

He clenched his jaw and stepped about five feet past her, then stopped and spun around. Irene apparently sensed it and swiveled in her chair to look at him face-to-face. He stared at her and wanted to wipe off her smug expression.

"Let's get something straight," he barked. "This is my firm, not yours. I can come and go as I please. So what if I arrived late today. I sometimes work late and on the weekends, and I carry my own load plus some of Marc's. I *don't* want to hear any more nasty, little comments coming out of your mouth. Do I make myself perfectly clear?"

Irene bowed her head and looked at the floor. "I was just having –"

"Having what, a little fun at my expense? Keep your crack comments to yourself."

Before she said anything else, David marched to his office. For the next thirty minutes, he worked on matters unrelated to Amanda Morelli, which gave him sufficient time to cool down. Then Marc appeared at his office door. David noticed his complexion had returned to normal and also spotted stubble on top of his head and where his eyebrows would grow back.

"How'd last night go?" Marc asked.

"How'd what go?"

"Hello! Didn't you have dinner last night with your sister and your future brother-in-law?"

David chuckled. "Sorry about that. It slipped my mind. Dinner went fine."

"Fine? That's it? No details? What'd you think of Chris?"

"Well … he seems like a good guy. I couldn't find any faults with him."

"And that's why you hate him."

"Exactly," David said with a grin.

AT THREE O'CLOCK, a notice flashed on David's computer, reminding him of his meeting with Amanda. By 3:15, she had not arrived. Since late arrivals were uncharacteristic of the Morelli family, David was somewhat concerned. He placed a call to Amanda's cell phone, and she answered after the fourth ring.

"Amanda, this is David. I thought you were coming to the office at three."

"Oh … right," she said as her voice cracked. "I'm, I'm sorry. Uh, I forgot." She sniffled and made a shallow cough.

"Hey, what's going on?"

"I, I can't talk right now. I'll call you tomorrow. Promise." Amanda broke off the call.

David did not know what to think. Perhaps a family member was seriously ill, or there had been a death in the family, and he hoped neither scenario was correct. David considered calling Valerie, but she might not have an answer. If that were the case, Valerie could become upset with Amanda for not reaching out to her, and David did not want to create friction between friends. He instead walked over to Marc's office, who was sitting behind his desk.

"Hey, David. I thought Amanda was coming this afternoon."

"So did I. Something's up. I called her, and she seemed really upset. She said she'll call tomorrow."

"That's weird."

"Yeah, I know," David said while still perplexed. "Anyway, I wanted to talk to you about something else. Any interesting emails from Amanda's old firm?"

"I haven't read all of them yet, but I've got the general idea. Even though no one else threatened to kill Simpson, it's really obvious he wasn't well loved. I set aside a few of the more notable comments. Get this. One paralegal called Big Bobby's death 'a gift from Heaven.'"

"Yeah," David said with a shrug. "It doesn't surprise me."

Marc leaned forward. "I found something else. Some emails reference a female attorney who was secretly organizing the women at the law firm. They didn't mention her by name, but I know the mystery woman was scheduled to meet with Old Man Thorton on Friday, the day after the murder."

"Any indication Valerie or Amanda knew about this secret group?"

Marc shook his head. "Not that I can tell. You know, this creates another issue for us. Jacqueline can show there were other options besides blowing away Big Bobby."

David crossed his arms. "Yeah, maybe. Someone must've identified her, and it should be somewhere in the discovery."

"I suppose you want me to go through all that?"

"Well, not just you. We need to figure out why the police eliminated everyone else as a suspect."

Marc let out an exaggerated, fake sigh. "Yeah, okay. I'll get to it."

EARLY WEDNESDAY MORNING, David finished breakfast and got ready for a meeting with a client who was housed at the federal jail in Brooklyn. Prior to leaving his apartment, his cell phone rang.

"Hi, it's Amanda. I'm really sorry about hanging up yesterday."

"No need to apologize. Is something wrong?"

"Yeah. Mom had a really bad accident and needed surgery."

David's mouth dropped open. "What happened?"

"We were in Savannah, and Mom tripped while walking down a flight of stairs. She came down hard on her left wrist and fractured it along with doing other damage. You could tell right away she was badly hurt."

He grimaced while an image of what occurred flashed in his head. "That's terrible. What were the extent of her injuries?"

"They told us at the local hospital. I was kind of freaking out and don't remember what they said. You can ask Dad about it. Of course, he stayed calm and asked the doctors a bunch of questions. Nothing rattles him. He kept reassuring me and Mom everything would be fine."

"Is she going to be okay?" he asked while putting his left hand on his head.

"She should fully recover, but it didn't seem that way at first. The doctors said Mom needed a hand specialist to operate on her immediately. So, they flew her to another hospital in Jacksonville. The surgery went fine, and she'll need another one once the swelling subsides. Mom told the doctors she'd been having pain in her left shoulder for about a month, and she thought it was arthritis. Turns out she has a partially torn rotator cuff, and we don't know how that happened. It can be repaired arthroscopically, which isn't as big of a deal. She's also going to need physical therapy for her wrist and shoulder."

David had difficulty processing a simple fall required emergency surgery, even though he knew stranger things have occurred. "Sounds like a long road to full recovery. Has your mom had any similar accidents?"

"Oh no, not even close. Mom's known for being scatterbrained, not a klutz. Anyway, I'm moving out of my apartment and back home to help out. Until Mom's wrist gets better, I'll do the cooking. Dad in the kitchen is maybe the one thing that could put a strain on their marriage. At least I won't feel guilty anymore over Dad paying my rent."

David was not certain what to say and remained silent.

"Do you want me to come to your office? We're still in Jacksonville, and we'll be back home in a couple of days."

"Are you sure?"

"Yeah, I guess so."

"Then why don't you …" David stopped himself. He needed answers regarding his client's statements to the police but could put the issue on a back burner for a while. "Never mind. It can wait. Go ahead and take care of your move and your mom. We'll talk later. Until then, I'll keep giving you and your dad updates over the phone and by email, okay?"

"Okay, thanks."

CHAPTER 14

Tuesday, October 13

DAVID WAS PLEASED to see Bev in the office and noticed she once again wore her usual stylish glasses instead of the ones with white rims.

"How was your vacation?" he asked.

"Stanley and I enjoyed ourselves, and it's always good to visit old friends. The wedding was tasteful and elegant, but the food at the reception was a disappointment."

"Well, overall, it was a pleasant trip. What's the status of your workload?"

"Thompson will be wrapped up in a couple of weeks. Same with the others except Nakahara, and we still anticipate an arrest. I assume you want me to start working on Morelli."

David gave a wry smile. "Am I that transparent? Marc and I've gone through some of the discovery. This week, he's reviewing all the documents concerning the law firm's employees. Could you give him a hand?"

"That's why I'm here," Bev said with no emotion.

"Marc's not yet 100 percent, and he's only working in the afternoons Monday through Thursday. Could you switch your hours from mostly mornings to mostly afternoons? That way, you and Marc can better coordinate your efforts."

"Can do except for a day here and there."

"Sounds good."

LATER IN THE day, David reviewed materials concerning another rich kid with more than a drug problem. The police and the district attorney's office claimed he had been dealing ecstasy on campus. While he had his head buried in paperwork, he heard a familiar baritone voice state, "Greetings."

David grinned, picked up his head, and saw Freddie Ferguson casting a wide smile. "Hey, how are you doing?"

"Very well and having an excellent day. Thanks for asking. Stopped by to drop off three reports. Got a few minutes to discuss?"

"Of course. Please sit down," David said as he held out his arm.

Freddie set the files on the desk and parked himself in a guest chair. "Before we get started on anything else, Helen wanted to know if you, Marc, and Bev can join us for our annual Christmas celebration on Sunday, December 20."

"I know I'm available but don't know about Bev and Marc. I'll find out."

Freddie nodded. "Alright."

"Why are invites going out so early? It's just a dinner party, right?"

Freddie chuckled. "Oh, no, not this time. Helen and her friends are making it a big deal this year, renting a hall and what not. They need a head count pretty early."

David leaned back and crossed his legs. "Sounds like fun. Anything I should bring?"

"Nah. Just be ready for a fun time with family and friends."

"Not a problem, but you're not here to deliver an invitation. I suspect your reports are the black and white version, which we'll turn over to the DA's office. You're about to give me the color commentary?"

Freddie chuckled in a register lower than his normal voice. "You know me a little too well."

David laughed and wished he and Freddie got together on social occasions more often.

Freddie rubbed his hands together. "Okay, let's get started. Simpson was first married to Nancy Hammond. I met her and her second husband, Brian, at their home in Westchester County. They're great people, a genuine pleasure. Nancy's the manager of the Crate & Barrel store in White Plains, and –"

David perked up. "Nancy works at Crate & Barrel? I love that place!"

Freddie's amiable demeanor disappeared. "Are you really going there?" His right hand brushed across his shaved head. "Another one of those. Next time Helen wants to go, you can take my place."

David chuckled. "Sounds good to me. Getting back to Nancy."

"Yeah. She married Simpson right after college. After he graduated from law school, they moved to New York. Nancy saw him slowly change for the worse, becoming increasingly obsessed with making money. Also, he started making inappropriate comments about women. Nancy disliked the man he became, but he was the one who filed for divorce. During the middle of it, Nancy met her current husband. Years ago, she regretted marrying Simpson. Now she believes without first marrying him, her life would've taken a different course, and she might've never met her 'soulmate,'" Freddie said while making air quotes.

"Okay. Was she ever a viable suspect?"

"No way. Nancy said she wasn't aware of her first husband's murder until the police contacted her. They hadn't spoken to each other in seven years. Nancy also said she worked on the day of the murder, and she gave me a copy of her pay statement. She also gave me a copy of a credit card statement, which had a charge for a restaurant in White Plains for that evening. Confirmed the place was only open for dinner on weekdays. Not enough time for her to pay the bill, get to Manhattan, and shoot Simpson, given his time of death." Freddie held out his arms. "Hey, anything's possible, but Nancy had no motive to kill him."

David tilted his head while leaning back in his chair. "Okay. What about Simpson's second ex-wife?"

Freddie shook his head. "Oh, you know the saying if you can't say anything nice, don't say anything at all?"

"Yeah?"

Freddie paused and then said, "I'm done."

David laughed and knew Simpson's second ex-wife was an awful person if Freddie did not care for her. He liked almost everyone.

Freddie chuckled at his own joke. "Man, got to laugh. She's absolutely horrible!"

"You got to meet her, and better you than me," he said with a smirk.

Freddie pointed at him. "Just for that, I'm telling Helen, and you might be disinvited to the Christmas party." He chuckled again.

"Why was she so horrible? What was her name, Victoria something?"

"Victoria Devereaux. Met her at her apartment, which set new standards for rich people throwing their money away on tacky and gaudy décor."

"Oh yeah?"

"Yeah. She was also arrogant and completely self-absorbed, bragged a designer created the outfit she was wearing just for her."

David grimaced. "How wonderful."

Freddie pointed to him. "That's one way to put it. Victoria said her marriage to Simpson lasted 'five long and difficult years.' Blamed him because he never fully catered to her needs. Simpson wrote the alimony checks, and she was upset the judge didn't make him pay more. At the time of the murder, Victoria was living with her boyfriend and refused to remarry so the alimony checks would continue to flow."

"What a piece of work!"

Freddie exhaled. "Tell me about it. Money's her only true love. Victoria said she was in her apartment during the murder. Tried to confirm it with the doorman, but he didn't remember. Victoria claimed she might've made a call or two from her home on that night. I asked to take a look at her phone records, and she refused to sign a release, very nasty about it too."

"Terrific," David uttered in disgust.

"Bottom line, don't believe Victoria killed Simpson or hired someone else to do it. She instead had a motive to keep him alive."

David nodded. "Makes sense. I imagine the third report concerns Simpson's prior law firms, the executives at Bennington, and so on."

"You got it."

"Did anyone give you a hard time?"

Freddie gave another wide smile. "Nah. Not after I told them who I was."

David chuckled. "You did it again, didn't you? In a slow and deliberate manner, you said, 'Hello, my name is Frederick … Douglass … Ferguson.'"

Freddie also chuckled.

"And when they didn't recognize the first two names, you politely made sure they caught a case of white guilt."

A QUESTION OF MURDER

Freddie continued to chuckle. "You know me too well."

"Yeah, and it's been a pleasure. Was there anything noteworthy regarding the lawyers and executives?"

"Nah," he said with a dismissive wave. "Just a bunch of mostly white people suing each other and no shady backgrounds. One disturbing thing, though. The executives at Bennington loved Simpson."

David's jaw dropped. "You're messing with me, right?"

"Nope. They thought he was a great lawyer for their company."

"Geez. Were all the executives men?"

"Guess what? One of them was a woman, and she sang praises of Simpson the most."

"What about all the sexual harassment?"

"Mentioned it, and they looked at me like I was some space alien who landed on Earth five minutes ago. They said he never did that stuff in front of them."

David shook his head. "So, he could behave himself but chose not to most of the time."

"Guess so. That's it for now. I'll get back to you in a couple of days about other stuff. We'll be getting together with Marc and Beverly for the meeting, right?"

"Yeah. Thanks for coming by, and please tell Helen I said hello."

"You got it my friend," Freddie said while casually pointing to David.

After Freddie departed, David strolled to the conference room to speak to Marc, who had documents and file folders spread over two-thirds of the glass-top table.

"Freddie was just here. As expected, we can't pin the murder on Simpson's ex-wives or former associates. How are things going with you?"

Marc exhaled through his nose. "Wading slowly through it all. I still don't have the drive or energy I had pre-leukemia, but I'm making progress.

119

So far, I've reviewed the files for about one-third of the attorneys and staff at Thorton, and I'm comparing their statements to their work emails. I'm also creating a spreadsheet and brief summaries to keep track of everyone."

"Okay. What have you determined so far?"

Marc shook his head. "What a bunch of bozos. Nearly all of them spoke to the police without counsel. One paralegal asked for a Thorton attorney to be present, which was a good idea, but not a great one, because they didn't practice criminal defense. One junior partner only spoke with the police in the presence of his criminal attorney. He already had a possession of cocaine conviction and was probably a little paranoid."

David smirked. "Yeah, maybe he was still snorting coke, which caused the paranoia. Anything else?"

"NYPD conducted background checks, asked everyone if they owned any firearms, and ran database checks for firearms registration. So far, I found six who owned guns. One attorney had owned a .38 revolver, and someone stole it about five years ago. We received a copy of the corresponding police report. Another attorney owned a .38. However, on the night of the murder, he was on vacation in California, and when he's here, he lives alone."

David frowned. "Any way we could point the finger at him?"

"Uh-uh. He's Mr. Clean. The detectives interviewed Old Man Thorton and inspected his firearms collection. He owned a variety of antique and modern weapons, which were on display at his home outside the city. The Old Man told the police since the onset of arthritis, he can't fire a gun and last held one about three years ago."

"Yeah … makes sense. Thorton's getting up in years."

"There's something else interesting about the Old Man. He said he was at his country home when the murder occurred, and his driver confirmed it. However, the driver didn't live on the property, and I doubt he stayed at Thorton's side night and day."

David was discouraged but not surprised. "Anything else interesting or noteworthy?"

"Yup. NYPD looked for evidence to back up alibis. Some people used their credit card around the time of the murder, and the location of their purchases put them too far away. Some made phone calls from their home phones, and others were simply home with family members. Having a loved one vouch for you isn't the most unbiased source, but it's better than nothing."

David frowned again. "I suppose so. Anyone without a concrete alibi?"

"Some had shaky ones, and for one reason or another, the police ruled them out. It's part of my summaries."

"Marc, any idea as to the mystery attorney's identity?"

"Two paralegals mentioned her to the police. It's Kelly Holcomb."

"What?" David said as he raised his eyebrows. "The former Cleveland Browns quarterback is now an attorney?"

Marc laughed a little. "No, it's a different Kelly Holcomb, and she's a woman. Then again, the former quarterback could've undergone a sex change operation. Want me to make a few phone calls to check on it?"

David smirked. "Let me get back to you on that. Anything else on her?"

"I haven't read Holcomb's file yet. I'm going through them in alphabetical order, and I'm finishing G."

"Alright. Keep wading through it."

CHAPTER 15

Monday, October 19

DURING THE MID-AFTERNOON, Frederick Ferguson returned, and from his office, David watched him give a pleasant greeting to Irene, who appeared to respond in kind. They also engaged in conversation, which David could not hear. Nevertheless, he surmised Freddie gave a compliment about her hair because she touched her gray shoulder-length locks. Irene then laughed at something. After Freddie and Irene chatted for about five minutes, David broke it up.

"Hey, Irene. It looks like there are no pressing matters for you. Why don't you take the rest of the afternoon off?"

"Huh?" she said with a quizzical expression.

"That's right. You can leave and still get paid for the entire day."

"Are you serious?"

"Of course. You mean you don't want to go home two hours early?"

"What? I mean yes," Irene said as her eyes brightened. Thanks." She placed a couple of items in her purse and hurried out the front door.

Once she left, Freddie chuckled. "That was fairly gracious of you. Perhaps I should work here too."

David smiled. "Not so generous of me. Think ulterior motive. You're here to talk about Paul Morelli, among other things, right?"

"That's right."

"I'd rather not have Irene around when you do. It's a long story."

"Whatever you say," Freddie said as he held up his hands.

"Before we get started, would you like some coffee?"

"No thanks. I'm good."

David gathered Marc, Bev, and Freddie in the conference room, and they took their seats. David noticed a large paper cup in Marc's right hand and detected the aroma of his latte. Bev brought a legal pad and pen, ready to take notes even though Freddie had always submitted written reports.

Freddie clapped his hands once. "Thought it'd be better to update you in person about Paul Morelli. So far, we've only got what's in the NYPD file. Reached out to my contacts in the department, and either they don't know anything, or they won't tell me. Best guess is the FBI never shared info on Paul, which is typical. Mike Stanton's a former partner on the force, and he knows a couple of FBI agents. Mike promised to contact them, but doubt he'll get answers. Haven't looked at Paul's phone records yet, and it'd probably be a waste of time. If he's connected, he won't be foolish enough to call a wise guy on his own phone. No pun intended."

David took the news in stride. "Okay, just keep looking, or have Mike keep looking. Do you have anything on Donna Conway, the paralegal who threatened to slit Simpson's throat?"

"Hey, about that." Freddie rubbed the back of his neck. "Sorry to tell you, haven't been able to contact Donna. Even in this day and age with everyone leaving a paper trail, no luck. It's not as if she vanished off the face of the Earth, but pretty close. Her last known address is an apartment in Brooklyn.

Spoke with the apartment manager, and he said she no longer lives there. Donna might be living with her parents in Philly. Three credit card companies and her cell phone company send bills to their address. Called her father, and he wasn't helpful, refused to tell me anything. Told me to contact their attorney and then rudely hung up."

Bev asked, "Did Donna's father provide the name of his attorney?"

"Yeah. Some guy in Philly."

Marc chimed in. "Should we tell the ADA about Donna and let the police track her down?"

David shook his head. "Let's talk to the Conways' attorney first. Anyone volunteer and possibly take a trip to the City of Brotherly Love?"

Bev briefly held up her right hand. "I'll do it. If the Conways will play ball, Stanley and I'll take the train to Philadelphia and visit with friends while we're there. I'll only bill the client for my round-trip train fare and one night's stay at a decent hotel. We'll cover our meals and local transportation. Approve?"

"How could I not?" David said. "Oh, Freddie, you don't mind, do you?"

He let out a wide smile. "Of course not! Do you have any idea how much business Beverly threw in my direction when she worked for her old firm? How could I possibly deprive her of a nice, little trip?"

Bev gave a nod of acknowledgment.

"Alright," David said. "Getting back to Freddie's to-do list. Except for further looking into Paul Morelli, what's left? Oh yes, building security, the videos, and the phone records."

"Right," Frederick stated. "I'll speak with security first and save the phone records for last, if you don't mind."

David snapped his fingers. "I almost forgot. There's one other thing. Eventually, you'll need to investigate the backgrounds of the detectives and other potential witnesses for the prosecution. You can put it on the bottom of the list, after the phone records. After all, at this point, we still don't know if we're going to trial."

CHAPTER 16

Tuesday, October 27

TWELVE DAYS LATER, David, Marc, and Bev again gathered in the conference room to hear Freddie's report about the O'Connell building, where the Law Offices of Thorton, Saxer & Caldwell had been located. He arrived with a long cardboard tube in his right hand. By this time, Marc's eyebrows had grown back, and he had a head full of short chestnut brown hair.

Before Freddie started, Marc blurted out, "Are you going to begin with a song? How about some Barry Manilow?"

Freddie appeared as if he had eaten the sourest pickle in the world. "Barry Manilow? Man, how bad is your taste in music? By the way, can't sing to save my life. If I could, you'd hear Al Jarreau or Otis Redding. Barry Manilow?"

"It was just a joke."

Freddie smiled. "And a terrible one."

"Gentlemen," Bev said. "May we please get started?"

Freddie nodded. "Right. Only asked for a copy of the first floor, and it's the most important one for today's discussion," he said as he opened the tube and removed architectural plans.

As Freddie rolled them out, Marc placed a book on each corner. All the markings on the plans were too much for David to absorb, and thus, he was glad someone could explain them to him.

"Okay," Freddie said. "As we can see here, the O'Connell building is a little longer going north and south than east to west. Streets run next to the east and west sides, and alleys run parallel on the other sides. The lobby is on the east side, and the parking garage entrance lies to the west. For the lobby," he said as he pointed to it, "there are two cameras. They were in place last June, when the murder happened, and there are no cameras anywhere on the building's exterior. In addition to the four elevators, there are interior staircases on each side of them." He motioned toward the middle of the drawing. "To enter these staircases on the ground floor, someone needs a key card to get in but not to get out."

David thought so far Freddie had provided no surprises.

"There are several law offices in the building. Since some attorneys work all kinds of crazy hours, security keeps a presence 24/7. Three guards are stationed in the lobby during the day and swing shifts. Only two cover the graveyard shift." Freddie shook his head. "Boy, hate to be on duty at three in the morning."

Marc chuckled. "No kidding. Do the guards patrol the higher floors?"

"Now they do but didn't last June. Near the entrance to the parking garage, another guard is stationed in this little booth." Freddie pointed to the location on the architectural plans. "It's right next to the driveway leading to parking on two lower levels. After the gate closes at seven p.m., a guard is stationed in the general area until it reopens at six a.m. When the gate's closed, someone needs a key card to open it, and that's how the cleaning crew gets in early in the morning. From the little booth, a guard should see everyone going to the parking garage, assuming he's paying attention, and a security camera records all entries by car."

"Okay," David said. "Let's get back to the elevators. I saw security cameras in them, both the regular ones and the freight elevator. Was that always the case?"

Freddie shook his head. "They were installed after the murder."

David made a half-frown. "That means back then, security wasn't aware of anyone's presence on any other floor, unless they patrolled the upper floors."

"Which they didn't at the time of the murder," Freddie added.

"When I was there, the freight elevator wouldn't work. I needed a key card, right?" David asked.

Freddie pointed at him. "You got it. Regardless of the time of day, it won't move without a key card, and it's been that way for years. You only need a card outside of normal business hours to use the regular elevators. Security told me the cards are programmed by floor. During the off hours, someone from Thorton could only access the parking garage, the first floor, and the two floors for the law firm."

Bev put down her notepad and asked, "Do you have anything else to report about the building? Perhaps other manners of entry and exit?"

Freddie smiled. "I was about to get to it. Let's examine the first floor's layout some more." He pointed to the top of the plans. "The north side has two fire exits near the northeast and northwest corners. The freight elevator is also near the northeast corner. Same thing for the south side, two fire exits and another freight elevator. No one can open the fire exit doors from the outside because there're no door handles, keyholes, or key card slots. Suppose someone can pry the door open with a crowbar, but building security and NYPD checked all the fire exits after the murder and found no evidence of tampering."

"What about the freight elevators?" Marc asked. "Can someone access them from the alleys?"

Freddie smiled and pointed at Marc. "Nice try, my friend. The freight elevators open on both sides. However, to access them from the street, someone first needs to roll up a large metal door. You can only open it from the inside manually or by pressing a button. Best guess, on the evening of the murder, someone left the building through a north side fire exit, but the police found no fingerprints on the inside door handle for either one."

Marc inquired, "Can anyone access the stairs leading to the fire exits from any floor?"

"I thought I told you about that," David said as he looked at Marc. "On the tenth floor, anyone can gain access to the stairwells. It's probably the same for the other floors above ground level. Right, Freddie?"

"Right. Now let's go over the videos."

With a remote, David turned on the television and video recorder in the conference room.

Freddie then stood, put a disk in the recorder, and let it play. "This is from a security camera in the main lobby on the night in question. Both cameras depict about the same thing from different angles. Watch the time stamp in the lower right-hand corner." He let the recording run for about one minute.

David leaned toward the television screen and watched Simpson enter the lobby and proceed to the elevator banks. At first glance, he observed nothing noteworthy and suspected he overlooked something significant.

Freddie stopped the recording. "Okay, let's watch it again with some commentary." He rewound it and played it again. When Simpson entered the lobby, he pressed the pause button and pointed at the screen.

"See, right there. It's 9:31 p.m. and change. A tall blonde woman accompanied Simpson, but you can't get a glimpse of her. You can only see a little bit of her hair, her arm, and her hand touching Simpson's shoulder, while our victim glanced back and smiled. He kept that grin on his face until he got to the elevators."

"Uh-huh," David said. "The police interviewed the security guards who recalled the woman's shapely legs and long blonde hair. Unfortunately, they didn't get a good look at her face. According to them, she told Simpson she needed to step outside to make a call. She also told him to go upstairs, and she'd be there shortly to have some fun. Any guesses how Big Bobby interpreted the comment?"

"Nope," Marc said. "It's loud and clear."

"According to the guards, the blonde woman stepped outside and never returned," David said. "Simpson had dinner with a tall blonde woman earlier in the evening. She must be the same person we sort of see. Any footage of her stepping back into the front lobby?"

Freddie shook his head.

"Was she seen at the building earlier in the day?"

"Checked the videos from all three security cameras, and never saw her."

Marc's eyes got wide, as if he had a sudden revelation. "Please play back the recording from 9:30 to maybe 9:32."

Everyone watched the video again, and David unsuccessfully tried to spot something unusual.

Marc pointed at the screen. "Did you see it? She stopped right before she got into the camera's field of vision. It's almost as if she'd been in the lobby beforehand and knew how to avoid them."

The wheels started spinning fast in David's mind. "A tall blonde woman … could've been there before … yeah … Wait a minute! I think I know who she is, sort of. Bill Saxer talked about a tall blonde messenger coming to the office about two weeks before the murder. Her appearance caught Simpson's attention, and his libido took over. He abandoned a meeting to speak with her.

I bet the messenger and the woman with him two weeks later are the same person. Does building security still have footage for early June?"

Freddie thumped the table once. "Good thinking, my friend, but no. Asked about old video footage, and security said they only keep the recordings for ten days. If nothing bad happened or no one filed a complaint, they recorded over the old video. That means footage for two weeks before the murder is long gone."

David frowned. "That's too bad."

Freddie shrugged. "Nothing we can do about it. Remember Simpson entered the building at 9:31. You don't see him getting into the elevator, but how else did he get upstairs? The woman went outside to make a call. The nearest cell tower handled several calls around the same time, and I reviewed the data. About one minute after Simpson appears, there's a fifteen second call from one cell phone, which I call Cell Number 1, to another cell phone, Cell Number 2. The same person bought both phones sixteen days before the murder, and coincidentally, the phone numbers end in 7881 and 7882. Seven minutes later, Cell 2 called Cell 1 for twenty-two seconds. Now hang onto your hats. Cell 2 was only in use during that evening and only for those two calls."

"So, Cell Number 2 sat for sixteen days, was used twice, and then dumped!" Marc exclaimed.

Freddie gave a wide smile. "Sure looks like it."

"What about the call history for Cell Number 1?" Bev asked.

"Good question. For two weeks, it communicated with only one other phone, which belonged to Simpson."

"What?" David said as his eyes got wide, and Marc's mouth dropped open.

Bev remained stoic and glanced in their direction. "Now, gentlemen. That should've come as no surprise." Returning her focus to Freddie, she asked, "Who purchased the cell phones?"

"Bonnie Parker or someone using the name. Probably an alias, and she paid in cash."

Marc laughed a little. "I'm sure the name was phony. Recognize it, David?"

"Yeah, I do. Bonnie Parker was one half of Bonnie and Clyde."

"Yeah, and it was also a great movie starring Warren Beatty and Faye Dunaway."

David held up his right hand. "Stop right there, Cowboy, and let's stay on track. Freddie, do you have anything else for us regarding the cell phones?"

"Nah. I spoke with two employees who were working the day Bonnie Parker bought the phones. For future billings, they needed a credit card number, and the one Bonnie provided was bogus. Neither employee remembered what she looked like."

"Huh, too bad," David said. "Did the cell phone store have any security cameras?"

"Afraid not."

Bev removed her glasses and tapped an earpiece on her cheek. "I believe we can make some reasonable assumptions. Bonnie Parker was the tall blonde messenger and the blonde woman with Simpson on the night of the murder. She basically escorted Simpson to his waiting assassin, who knew how to get in and out of the building undetected. Anyone want to dispute my theory?"

Three heads shook, indicating no disagreement.

David crossed his arms. "So far, none of this clears Amanda. Any other good news, Freddie?"

"If you mean more bad news, getting to that." He switched out the disks and played another one. "This is footage from a camera pointing north and attached to the building directly south of the O'Connell building. It recorded the area in front of both buildings on the west side. There's a lot of foot traffic. Keep your eyes on the far corner … and we're coming up on 9:43." Freddie paused the recording and pointed at the screen. "An older woman with a cane exited the alley north of the O'Connell building. She turned right and disappeared into the crowd."

David furrowed his brow in frustration. "I couldn't see her too well. There were too many people on the street, and she was too far away from the camera. I'm surprised you noticed her."

Freddie grinned. "Didn't the first time around." He switched disks again. "Someone at NYPD must've stared at the last video too long and finally noticed her. They made another one with some enhancements and focused on the older woman." He pushed the play button. "The camera never captured her face. She could've shot Simpson and hurried down ten flights of steps. Best guess, she had a key card, took the freight elevator, and got outside through a fire exit." Freddie then stopped the recording.

"Hang on," Marc said. "Why not go downstairs in the freight elevator, open the metal door, and leave?"

Freddie gave a thin smile. "Another good guess, my friend, but no. Opening the rolling door next to the freight elevator would've triggered an alert on the security board. Why were the rolling metal doors alarmed and not the fire exits? No clue. Plus, once she gets outside, she couldn't close the door, and it was closed when the police arrived. Did you get a good look at this woman?"

"Not her face, but overall, yeah," David said. "Long gray hair in a bun, frumpy clothes, a large purse, and a cane. I think she's five-three or five-four."

Freddie pointed at David. "Right. Anything else?"

"Like what?"

Marc perked up. "She didn't fit in with the rest of the crowd?"

Freddie shook his head. "That's not it. Let me play the enhanced video again."

While the recording played on the television screen, Bev leaned forward and then a moment later said, "She's not using the cane correctly, and it's only a prop."

Freddie clapped his hands once and pointed to her. "That's right! You got it!"

David groaned. "Ah crap. So, here's the DA's theory of the case. The tall blonde woman, also known as Bonnie Parker, arranges for Simpson to take her to his office, and it's a setup. She ducks out to call the killer, who's somewhere in the building. After Simpson's shot, the killer calls her back, but why? Just to say she did it? Maybe Bonnie was also the getaway driver, and if so, where was her car? The killer's a short woman who wore a disguise to make herself look older, and the DA believes it was Amanda. Since Amanda worked in the building, she knew how to avoid the security guards and cameras. We also know she went home early, and no one can vouch for her whereabouts until the following day. Did the cameras in the lobby catch her leaving?"

"Absolutely," Freddie said.

"Any footage of her coming back later that day?"

"Nah. Checked the footage from the lobby, the parking garage, and the other camera."

"Did any camera spot an elderly woman entering the building through the lobby?"

"Strike two."

David rubbed the back of his neck and considered other possibilities. "What about Bonnie Parker driving into the parking garage? If so, did she have any passengers?"

Freddie nodded. "Looked for that too. Quite a few women drove into the building. Some had passengers, but nobody had long gray hair. Two female drivers who arrived late in the afternoon might've been taller. One was Asian, and the other one was a white brunette with large sunglasses. Could've been Bonnie with a wig, but she had no passengers."

David crossed his arms. "Well, assuming the woman with the cane was the killer, she could have gained access to the building by someone on the inside opening a fire exit door. Security would've been unaware because the fire exits don't have alarms."

"Right. Unless you have more questions, that's it for now. I'll get back to you soon enough on the other matters."

CHAPTER 17

Friday, October 30

THE BLARING ALARM caused David to wake up startled. He glanced at his clock, which stated it was 6:30, and he forgot why he needed to get up so early. He grabbed his cell phone on the nightstand and found a text message Bev had sent late yesterday:

> *Spoke with Conway and her attorney.*
> *Email to follow.*

David coughed and then shuffled to his small dining room table, where his laptop sat. He turned it on and then accessed Bev's email.

From: Beverly Cohen
Sent: October 29, 2009 9:58:07 PM
To: David Lee, Marc D'Angelo, DAL firm
Subject: Donna Conway

I met with Conway and her attorney, and her contempt for Simpson was obvious. Conway admitted after he made another crude comment, she threatened to slit his throat and only wanted to scare him so he would leave her alone. Conway claimed in hindsight, she knew the threat was inappropriate and alleged she had been in a considerable amount of pain (which is not a sufficient excuse in my book). While on active duty with the Air Force, she suffered a significant injury and never fully recovered.

Conway said after she was fired, she moved back to Philadelphia, and eight days prior to the murder, she had back surgery at the local VA hospital. Four days later, she was discharged to a rehabilitation center and claimed she was still there when the murder occurred. Conway's attorney promised to send copies of her medical records once he obtained them.

I asked Conway whether she would testify for us if Morelli went to trial. She said she would think about it, but given her body language, I sincerely doubt it. As you know, we cannot compel a person who lives out of state to appear in court.

David groaned upon reading the last paragraph. If Conway were a viable suspect, he would have been tempted to file a motion to dismiss, which was no longer a reasonable option. He also believed if Conway refused to testify, the jury would never hear about her death threat, and her testimony was necessary to counteract the impact of Amanda's "Let's kill him" email.

LATER IN THE morning, David watched security footage from the O'Connell building in the conference room. Marc's arrival provided a somewhat welcome reprieve.

"Geez, Davey. You look terrible with those bloodshot eyes."

"Thanks a lot. Aren't you in the office a little early today?"

"It's not early, about 10:30. Besides, I'm getting better and almost back to my old self."

"Oh really? Your old self? Is that a good thing?"

Marc chuckled. "How long have you been staring at that screen?"

"Too long."

"Learned anything interesting?"

"Not really. I watched the videos from the lobby and tried to get a glimpse of the blonde woman's face. When you can see some of her, I reviewed the videos frame-by-frame and saw nothing except her arm and a few strands of hair."

"Anything else interesting?"

"Well, during the thirty minutes before Simpson arrived, there were three food deliveries. One of them was definitely pizza, and the other two were probably deli food and Persian. Exciting enough for you? On another note, did you read Bev's email?"

"Yeah, I did. I guess we'll have to rule out Conway as the killer. Oh well."

David stared at Marc in disbelief. "Oh well? What if Conway doesn't testify at trial? It could really hurt our case."

"You've been staring at the TV too long, and your brain's turning to mush. Think about it. How can we get Conway's threat into evidence?"

David threw up his hands. "Okay, I'll play along. Two people were present when the death threat was made. One is dead, and the other probably won't testify. Now what?"

Marc bent over and used his right hand to make the motion of a wheel turning round and round. "Come on. Get the hamster moving and think it through. Who else knew about the death threat?"

David stared at the wall. "Bill Saxer saw something but didn't hear it."

"Keep going."

After a couple of moments, David smiled as he determined a senior partner could testify they fired Conway due to the death threat.

Marc patted him on the shoulder. "And now we're up to speed." He then took a seat and with a serious look, he said, "There's something else we need to discuss. I haven't been looking at our finances recently. How are we doing?"

David chuckled. "Is that all? You had me worried for a minute. We're doing fine, much better now thanks to racking up billable hours for Morelli, and her parents have been making timely payments. We took care of Bev's husband's bill for his financial report a long time ago, and we've paid Freddie in full for everything he's done so far."

"That's good, really good. Are Paul and Lorraine still paying in cash?"

"Yeah. It seems fishy, but I haven't asked them where it came from."

Marc smirked. "Isn't that defense attorney 101? Don't ask how you're getting paid."

"It might be in the manual, and I've never read it," David joked. "Anyway, for Amanda's initial appearance, her parents showed up with a bank statement showing over $163,000 in savings. The money could be coming from there, and if so, they could give us cashier's checks or wire the money into the firm's bank account. I don't get it."

"Maybe it's coming from *those* people," Marc said with a grin. "You know, bada bing, bada boom."

David chuckled. "Who knows? Freddie and his old partner never came up with anything to show Paul has mafia ties, but I'm still not ruling it out. Why the sudden interest in our cash flow?"

"Nothing much," Marc said as he waved his right hand. "Steph and I are thinking about buying a house, and I want to make certain we'll be able to afford a mortgage."

CHAPTER 18

Monday, November 16

A NOTHER RICH KID *with a drug problem,* David thought as he watched Marc usher a pretentious teenager and his parents into the conference room. David was relieved he could take a break from the steady stream of the privileged and entitled. More importantly, he was glad Marc was regaining his strength but still did not have the endurance for the rigors and stress a full-blown trial presented. On the other hand, Marc was working almost full time and could handle most of the firm's clients, which meant David could focus almost exclusively on Amanda Morelli. Unless a significant development occurred, which seemed unlikely, he and Bev would soon be high and deep in pre-trial preparation.

Despite the best efforts of Frederick Ferguson, no new leads presented themselves. David, Bev, Marc, and Freddie had reviewed all sixteen boxes of discovery from the district attorney's office and found no decent basis to support a motion to dismiss. In addition, Freddie's examination of the phone records revealed nothing noteworthy, except for Simpson's communication with "Bonnie Parker" during the last two weeks of his life.

By this time, David understood NYPD detectives had narrowed down their list of suspects through a process of elimination. The police had obviously concluded Amanda was the best one but uncovered no direct evidence linking her to the murder. David's team could not identify any other possible suspect, but this did not faze them. The prosecution had to prove its case beyond a reasonable doubt, and the defense did not have to prove anything. If necessary, the defense would only need to discredit portions of the DA's case, and David saw multiple possibilities.

LATER IN THE morning, David arrived at the courthouse for another status conference with Judge Perkins. He had looked forward to it because he had seen no member of the Morelli family in several weeks. He had instead given them updates over the phone and via email. While David had initially dreaded dealing with Amanda's parents, their personalities had grown on him, even though he still did not trust Paul, who had falsely claimed Marc was "a nephew of a good buddy of mine."

As usual, David arrived at the courthouse well before the scheduled hearing time. While waiting to pass through security, he observed a petite woman in line ahead of him. Her dark brown hair flowed down past her shoulder blades, and she wore a burgundy business suit with a knee-high skirt and matching two-inch heels.

David also noticed the woman was alone. She carried a purse, as opposed to a briefcase or satchel, indicating she was not an attorney making a court appearance. David checked his watch and confirmed he could spend a moment or two with this woman. If she made a good first impression and they seemed to click, he would give her his business card. After all, he was single and unattached, and there was no harm in introducing himself.

Once David passed through the metal detector, he strolled toward the woman, who stopped in front of Judge Perkins' courtroom. She glanced left and then right, as if she were searching for someone. When David was about ten feet away, she turned around. It was Amanda! She saw David and released a big smile. She also put her hands on her hips and made a pose stating, "Look at me now."

With a gleam in her eye, Amanda said, "Howdy, Stranger. You come here often?"

David chuckled. "Good morning. Did you go back to your original hair color?"

"Yes, thanks for noticing. We really need to catch up. How about lunch after the hearing?"

"Sure, I'm available." He believed there was no other reasonable answer to the question. "Where are your parents?"

Amanda gave a dismissive wave. "They're not coming. They figured not much would happen today, and Dad had a doctor's appointment this morning."

ONCE DAVID AND Amanda entered Judge Perkins' courtroom, the same three elderly men sat in the gallery's last row. The one on the right put his index finger in front of his mouth and said, "Shh!"

David smiled and whispered, "I know. Thanks." As he sat down, he wondered why the retired men chose to sit and watch in this courtroom, as opposed to any other, where the judges created a more tolerable atmosphere. He once again noticed the painting of His Honor casting an eye on him from above and hoped his ego would never become as inflated as the one the judge possessed.

As expected, the hearing was brief.

Judge Perkins asked in his raspy voice, "What's the status of the case?"

"The People have provided no additional discovery to the defense," Jacqueline said, "and we don't anticipate providing any more before trial."

The judge turned his gaze toward the defense table.

"Your Honor, the defense has reviewed all the discovery from the prosecution and has complied with our obligations by serving reports concerning our investigation. The defense will file pre-trial motions shortly."

Judge Perkins remained expressionless except for his droopy eyelids making him appear disappointed. He had no questions, comments, or scathing remarks, which meant he was satisfied. No attorney would ever hear the slightest bit of praise from him.

"We'll meet again for another status conference on December 14," he said. "Hearing is adjourned."

David and Amanda decided to eat at a Japanese restaurant two blocks away. As David left the courthouse, he checked his phone for any messages and then turned it off to give Amanda his undivided attention. After a server took their orders, he studied her large brown eyes and high cheekbones. He also noted she was wearing make-up but did not need it.

After they gave their orders, David said, "You know plenty about what I've been doing lately, and you know Marc's back in the office. It's not a good idea to talk about the case right now, because others might try to eavesdrop. So, please tell me what's new with you."

"What's new?" Amanda smirked. "Does anyone really talk like that?"

David was amused and raised his hands and eyebrows.

Amanda gave a light chuckle. "As I said before, I thought about getting into shape and got tired of sitting around and doing nothing. I've been running and working out at a gym, and I've lost about ten pounds. I now fit into my skinnier clothes, including this outfit. It's almost like I'm back to my college days when I was in shape."

"That's great. I'm glad to see you're in a better mood, and I'm really sorry about your mom's accident. How's she doing?"

Amanda's smile disappeared. "It's been a tough road for her. Both surgeries on her wrist went okay, and she recovered from the arthroscopic on her shoulder sooner than expected. She's still in physical therapy for her wrist. She won't admit it, but the exercises have been painful. A couple of times, I took her to therapy and could see she was trying to hide the pain."

"Sorry about that. I guess it's a good thing your mom already sold the travel agency. That's one less thing to worry about."

Amanda shrugged. "Yeah, suppose so. The doctors also advised Mom to get regular exercise, and now Mom and Dad walk together every morning."

David nodded and acknowledged he needed to exercise more often. "Sounds good. What about when winter sets in?"

Amanda perked up. "Dad already planned for it. He bought a matching set of exercise bikes and put them in Daniel's old bedroom. It's kind of cute: his and her bikes." Her eyes got wide. "Oh, there's been one good thing. Since Mom's accident, we've had many guests over to the house, and of course, Pete and Debra are the most frequent visitors. All of them have helped to lift Mom's spirits, and she really enjoys entertaining. As a bonus, their friends frequently bring food or invite us over for dinner. That's a little less time in the kitchen for me."

David chuckled. "I'm not much for working in the kitchen either."

"It's not so bad if you don't have to cook every meal," Amanda said with a wave of her hand. "Another thing. Believe it or not, Daniel and I are on better terms, and his family's been over to the house more often. We finally coaxed Mom to go with us to a hockey game. The Rangers lost, but it was still fun. Mom said she liked it, and I suspect she was just humoring us. Dad and I hope to see a few more games this season."

"That's nice. So, your folks are enjoying themselves as best as they can."

"Yeah. Halloween helped too. I thought after Mom's accident, they would've cancelled their annual party, but they threw it anyway, and this time, they hired a caterer. You won't believe what Mom and Dad chose as their costumes."

"I have no idea."

"Indiana Jones and Marion Ravenwood, an injured version of Marion with her arm in a sling."

"From *Raiders of the Lost Ark*, right? So, what was your costume?"

"I didn't have one," Amanda said. "It was an older crowd, and I didn't want to stick around. I went over to Valerie's place, and her kids wanted to watch a very scary movie. So, Valerie rented *The Exorcist*."

"I'm not into horror films. Is it really scary?"

"If you believe in Heaven and Hell and were raised Catholic, oh yeah," Amanda said as she raised her eyebrows. "It's probably the most frightening movie of all time. Think you can handle watching it with me, Big Boy? I've never seen a grown man completely freak out." She flashed a devilish grin.

David chuckled and raised his hands. "No thanks!"

Despite the creepy look, David was pleased to see Amanda in a better mood. Perhaps her true personality was coming through. More than once during lunch, David had to remind himself Amanda was a client, and he did not date them. Nonetheless, he appreciated her company in more ways than one. After they finished eating, the conversation continued.

"Getting back to you and your family. Anything else interesting at home?" David asked.

Amanda's eyes got wide. "Yeah! After I read Beverly's book on jury selection, Dad read it twice. Sorry, I forgot to bring it with me. Dad's been asking me many questions about lawyers and trials. He always supported my decision to become a lawyer, and he's more interested now for obvious reasons. He really wants to know what could happen during a trial, and I've been teaching him the rules of evidence."

David shook his head. "The rules of evidence? Really? I found them confusing the first time around and the second."

"Yeah, I know. It was the same for me. However, Dad's a pretty sharp guy, and he's picking it up fast. I don't know if it was intentional, but it was a brilliant idea to show Dad the boxes of discovery. It made him realize the case wasn't going away in short order. He hasn't kept asking the equivalent of 'are we there yet' over and over, right?"

"Nope. He asks questions, but not that one."

The check arrived, and Amanda reached into her purse.

"Don't even think about it," he said. "I don't make clients pay for meals with me."

She smirked. "At least not directly. We're paying your fees."

"*Touché*," he said with a grin while placing a credit card on top of the tray holding their bill.

Amanda laughed a little. "Hey, did my parents tell you the reason they hired your firm? Marc was a nephew of a good buddy, right?"

David was amused and anticipated the punch line for a joke. "Yeah. We checked it out, and it's not true. So, you know the real reason?"

Amanda laughed some more. "Uh-huh. Dad told me yesterday. He and Mom checked the phone book for defense attorneys with Italian last names, and D'Angelo must've been the first one they spotted."

David laughed as well and had difficulty stopping.

"I guess you're not mad at my folks?"

"Gee, I wonder why you said that?" David then chuckled. "Well, they could've hired a lot worse. I know some attorneys with Italian last names who are so dumb I'm surprised they passed the bar exam. No offense. I also know attorneys from other ethnic backgrounds who are complete morons."

Amanda smiled. "I didn't take offense, and I know some of those attorneys. Maybe someone took their bar exams for them."

"Yeah, maybe. Anyway, about your case. I need to talk to you and your parents about a public relations strategy, and we need to discuss other matters alone. Can all of you stop by the office tomorrow afternoon at three?"

"Uh, sure. I'm off Mondays and Tuesdays. What public relations strategy?"

"Sooner or later, your case will be in the news, and we should set the agenda." David's mind stopped in its tracks. "Wait, what? What do you mean off Mondays and Tuesdays? You're working?"

"Oh yeah, I forgot to mention it. I've been working the lunch shift at a Greek restaurant not too far away from the house. The owner's another good buddy of my dad's, of course." Amanda smiled and rolled her eyes.

"How's that going?"

"Not too bad. I don't want to work in a restaurant forever, but it's better than sitting around doing nothing."

"Does the owner know about your situation?"

"Oh yeah, and he thinks it's good for business. According to him, lunchtime has been busier since I started."

David suspected the uptick in business had less to do with Amanda's criminal case and more to do with her being very attractive. He wanted to give her the compliment but did not do so, as he did not want to run the risk of her feeling uncomfortable around him.

CHAPTER 19

Tuesday, November 17

F OR A GOOD part of the day, David worked on mundane matters. Over the past few months, he had read about the federal government's new law enforcement priorities, including mortgage and health care fraud. He expected many attorneys would become busy representing white-collar defendants, but no such individuals had been knocking on his law firm's door.

As expected, the Morellis arrived early for their meeting, and they briefly chatted with Irene. David noticed the brace on Lorraine's wrist and a tray covered with aluminum foil in Paul's hands. Since he had not seen Paul and Lorraine in several weeks, he had forgotten the extreme difference in their sizes. Paul was about one foot taller than Lorraine and outweighed her by at least 120 pounds.

David went to Marc's office, where his law partner stared at his computer screen. "Hey, Marc, the Morellis are here. I want to introduce you."

Once they reached the front desk, David said, "Paul, Lorraine, and Amanda, this is Marc."

"It's nice to meet you," Marc said and could not take his eyes off the tray.

Paul said, "Yes, it's nice to finally meet you."

"Likewise," added Lorraine.

Marc pointed to the tray in Paul's hands. "What'd you bring?"

Lorraine giggled. "Why don't we show you. Where can we set it down?"

David gestured toward the conference room. "Over there."

As Lorraine passed him, he noticed her lavender perfume.

Paul set down the tray and removed the aluminum foil.

"Cannoli!" Lorraine said. "There's plenty for everyone. I should've brought something sooner, but uh, I don't know why I didn't. Since we're coming anyway, I thought why not? Enjoy!"

Before David and the others lay stuffed shells with ricotta cheese and dusted with powdered sugar. He was not fond of any dessert containing cheese but tried one cannolo to be polite. Upon his first bite, his knees nearly buckled. The shell had a nice crunch, and the powdered sugar added sweetness. The ricotta had a smooth texture and was just sweet enough. David also tasted hints of vanilla, lemon, and orange.

"Lorraine, this is spectacular!" he said.

Marc's closed eyes and the "mmm" coming from his mouth indicated he was impressed. Paul and Amanda had their mouths full, and both gave a thumbs-up. Irene's rapid consumption of one cannolo and then another reflected her approval.

Lorraine was beaming. "Thanks."

"You were able to make this with your banged up wrist?" David asked.

"Oh sure. It was really nothing."

"Oh no, it's a lot more than nothing," Marc said. "This might be the best cannoli I ever had, and there are some excellent cooks in my family. It's too bad Bev took the day off and can't have any."

"Are you kidding?" David uttered. "With her super healthy diet, she wouldn't touch them."

Marc smiled and grabbed another cannolo. "True, true. Too bad for her, and more for the rest of us."

After the last piece had disappeared, Irene returned to her desk. Everyone else sat down, and David was ready to discuss more important matters.

"So, Paul. I heard you went to the doctor yesterday. How'd it go?"

Paul waved his right hand. "Fine, fine. Don't worry about it."

David saw Amanda shake her head, which her parents apparently did not notice. She also mouthed, "Tell you later."

Paul shifted in his chair. "Before we get started, we wanted to … Ah, Honey, why don't you just show them what else we brought."

Lorraine opened her purse, which revealed a stack of hundred-dollar bills.

David estimated she had about $30,000, which surprised him, even though another wad of cash was nothing usual for Paul and Lorraine. He politely said, "Look, I already told you not to carry so much cash around. When you withdraw it from the bank, you can ask for a cashier's check or wire it to us. I mean, aren't you afraid of muggers?"

Lorraine beamed at her husband like a teenager girl having her first crush. "Now who's going to mug us with my big, strong husband around?"

Paul smiled back at her, while Marc shook his head, and Amanda raised her arms, indicating, "I give up."

David finally acknowledged there was no use telling Paul and Lorraine how to handle their money. "Alright. Let's talk about the case. Simpson's murder was in the news a little bit. Marc and I searched for any coverage of Amanda's arrest or indictment and found nothing. Amanda, I take it the police never did a perp walk."

"A perp walk?" Lorraine asked.

"Yeah, perp walk, Mom. It's when the police parade someone in front of the cameras right after an arrest. No, it didn't happen."

"Okay, good," David said. "Jacqueline Marshall doesn't like to cozy up to the media, but her boss, the district attorney, is another story. I'm a little surprised the DA's office never issued a press release. We're not sure what to make of that. Anyway, sooner or later, there'll be media coverage, and many people follow murder trials. Besides, Amanda's case is more interesting than one gang member killing another one."

David noticed Paul and Lorraine were paying close attention.

"This type of case sells newspapers and drives up TV ratings. So, I suggest we get Amanda's name and face out there, and we could set the agenda. Any coverage should reach some potential jurors, which will work in our favor. During jury selection, they'll be asked if they have any prior knowledge about the case, including whether they heard about it from any TV show, the radio, the *New York Times*, whatever. Even if someone says 'no,' he or she will still be on notice of Amanda's celebrity status, and celebrities receive more favorable treatment from juries. So, what do you think?"

Paul tilted his head and raised the left side of his mouth. "Have you done such a thing before?"

"To an extent, yes, but not the massive exposure I have in mind. I plan to contact many media outlets, and we'll see who's interested. We'll give as many interviews as possible, within reason, of course. Marc and I already have some contacts, and Beverly has a few more."

Paul nodded while in thought. "Uh-huh, uh-huh. What would you say?"

"More like what would Amanda say," David said. "We'd present her side of the story. She was sick and in bed when the murder happened. The police and the district attorney made a terrible mistake and went after the wrong person. I also want to provide Amanda's backstory, which means telling the public where she grew up, her family, that kind of thing. Her life will make a good human-interest story, and she'll become likeable in the eyes of potential jurors."

The big man tapped his right index finger on the table. "And you think this can help Amanda during a trial?"

"Absolutely."

Paul turned to his wife. "Honey, what do you think?"

Lorraine shrugged. "I guess so. I can smile and wave at a camera if I have to."

David nodded. "Paul, okay to proceed with a PR strategy?"

"Okay by me."

"Amanda?"

She smiled. "Sure, why not?"

"Great!" David grimaced and snapped his fingers. "Oh yeah, there's one other thing I forgot to mention. Amanda, since you're attractive, some members of the media will play up that angle *a lot*. You're probably going to hear or read many comments about your appearance. Some will be favorable or rather innocuous, while others will be demeaning and sexist. Even if you try to ignore all the buzz, you won't be able to tune it out completely. Can you handle it?"

Amanda pursed her lips for a few moments while looking at the conference room table. She then raised her head and replied, "I guess it's better to be viewed as a sex object than a cold-blooded killer. I'm still in. When do we get started?"

"Today. I'll start making phone calls, but first you and I have a few things to discuss."

Paul slapped the arm of his chair. "I guess that's the cue for Lorraine and me to leave."

"Oh sure," Lorraine added. "Next time, I'll bring another dessert."

"Please do," Marc said. "If you can't, I can make the sacrifice and come to your house to eat them."

The Morellis laughed, but as on other occasions, David found Marc's humor inappropriate. Once Lorraine and Paul departed, Amanda gave the correct information about her father.

"Here's what's happening with Dad," she said while leaning toward David. "A little while ago, he had a check-up, which revealed he has high blood pressure. His doctor ordered blood tests and an EKG, and yesterday, he went back for the results. His heart is fine, which is great. However, Dad has high cholesterol, really high. Exercising helps, and he has to take medication. Of course, with him, it's always 'Don't worry about it,' and he'd like to ignore his doctor's instructions." Amanda tapped the table with her right index finger. "I'll make certain he takes his medication every day until it becomes routine for him. The Italian desserts don't help matters. Hopefully, the medication will work, and Dad doesn't have to take what he'd consider more drastic measures, such as eating healthier."

"I'm sure he'll be fine," David said. While not mentioning it aloud, he was not pleased Paul had lied to him a second time. Lying about one's health was not the greatest sin in the world, but it gave David one more reason not to trust him. "Now, for another matter ... we need to have a trial prep discussion."

Amanda's pleasant demeanor disappeared. "I've been trying not to think about it. When I do, I get a little sick to my stomach. It's really going to happen?"

David nodded. "It certainly looks that way, and I'm confident the jury will rule in your favor."

Amanda sighed. "Yeah. Trial prep ... okay. I know you talked to Valerie about that email and what we said at the restaurant. I guess we both have sick senses of humor and were only blowing off steam."

"Yeah, I know," David said. "I want to cover a few other things. Let's start with the gun. You told the police you didn't own a gun, but they found one in your apartment. How do you explain that?"

Amanda looked down and exhaled through her nose. "At the time they asked me, I had forgotten about it." She looked David in the eyes. "Really, I did. When the police executed the search warrant, they never mentioned finding it. I didn't realize I had it until I was packing up to move back home with Mom and Dad. I sold it to a gun store, and I think I still have the receipt if you need it."

"How'd you end up with the gun in the first place?" Marc asked.

Amanda scoffed. "My crazy ex-husband gave it to me after we broke up about … five years ago." She shook her head. "What a mess it was. My ex came over to my place shortly after we separated, and he gave it to me. He said I needed it for protection. I didn't need it, and the gun wasn't much of anything. It was a .22 semi-automatic: a tiny little thing. If I wanted a gun for protection, I would've bought a larger caliber revolver or a shotgun. I just took the .22 to avoid another argument and threw it in the back of my closet. I guess I forgot about it."

David thought Amanda gave a credible explanation. "Why didn't you tell me about the pistol?"

She shrugged. "I thought it didn't matter because it wasn't the murder weapon."

"Okay. When you were a kid, you learned how to fire a variety of guns, right?"

"Yeah," she said with a confused look. "What's your point?"

"Do you still go shooting?"

Amanda frowned and rolled her eyes. "You've got to be kidding. I really hate guns and told the police that. Isn't it in one of their reports? I haven't fired a gun in over ten, maybe fifteen years."

"Do you still keep in touch with your ex?" Marc asked.

"No way. His presence only brings up bad memories, such as the times when he was completely neurotic. Would you believe he was a stockbroker? He probably had a complete meltdown when the market went into panic mode last year."

David nodded. "I'm sure the same thing happened to many stockbrokers. On to the next topic. According to one detective's report, you said you never went into Simpson's office, but they found your thumbprint on his desk."

Amanda's mouth opened. "What? That's not right. I don't remember exactly what I told the police, but I never would've said that. I was assigned to Bennington, you know, the pharmaceutical company, which meant I had to work with Simpson. Sometimes I spoke to him in his office, and when I did, I made certain the door was always open. Other times, I dropped off paperwork early in the morning, before he arrived, so there would be one less opportunity for him to make a crude comment."

David nodded again. "Okay. Sounds reasonable. How'd the police match your fingerprint to the one found in his office? Did you have a prior arrest?"

"No. The police asked several of us at the firm for our fingerprints. I didn't see the harm, and they brought a fingerprint kit."

Despite everything he had heard and read, Marc's eyes got wide, indicating he could not accept Amanda's last comment. Meanwhile, David kept his poker face.

"Anything else?" Amanda asked.

"A few things," David said. "The police asked the attorneys and the staff their respective opinions of Simpson. Many comments were rather unkind, and apparently, you said, 'He wasn't so bad.' Is that true?"

Amanda looked at the table for about five seconds. "Not sure. I don't remember exactly what I said … it could be right. He was a really awful person, but he wasn't so bad that I thought someone should've killed him."

"And you told someone at the EEOC Simpson was better off dead."

Amanda sighed. "Yeah, I said it. I was pretty mad and didn't want to deal with him anymore." She grimaced. "All of this doesn't look good, does it?"

"Not on the surface," Marc said. "However, it doesn't mean you shot Big Bobby twice in the head. A trial won't be fun, but I really like our chances."

"*Our* chances?" Amanda asserted. "You're not the one on trial. Care to switch places? You'll probably look fabulous in prison stripes."

Marc grinned and turned his head towards David. "I like this one. Can we keep her? You know, make her a partner?"

"Cute," David said.

Amanda asked, "Anything else?"

"Nothing from me," David said. "Marc?"

"More cannoli, please."

Amanda smirked. "I know! They're delicious. I have to stop Mom from making them all the time, or I'll blow up like a balloon."

CHAPTER 20

Thursday, November 19

DAVID ARRIVED AT the Morelli residence in Bensonhurst, Brooklyn. Despite the cool, brisk weather, he took a minute to view the neighborhood, consisting mostly of row houses with the same facades and color scheme. On the other hand, the Morelli home was a two-story, single-family residence with no common walls. It was also long and narrow, and driveways ran on both sides. The home's exterior had a hodgepodge of architectural styles. Bricks covered the first story, and a brick chimney rose above the left side. A bay window jutted out to the left of the front door and clashed with the brick. The second story's exterior was made of gray horizontal boards, which did not match anything else.

David spotted a low, white metal fence, and when he opened the corresponding white metal gate, it made a faint squeak. To the left of the walkway laid faded red brick surrounding a bare area, which was probably filled with flowers during the spring and summer. He approached the white front door and rang the doorbell.

About thirty seconds later, Paul opened the door as he held out his right arm. "David!" he said with a wide smile. "Please come in."

"Thanks."

"We'll talk at the kitchen table."

The big man escorted David through the living room, where the tan carpet showed years of wear and tear. The room also featured aging and overstuffed furniture, and the wallpaper appeared faded. If plenty of natural light did not fill the room, its ambience would have been too depressing. Paul and Lorraine's wedding photo sat inside an elegant silver frame on a small table next to the couch. David also noticed many family photos on the walls, including those depicting Amanda and her brother Daniel from early childhood to various graduations.

A round table and four metal chairs with a yellow flower pattern on the seat cushions sat next to the kitchen. Cheap plastic with more flowers pretended to be a tablecloth. David took a seat opposite Paul and wished they would have sat at the dining room table. Given its apparent quality, David suspected it had been imported from Italy, and its top shined after a recent polishing. A modest chandelier hung above the table, and David could not see a speck of dust on it. In fact, everything within his field of vision appeared clean and tidy.

David also noticed the dated kitchen and its cabinets needing an extra coat of paint. The dishwasher was new, but the avocado green oven featured a mechanical clock, not a digital one. Even though David's legal fees were reasonable, he felt guilty over taking the money that could have been used to remodel the house and buy new appliances and furniture.

"What do you think of the place?" Paul asked.

David wanted to be positive and still honest. "It looks like Lorraine keeps up the house as well as she makes Italian desserts."

Paul smiled. "Thanks. It's mostly Lorraine, and I help a little. Amanda left for work, and Lorraine went out shopping with Debra, which means we're free to talk. What's on your mind?"

David tried to be as diplomatic as possible. "We need to discuss some things that came up during the police investigation, okay? I believe you told a detective or two you previously owned a .38-caliber handgun."

Paul appeared at ease and leaned back in his chair. "Oh sure, sure. I owned a Smith & Wesson snub-nose .38. I bought it for protection, for burglars or something like that. Have you ever fired one?"

"No, not yet. According to the police, you got rid of it some time ago. Is that right?"

"Oh yeah, sure, sure. Amanda bugged her mother and me to get it out of the house for the longest time. I don't know why she worried about it so much. I finally gave in and got rid of it … when was that?" Paul gazed at the ceiling as if it would help him remember. "Got rid of it three or four years ago."

"Did you sell it or give it away? Did you throw it away?"

Paul gazed at the ceiling again. "Huh … what happened?" He then looked at David. "I think I gave it to a good buddy who wanted it as a present for a nephew or a cousin. I'm not sure."

"Do you remember which buddy got the gun?"

Paul smirked. "No, not really. I've got a lot of good buddies."

While David liked Amanda's father, he could not discern when Paul was telling the truth and when he was lying. During their conversation, Paul's posture and body language never changed, and he gave no hint of deception.

"Do you know why I'm asking about the gun?"

The big man nodded while continuing to lean back in his chair. "Oh sure, sure. The murder weapon was a .38. It's a coincidence but not much of one. There are probably thousands of them in the city, even more in the state."

David needed to move onto another topic but was uneasy about it.

Perhaps Paul noticed it. "Anything else? You can ask me anything. This is all about giving Amanda the best defense possible, right?"

David gave a half-smile. "Yes, it is. The police asked you about another matter, which we need to discuss."

The big man leaned forward and rested his arms on the table. "Yeah, I know what you're talking about. The police asked about the mob, right? They wanted to know if I knew any wise guys or ever worked for them."

"So, you're not offended about my asking?"

Paul chuckled and gave a dismissive wave. "No, no. I knew you're going to get around to it, eventually. Like I told the police, I was a union rep, and I dealt with all kinds of people. I knew quite a few wise guys, especially in the old days. They took their cut, and everything was fine. Just because I knew some of them doesn't mean I was in bed with them."

Paul leaned back again. "You know, back in the day, life was better and less complicated. Suppose one of the families protected a construction site. Nothing unusual about it. The building owner and the construction company paid the mob protection money, and that might sound bad, but in return, *nobody* dared to touch the job site." He chuckled. "It would've been suicide. Do you know what I'm talking about?"

"Yes, I've heard about it."

"Now, it's a lot different." Paul waved his arms in the air.

David also noticed him speak in a more negative tone.

"Now, an owner pays a private security company to protect a job site. The guards are supposed to watch the area when the construction crew isn't around, but who knows when the graveyard shift will be absent or asleep on the job? Thieves take whatever they want, lumber, pipes, copper wire. Don't forget drug addicts are looking for anything to steal and sell, and the guards could be crooks too. Many of them are ex-cons who have no decency, no honor." Paul shook his head with a disgusted look.

"I guess so," David said even though he was unconvinced. "So, if you weren't part of the mob, why does the FBI have a file on you?"

Paul's eyes lit up. "No kidding? Did you see it?"

"No, I haven't. The FBI didn't turn over a copy to NYPD or the district attorney's office. Sometimes, the feds don't work and play well with others. Back to my question. Any idea why they have a file on you?"

The big man made his lower lip pout while he shook his head. "Not really. I knew some wise guys, and maybe the feds did surveillance. You know, they targeted some guy, and I'm in the same photo. It could've happened a few times, and they opened a file on me. No big deal. Hey, wouldn't it be fun to get a look at my file, right?" Paul lightly punched him in the arm.

"Of course." David was hesitant to ask his next line of questions but believed he had no choice. "How well did you know the wise guys?"

"Some better than others. You know, I'd see them from time to time."

"What about more recently?"

"Oh, sure," Paul said as he flicked his right hand. "You're probably too young to remember when the feds went after the five families back in the eighties. They got a bunch of convictions, but they didn't get rid of the mafia altogether. They're still out there, just not as powerful."

"Okay. Did Amanda ever tell you about Big Bobby's personality?"

"Of course, Amanda and I are really close, and ..." Paul's genial demeanor turned more serious. "You want to know if I told any wise guy about Simpson."

"Well, yeah," David said sheepishly. "Sorry about that."

Paul held up his right hand with the palm facing out. "Don't worry about it. You've gotta to do what you've gotta to do." He put his hand down. "Amanda shared her feelings about Simpson with me in confidence, and I never told anyone, not even our good friends and neighbors. No wise guy did me a favor by whacking Simpson. I didn't like the guy, but I never wanted him dead."

"Okay. I get what you're saying." Although David was uncertain it was the truth.

"Anything else?" he asked without a hint of anger or bitterness.

"No, that's it. We might have to chat again at a later date."

"Fine, fine." Paul's eyes lit up again. "Hey, it's about lunchtime. How about Santorini? That's the Greek place where Amanda works. The food's excellent, and if I see anyone I know, I'll introduce you."

"Sounds good."

"Santorini's only a few blocks away. Let's walk."

NORMALLY, DAVID WOULD have not minded travelling on foot. However, on this day, a stiff breeze blew as he and Paul crossed two larger streets. Between the wind and the cool temperature, David was miserable, while Paul appeared unfazed.

When they arrived at the restaurant, David noticed it was small and nicely furnished with white tablecloths, and it had views of various Greek vacation spots hanging from the walls. He also detected the aromas of olive oil, garlic, and onions wafting from the kitchen. Elderly customers filled most tables, which made sense because it was the middle of the week, and Santorini was in a mostly residential area.

A large man with thick, wavy gray hair spotted Paul and greeted him with open arms. "Paul!"

"Hey Nico! How's it going?"

They acted as if they had not seen each other in years, and David suspected only a few days had passed.

Nico chuckled. "Business is good, really good, thanks in part to your daughter."

"Great!" Paul said. "Speaking of my daughter, this is her defense attorney, David Lee."

Nico shook David's hand forcefully. "Oh, yes. I've heard about you. Starting a media blitz, huh? Why don't you hold a press conference or do some interviews here, huh? Huh? It'd be good for business!"

David was not certain how to respond to the gregarious man. So, he merely smiled and uttered, "Uh-huh."

Nico clapped his hands once and rubbed them together. "Okay! Paul, I have a very nice table for you."

"Fine, fine. First, I want to say hello to a few familiar faces and to my daughter." Paul looked to his left. "Oh, there she is."

Amanda came out of the kitchen with two plates of food and wore the standard attire for the staff: a white top and black pants. Even though she sported a casual look with little make-up and a ponytail, David thought she was stunning. Amanda could have dressed up for a walk on a red carpet, and he would have not been more impressed. Amanda appeared to be enjoying herself, and her people skills were on full display. With her personality, a pleasant atmosphere, and apparently excellent food, all the patrons were happy.

Paul took David around and greeted those he recognized, which was at least one person at every table. As expected, he was engaging and introduced David. Paul occasionally made a comment such as, "Hey, give this one your business card. He's a troublemaker, and his luck's about to run out." Laughter followed such remarks.

Once they took their seats, David realized they were sitting at one of Amanda's tables. She chatted with them before handing out the menus, which caused David to wonder if she was flirting with him in front of her father. He told himself it was wishful thinking and needed to focus on his priorities. After all, she was a client, not a potential date. Nevertheless, during lunch, he glanced in Amanda's direction multiple times and noticed all the customers treated her well.

"Hey, Paul. Has Amanda had any problems with a customer?"

Paul chuckled. "Are you kidding me? No way! If someone did that, he'd have to answer to me, or worse, he'd have to answer to Nico Junior."

"Nico Junior?"

"That's right. He's not here right now, and he usually works in the back," Paul said as he pointed his thumb over his shoulder, "while his father works the front of the house. If he were here, you wouldn't miss him. He's a really big guy, bigger than his father or me. He's really great with the staff and the customers, but don't get on his bad side."

Paul leaned forward and in a quieter voice said, "I heard about one jerk who gave a waitress a hard time. Nico Junior wasn't working that night, but he and his family live about a block away. Somebody called him, and he got over here in a big hurry. He remained calm and politely asked the guy to step outside. What happened next?" Paul held up his hands. "Nobody told me. All I know is the jerk never came back. You know, they have a saying here. 'If anybody acts up, don't call the police. Call Nico Junior.'"

David mulled over his recent conversations with Amanda's father, both of which raised red flags. Paul was nostalgic for the old days, when the mafia had a freer rein in the city. Despite being a defense attorney, David was not a fan of organized crime and did not buy into its hype and supposed glamour. Paul also favored taking the law into one's own hands.

David then considered whether Paul could have been involved in Big Bobby's murder. The physical evidence pointed to a shooter who was a shorter person, and Paul was too tall. He could have shot Simpson from a sitting position, but as Freddie said, that scenario was unlikely and would have been too awkward. Despite his denial of any involvement, Paul could have hired a contract killer. However, the police had subpoenaed his bank records and had found no suspicious payments to anyone. On the other hand, Paul could have paid someone in cash, the same as he had paid the bills from his firm. So, David could not rule out Paul from being part of a conspiracy to murder Simpson, but, with each passing day, he was more convinced Amanda was innocent.

CHAPTER 21

Monday, November 23

D AVID ARRIVED IN the office shortly before 9:30, as he had a meeting with Marc and Bev regarding the Morelli case, perhaps the most important meeting of his legal career. They intended to discuss where they stood on the evidence, what steps they should take, and whether they would recommend taking the case to trial.

While Irene was normally at her desk by 8:30, David saw no evidence of her arrival. She had not draped her jacket on her chair instead of hanging it in the closet, as he had repeatedly asked. Her coffee cup was not sitting on her desk, and her usual coaster was missing. David did not ask Marc about Irene's whereabouts and hoped she had taken the day off. Even after his law partner had returned to work, she had continued to get on his nerves, and he was uncertain how much longer he could tolerate her poor attitude.

The local media had begun to report on Amanda, largely as David had fed information to them. For many criminal cases, a certain catch phrase or nickname circulated, but from what David had read, the media had not yet settled on a moniker. One reporter had used the term, "*La Femme Fatale*," which he did not appreciate, as it implied Amanda was guilty.

Many media outlets made comments about Amanda's appearance, and a few called her "The Bensonhurst Babe." David acknowledged the nickname was catchy and would probably stick. While it was rather sexist, he reasoned it was better than other nicknames referring to violence or murder. As far as making Amanda likeable in the eyes of the public, he believed there should be no problem provided she did not become nervous in front of the cameras. David would find out soon enough given that her first interview was scheduled for the next day.

One commentator had opined J. Robert Simpson's murder was a victory for feminism. She had discussed how women had suffered and had claimed sometimes they needed to resort to violence to stop the oppression. However, David believed such action was acceptable in only the most extreme circumstances. A woman could respond to sexual harassment in other, less violent ways, including suing the pants off the offender. Besides, if the case went to trial, the defense would argue Amanda did not commit the crime, which means David and Bev would not claim self-defense, justifiable homicide, or diminished capacity due to constant sexual harassment.

Once Bev arrived in the office, David led her and Marc to the conference room.

Marc took a seat at the glass-top table with a latte in his hand. "Okay. Where do we start?"

David passed a sheet of paper to each of his colleagues. "I thought I should hand out an outline to provide some structure to the meeting." As he turned his head towards Bev, he added, "A wise sage once suggested it to me. The first item is Amanda's statements to the police. I don't see how we can get them excluded."

Bev put a check next to the first line on the list. "We could file one motion after another, and it wouldn't make a difference. Morelli gave consensual interviews."

"Agreed," Marc uttered and shook his head. "Would someone explain to me again why she did that?"

"Never mind," David said. "We can't travel back in time and stop her from talking. The next item is Amanda's comments to an EEOC employee, which included 'Simpson would be better off dead.'"

Marc groaned. "Another bad decision. It's really damaging and fair game because she gave a voluntary statement."

"Correct," David said with a half-frown. "Then there's fingerprint evidence, Amanda's thumbprint on Simpson's desk and the exemplars she provided to the police. They're admissible."

"Agreed," Bev said as she checked off another item.

"Yeah," Marc added. "I can't remember a judge ever excluding prints found at a crime scene or an exemplar from a defendant." He was about to take a sip of his latte and then paused. "What about Bonnie Parker?"

David smiled. "She's further down the list. We don't know the real identity of the tall blonde woman and have no leads. The authorities don't know her identity either, which might work to our advantage. Going back to the list, the next item is pre-trial motions."

"Mine," Marc said as he briefly raised his hand. "I'll draft a motion to exclude the autopsy photos and the more graphic images of the murder scene. They're too shocking for the jury and too prejudicial to the defense."

"We should attempt to exclude the medical examiner's report in its entirety," Bev stated.

"What?" Marc said as his eyes got wider. "It always gets presented to the jury."

Bev raised an eyebrow. "Think a little more creatively. The forensics expert can testify how Simpson was killed, and thus, the autopsy report and corresponding testimony isn't necessary. The only significant fact the medical examiner could add is the estimated time of death, which we're not contesting. We could stipulate to it or allow another witness to inform the jury."

David was impressed. "If the medical examiner's report is excluded, the jury might focus less on Simpson's death, which could help us."

"Exactly," Bev said.

Marc smacked the table. "Okay! I'll write it up. Beverly, could you review the first draft?"

"My pleasure," she said stoically.

David nodded and read the last item. "Finally, we get to the topic of any other motions."

"I've given it some thought," Marc said. "We could draft some of the usual motions filed by defense attorneys, but what's the point? Judge Perkins won't grant them."

"Agreed," Bev uttered.

David added, "I know filing frivolous motions irritates Judge Perkins to no end, and I'd rather remain in good standing with him. If there's a close call for a ruling, any little bit might help. Even though Perkins tries to remain neutral and objective, his emotions could sway him one way or another."

"True," Bev said. "I'm fairly certain I know the answer to my next question, but you two know Jacqueline Marshall better than I do. Do you believe she'd hide anything?"

David shook his head slightly. "She was a straight shooter during my prior cases against her. Marc?"

"That was her reputation in the office. NYPD could have held something back, but I doubt it. Nothing gets by her."

"Okay," David said. "We need to present options to Amanda. We could start up plea negotiations with Jacqueline, but I believe we have a very good chance of winning at trial. Anyone disagree?"

"No," Bev and Marc said in unison.

Marc then held out his hands. "So, here's where we are. We're ready to prep our witness and prepare for cross-examination of Jacqueline's. We'll need to make copies of our exhibits, which Irene can take care of and won't take much time. We can be ready in about a month. However, the Speedy Trial Act gives the DA six months to prepare, which means no trial until March. Are we just supposed to do nothing but spin our wheels for a while?"

"Not necessarily," Bev said with another raised eyebrow. "You should've done your homework on Judge Perkins, who's a stickler for the rules, but not all of them. The glaring exception is the Speedy Trial Act. In his opinion, the prosecution should be ready for trial immediately after the case is indicted. It might not take much of a push to force an earlier trial date."

"Nice!" David said with a wide smile. "I'll let a few reporters know that during the next hearing, we'll announce we're ready for trial. Jacqueline doesn't care about her public image, but the DA does. He'd look foolish if we say we're ready, and Jacqueline says she isn't."

Marc chuckled while Bev remained expressionless.

David continued with his train of thought. "If we start preparing for trial now, we'll probably give ourselves a little more time than Jacqueline. Given most defense attorneys drag things out, she probably hasn't gone into full trial mode. With less time, she might make a mistake during trial preparation. It's unlikely, but it could happen. Anyone mind putting in extra hours around the holidays?"

Marc and Bev shook their heads.

"Good. We also need to consider the rest of our caseload. Marc?"

"I'll take the steady flow of rich kids while you and Beverly work on Morelli."

David nodded. "Okay. I'll handle the sentencing hearing for Morales. Marc, what about Nakahara?"

"Sorry, I forgot to tell you the latest. A little birdy told me late yesterday that she and her co-conspirators are about to be indicted. Nakahara's interested in pleading guilty if we can get the DA to agree to probation, a fine, and community service. It's a realistic possibility since she was a minor player. I can handle the case solo, no problem."

"Sounds good. By the way, how did Karen Nakahara get mixed up in a phony sports memorabilia scam?"

Marc rolled his eyes. "I know."

"Did we cover everything?" David paused momentarily. "Not quite. What about the indigent defendants? I suggest we inform the federal and local courts we can't accept new indigent clients for a few months. Marc, are you okay with that?"

"Yup."

David scoffed. "I'll also be glad when we don't have to rely upon those cases and can pick and choose all of our clients."

"You'll get no argument from me," Marc said.

"Okay. Getting back to *The People versus Morelli*," David said. "Once we get Amanda's approval to push for an early trial date, which I'm sure she'll give, we're officially going into trial mode. Her father wanted a quick resolution and might get it. We'll ask Amanda, Valerie, and maybe Bill Saxer about other Thorton refugees who might make good defense witnesses."

Marc raised his hand. "Could you also ask Lorraine to bring us more desserts?

CHAPTER 22

Tuesday, November 24

P AUL OPENED THE front door for David and remarked, "I was getting worried you wouldn't get here before the show started."

"Yeah, I know. I took a cab and rush hour traffic was worse than usual."

"Please come in and have a seat," Paul said as he gestured toward the living room, which appeared sadder without natural light streaming through its windows.

Amanda and Lorraine were seated on the couch. Amanda waved to David with a smile as he approached the chair further from the front door. He believed it was more polite to allow Paul to sit in the closer one.

While displaying her usual pleasant mood, Lorraine said, "I'm sorry Paul and I couldn't make the … what's it called?"

"Taping," David replied.

"Taping of the show. I had to see the doctor about this," Lorraine said as she held up her wrist and the brace around it.

"I know. Amanda told me about it, and it's fine." David winced in his mind over Lorraine still undergoing a long and painful recovery.

Paul pointed the remote at an old television and turned up the volume. A commercial ended, and *Out and About* appeared on the screen, the name of a low budget show on a local cable station. The opening scene depicted the show's host, an attractive woman with shoulder-length black hair, Amanda, and David sitting in director's chairs in one corner of Santorini. David wore a suit and tie, while Amanda was again dressed in the restaurant's standard attire: a white top and black pants.

"Hello, welcome again to *Out and About*. I'm your host, Poppy Bradshaw," she said too enthusiastically. "We're here at Santorini, a fabulous Greek restaurant in Bensonhurst, with my guests today, Amanda Morelli," Poppy gestured with her right hand toward her, "who works here, and her attorney, David Lee."

Both Amanda and David smiled, and he also gave a brief wave.

"We're here because Amanda has been charged with murder." Poppy gave an obviously fake grimace and shook her head. "It's so hard to believe. I mean, you seem like such a nice person."

"Thank you," Amanda said.

David stopped paying attention to the dialogue and focused more on Amanda's body language and mannerisms. Meanwhile, Poppy supplied a brief description of the murder case. She and Amanda then discussed various aspects of Amanda's life. To David's delight, Amanda appeared comfortable and charming.

"Where were you when Simpson was killed?" Poppy asked.

"I was sick and asleep in bed."

"Huh … Then, why in the world are you charged with this horrible crime?"

Amanda shrugged and held out her hands. "I guess the police made a big mistake. What can I say?"

After the first commercial break, Amanda gave praise to her attorney.

"So, David. Why are you here?" Poppy asked with a gleam in her eyes.

"To provide atmosphere, and I'm trying to score a free meal."

Everyone on camera laughed, and David heard light chuckles coming from Paul and Lorraine.

Poppy then asked, "Amanda, you were an attorney. Please tell me why you're working in a restaurant?"

She raised her hands. "That's the way it is. With an indictment hanging over my head, no law firm will hire me. That's okay. I really enjoy working here, and I have a great boss."

That was Nico's cue to enter "stage right," and he put his charismatic personality on display. He stood to Amanda's left while the interview continued.

"Poppy's very pretty, right?" Lorraine asked.

David did not respond because the show had his full attention, even though he knew every line delivered.

"Please tell me something," Poppy said. "Some people are calling you the Bensonhurst Babe. Are you okay with it?"

Amanda paused and then cracked a smile. "Since I work here, I prefer the Greek Goddess, even though I'm Italian."

David, Nico, and Poppy laughed again along with others off camera.

David turned his head toward Paul and Lorraine and said, "I have to confess my laugh was fake. We planned that line before the cameras rolled."

Poppy and Amanda engaged in light banter, which David ignored. All he noticed was Amanda making a favorable impression. He also concluded it was safe to have her appear on other television shows with better hosts and larger audiences.

At the end of the second segment, Poppy said, "Coming up after the break, Nico will make a couple of his favorite Greek dishes."

Paul used the remote to turn off the television. "We've seen Nico in the kitchen plenty of times. I knew my Amanda would come through. Right, Honey?" he asked as he glanced at Lorraine. "David, you looked good too, but I wasn't too sure about you before watching the show. No offense."

David smirked. "None taken. Actually, I was a little bit nervous before we got started. Would you believe we did the whole thing in only two takes?"

"What's next?" Paul asked enthusiastically.

"Amanda and I have another interview scheduled for Friday. We'll be taping an episode of a show called *Newsmakers*, or something like that, and it airs on Sunday afternoon. Later on Friday, a reporter from the *New York Post* will interview Amanda and you two right here. Of course, I'll be on hand."

"Okay, okay," Paul said. "I've been reading about the case on the internet."

"Really?" David asked.

"Sure," Paul replied with a chuckle. "I know how to use a computer. People are saying good things about you and Amanda, but I also read many jokes about lawyers."

"Yeah. I've heard plenty of them," he said while disappointed. "They used to bother me. Too many unethical attorneys have reinforced the profession's reputation as a bunch of slimy operators. There's nothing I can do about it, except not follow their example."

Paul held out his arms. "I guess that's all you can do."

"Are you sure you can't spend Thanksgiving with us?" Lorraine asked.

"Yes, I'm sorry. I'll be with my family."

"Will your sister and her fiancé be there?"

David grimaced. "Oops. I forgot to ask. I guess I'll find out soon enough."

CHAPTER 23

Friday, December 4

DAVID HAD AN unpleasant visit with an indigent defendant housed in the federal jail in Brooklyn. Afterwards, he thought he would save money by taking the subway. Unfortunately, his train had a mechanical problem between stations and did not move for over twenty minutes. So, when he arrived at his law office, he was in a foul mood.

From her desk, Irene tilted her head down and bore her eyes into him. David had the clear impression she disapproved of his late arrival but did not inquire. If he did, he figured his rotten day could turn even worse. After working in the office for a couple of hours, he left for lunch. When he returned, he headed straight to Marc's office.

"Hey, Davey. I'm almost at full strength right now. Are you ready to get your butt kicked in Nerf basketball?"

David chuckled. "Maybe. You might be getting better, but the Julius Caesar look must go. Your bangs look ridiculous."

Marc smirked. "Thanks, and I love you too. Is that why you came to my office, to criticize my haircut?"

"No, not really. It's something else. Do you want to attend a wedding?"

Marc feigned surprise and put his right hand to his chest. "Oh wow! Are you proposing? I didn't know you loved me that much. You know I'm married to Steph and divorcing her will take a long time and get really messy. Can you wait?"

David chuckled again. "Hey, sorry to spoil your hopes and dreams, but I'm not proposing. I just had lunch with my sister, and we talked about her wedding."

"And?"

"Courtney and Chris want something simple and small, and they would pay for it. Well, with Courtney's signing bonus from Peabody, they could afford a bunch of small weddings and four or five honeymoons. Anyway, my sister was concerned about the families fighting over who would pay for it. Even though Chris' family is Chinese, they act like Americans, and in this country, the bride's side pays, which means Mom and Dad. In Chinese culture, the groom's side pays, which means Chris' family."

"Yeah, I know. I'm Asian by proxy."

Marc's comment was so out of left field it stopped David in his tracks.

"Come on. I've known you for a long time, and I know other Chinese people. I don't live in a social coma. So, who's paying for it?"

"Would you believe my parents?" David said as he held up his arms and widened his eyes. "Maybe they're doing it because they're thrilled with Courtney's so-called choice for a husband. They said this is America, and the bride's side pays. They're going all out. Even though the wedding is scheduled for early June and most places are already booked, they still found a church and a large hotel ballroom for the reception. Both sides will invite a ton of people, maybe 300, 350 in total."

"You said Courtney wanted a small wedding. Doesn't she have anything to say about it?"

David shrugged. "What can she say? Even if she objects, our parents won't listen. It's not all bad as they mean well, I guess. Getting back to my question. Would you and Steph like to come to the wedding? I need at least a couple of familiar faces in attendance."

"Sure, and you want me to be there so you can engage in pleasant conversation."

David tilted his head. "No ... that's why I'm inviting Steph. Since she's married to you, I guess you have to be there as well."

Marc smirked. "I'll talk to Steph, and I'm sure we have no plans for June. By the way, while you were having lunch, Bill Saxer called. He said Jacqueline wants to interview him next week, and he asked me what he should do."

David frowned and shook his head as he found Marc's comment hard to believe, even though he knew it was the truth. "He's a law professor and was a partner in a law firm. Now he wants to know what to do. Give me a break. What'd you tell him?"

"Same thing you would've, it's up to him. I told him if he talks to Jacqueline, that's fine. Tell the truth, don't leave anything out, and then tell us what you told her."

"Did Saxer give you any more details about his conversation with Jacqueline?"

"Nope. Maybe there weren't any."

David mulled over what he had heard while staring at a wall. "Yeah, maybe. Perhaps Jacqueline has gone into trial mode already, and she intends to call Saxer as a witness. We've talked with a few potential witnesses, but I didn't tell them about our big announcement during the next hearing."

"Neither did I. I'm sure Bev didn't, and we're keeping Irene in the dark."

David was lost in thought. "Yeah … right … probably doesn't matter. I'd still want to know what's happening at the DA's office. Got any spies you can call?"

"I left on good terms, and I still have friends over there. However, I doubt they'll tell me anything because I went to the dark side."

"Suppose so. Have you had any luck setting up an interview with Old Man Thorton?"

Marc exhaled. "I'm still trying because he's hard to reach. Someone will probably have to interview him at his place. Want me to do it?"

"No. I should talk to him because if we have to put him on the stand, he'll be my witness."

CHAPTER 24

Monday, December 14

D URING THE PAST few weeks, the Law Offices of D'Angelo and Lee had been a hectic place. Marc had been dealing with most of the firm's caseload, while David and Bev had prepared for the Morelli trial, which included interviewing potential defense witnesses. They even brought in Valerie Fernandez to take part in a mock session. David questioned her on direct examination, and Bev played the role of Jacqueline Marshall and grilled her on cross. Despite Bev's pretend assault on her character and credibility, Valerie never lost her composure. Just in case Jacqueline's co-counsel questioned her, Marc played that role, and he was intentionally too forceful and aggressive. She still remained cool as a cucumber.

Even though practice was no substitute for testimony in court, David believed Valerie would make an excellent witness. She could testify at length about Amanda's character, explain away the "Let's kill him" email, and discuss what transpired the following evening at the restaurant, when she and Amanda joked about killing Big Bobby.

David had usually asked witnesses to be themselves on the stand, but Valerie had referred to Simpson in harsh and vulgar terms. David had repeatedly reminded her not to swear on the stand. Even if Valerie let a curse word slip out, he believed her testimony would come across as natural and credible.

On Monday morning, David and Amanda arrived in court for another status conference with Judge Perkins. Even though he had seen it enough times, David still could not believe the judge kept a self-portrait in the courtroom. Before the hearing began, he amused himself by wondering whether he could sneak into the building at night and deface the portrait. Perhaps he could "improve" His Honor's appearance with a pirate hat, an eye patch, and a hook in place of his right hand.

Amanda's parents and their good friends, Pete and Debra, sat in the first row behind the defense's table, while the elderly court watchers and the media filled the back half of the gallery. Given the judge's quiet rule, David only heard murmurs in the back instead of the usual buzz before the start of a high-profile hearing. Meanwhile, microphones stood on the courthouse steps and were ready for a press conference.

Prior to the hearing, various media outlets had discussed Amanda's case, and overall, the coverage was favorable to her. For better or worse, most commentators were calling her the "Bensonhurst Babe." In response, the District Attorney had launched his own media campaign and had sat for interviews. David noticed Jacqueline's name rarely appeared in the news, which was not surprising, as she did not crave attention and was not fond of reporters. Nevertheless, Jacqueline caught his attention by changing her hairstyle again, back to a short afro.

Last week, an unnamed source (David Lee) had told a handful of reporters the defense would announce it was ready for trial, which had been an indirect message to the DA's office. David anticipated the District Attorney would place too high a priority on his political image and order his star prosecutor to state she would be ready as well. Further, David believed the media only wanted a good story, and to them, allowing the prosecution six months to prepare for trial, as permitted under New York state law, was irrelevant.

As usual, Judge Perkins took the bench at the scheduled time. His facial expression and body language gave no sign the larger than normal number of court observers made any impact on him.

At the outset, Judge Perkins said, "The defense filed a motion *in limine* to exclude some of the crime scene photos and all those taken during the autopsy. I've read your response, Ms. Marshall. Do you have any further comments?"

"Yes, Your Honor," Jacqueline said while standing straight with her clasped hands behind her back. "It's customary to present photos to the jury to demonstrate how the victim died. Relevant case law clearly indicates such photos aren't too inflammatory or prejudicial."

Judge Perkins had no reaction, and his eyes shifted towards the defense table. "Mr. Lee?"

"Nobody's disputing the deceased was shot twice in the head. We don't need one extremely graphic photo after another to drive the point home. As stated in the defendant's motion, a few crime scene photos would be sufficient."

The judge cleared his throat. "The defense's motion regarding the more graphic photographs of the crime scene and the autopsy is granted."

"Your Honor," David interjected. "We also moved to exclude the medical examiner's testimony and his corresponding report."

A vein on the side of Judge Perkins' neck bulged while the muscles in his face became tense. He growled, "Mr. Lee, the prosecution should be allowed to establish the approximate time of death."

David did not flinch. "That's true, Your Honor, but in this case, there's no dispute. The defense will stipulate to the estimated time of death, as stated in the examiner's report. In the alternative, a crime scene investigator may testify about it without objection."

Judge Perkins pivoted to the right, while his neck vein and facial muscles returned to their normal states. He then turned his gaze toward Jacqueline and did not need to say another word.

"That's fine, Your Honor," she said.

"Very well. Does the defense anticipate filing any more motions?"

"No, Your Honor." David paused for dramatic effect. "And we're ready for trial."

Judge Perkins remained expressionless. Perhaps the announcement did not catch him off guard because he had read a news article quoting the unnamed source. "Ms. Marshall?"

Jacqueline tilted her head down, and her eyes drifted toward her forehead. David had seen this body language beforehand and thus knew she was upset.

"Your Honor, the People are ready. However, I'd like to note the holidays are approaching and –"

"Yes, I'm fully aware. If we start the trial before the first of the year, we'll have difficulty seating a jury. Trial is scheduled for January 4, 2010."

"I'm sorry, Your Honor," David said. "I have a sentencing hearing in federal court that morning."

Without skipping a beat, Judge Perkins proclaimed, "Trial is scheduled for January 11, 2010. Both parties shall follow the Court's standing orders regarding any further motions, exhibits, witness lists, and jury instructions. Given the expected length of trial, we'll seat four alternate jurors. Anything else from either party?"

"Nothing else," Jacqueline replied.

"No, Your Honor," David said and believed the hearing was over. He was ready to bolt outside and step in front of the microphones on the courthouse steps.

However, Judge Perkins did not rise from his chair and instead examined all those in attendance, one at a time, which made David feel uneasy. After about twenty seconds of awkward silence, the judge gave his final orders for the day.

"Everyone in this courtroom needs to listen very carefully. The Court acknowledges members of the fourth estate are present, and the parties have already been trying their cases before the public. It … stops … today. From this moment until the end of trial, a gag order is imposed upon the District Attorney's Office, defense counsel, all potential witnesses for both sides, the defendant, and her family members. There are no exceptions."

The judge leaned forward, and the courtroom was so quiet that a faint squeak from his chair seemed much louder.

In a raspier than normal voice, he said, "If anyone is foolish enough to violate the gag order in the slightest, the Court *will* respond swiftly and harshly."

David knew Judge Perkins was not bluffing as he did not make empty threats.

"The reporters want cameras in the courtroom during the trial, and someone might file a motion to allow them. Don't bother because the Court will deny it. The trial shall be open to the public, and that's enough."

Judge Perkins continued to lean forward, rested his arms on the bench, and clenched his jaw. "One final matter for the prosecution and defense. Given the nature of this case and the accompanying publicity, you might be tempted to push the ethical envelope. *Don't* even think about it. *This* Court will make certain you don't even see the edge. If you try, you *will* get slapped back. Let me make this perfectly clear. Both sides shall follow the rules of ethics, evidence, and trial procedure to … the … letter. We're adjourned." Judge Perkins then stormed off the bench.

Following his departure, David heard the buzz in the back, turned around, and noticed several looks of bewilderment.

One reporter spotted David and mouthed, "What the hell?"

In response, he shrugged and said, "Sorry."

As Jacqueline left, she gave David an icy stare. David, the Morelli family, and their friends waited for everyone else to file out. While doing so, Paul gave David a thumbs-up. The twitch in Amanda's left leg and the tension in her face indicated she was less secure.

David put his right hand on her shoulder. "Are you alright?"

"I guess so ... not really. I gave the green light, but I'm not ready for a trial."

He removed his hand and nodded. "I know. Give it a little time to sink in. It's still a month away."

"Yeah, but ..."

"Don't worry about it," Paul said. "You'll get through this. You'll win, and you can go on with your life."

Lorraine chimed in. "Sure, it'll be fine."

"Don't think about it right now," Paul said. "How about we all go to lunch?"

Amanda groaned. "Not me. I don't think I can hold anything down right now."

"Sorry, this time I have to pass," David stated. "Too much to do today. Amanda, we'll talk again really soon, okay?"

DAVID MADE A beeline back to the office, and as he sat down at his desk, Marc needed to talk to him.

"Remember when I tried to reach Donna Conway and left messages? While you were out, she finally got back to me and said she won't testify. Sorry about that."

David sighed. "Yeah, we figured she wouldn't, and it's not a big deal. We can work around it, and the jury will still hear about her death threat to Simpson."

"What happened during the hearing?"

"Judge Perkins scheduled trial for January 11th and imposed a gag order."

Marc chuckled. "Uh-oh. That means no more Mr. TV Celebrity for you."

David smirked. "Guess not, but it's fine. We'll get some coverage today, and it'll pick up again right before trial."

OUT OF CURIOSITY, David watched the local evening news and surfed the internet for articles discussing the court hearing. Many commentators made frivolous remarks, including those concerning Amanda's outfit, and others claimed the gag order violated freedom of speech and freedom of the press. A more knowledgeable commentator believed Judge Perkins wanted to avoid a repeat of the media circus surrounding the O.J. Simpson trial. David also noted he could not find one article that took an in-depth examination of the case. The media only took what he fed to them, and he had no issues with it.

CHAPTER 25

Monday, January 4, 2010

B EFORE LEAVING HIS apartment, David checked the weather report and groaned. The high temperature would hover just below freezing, and a stiff breeze blew through the streets of Manhattan. As he had every other winter of his adult life, he kicked himself for not moving to a warmer climate. He would have preferred to stay in bed yet braved the elements to attend a sentencing hearing in federal district court.

Once the hearing concluded, David went to the Morelli home in Bensonhurst. Once again, Paul greeted him at the front door and brought him to the awful kitchen table with the plastic flower-print cover, where Amanda and Lorraine were waiting. He took a seat and skipped any small talk.

"Just before going to court this morning, I received a phone call from Jacqueline Marshall, and she offered a deal. If Amanda pleads guilty to manslaughter, Jacqueline will recommend a sentence of twelve-and-a-half to twenty-five years in prison. It's not good, but it's better than twenty-five to life, which comes with a first-degree murder conviction."

Amanda bit her lower lip and turned her gaze to a wall.

Paul asked, "Do you know why the DA made the offer?"

"She didn't say. Early on, Jacqueline said she might drop the charge to murder two, and now she's offering manslaughter. Perhaps she believes the jury will see Simpson as the bad victim, which won't go over very well. Maybe her boss wants to make the case go away, or maybe it's something else. Who knows? Jacqueline doesn't have to show us all of her cards."

Amanda continued to look away, and David tried to draw her attention by touching her hand. She glanced at him and then stared at the floor with a distressed expression.

David sighed. "I'm sorry. I know this isn't a fun conversation, but we must have it. We have some options, and it's ultimately your call, not mine. You can take the deal, or we can make a counteroffer of a plea to manslaughter in exchange for a recommended sentence of six to twelve years. If the DA's office really wants the case to go away, they might take it."

Tears welled up in her eyes. "Why are we talking about deals? Do you believe I killed Simpson?"

David shook his head, and in a soothing voice said, "No, I don't. I also don't believe Jacqueline can convince a jury beyond a reasonable doubt you committed any crime. Unfortunately, there's always a risk of conviction, and that's why I suggested a counteroffer. However, I'm recommending no deal, and we go to trial. What do you think?"

Amanda grimaced as a tear fell down her cheek. "Uh, this is too much right now. I didn't do it, and I really don't want to go to prison for twenty-five years. Even six years sounds really awful. Mom, Dad, what do you think?"

Paul puffed out his chest. "Your mother and I know you didn't do it. The jury will agree. Don't take any deal. Right, Honey?"

Lorraine nervously shook her head. "I, I don't know. Is there another way out of this?"

Paul patted her hand. "We already talked about this, remember? The DA won't drop the case. Amanda will win. You'll see."

Lorraine grabbed Paul's hand and nodded.

"Look," David said as he addressed Amanda. "We've gone through all the discovery and conducted our own investigation. While some things don't look good, the DA has no direct proof against you. I can't absolutely guarantee the jury will return a not guilty verdict because we don't live in a perfect world. However, I'm very confident we can win at trial. So, what do you want to do?"

With a worried expression, Amanda asked, "Can't I just click my heels three times and keep saying there's no place like home?"

"I'm afraid not, and we need to give Jacqueline an answer this morning."

Amanda sighed. "Yeah, right. Okay, okay. Give me a minute." She wiped away a tear and then stared at the kitchen table. The Morelli home became silent while seconds passed as if they were hours. Amanda then raised her head. "No deal. Let's go to trial."

David slapped the table. "Good. I'll let Jacqueline know."

Amanda grimaced again. "It felt good for a second, but now I feel sick to my stomach again."

"It'll pass, Pumpkin," Paul said. "Don't worry about it. David, anything else you need from us before the trial?"

"Not really. On Wednesday evening, I'll give a mock opening statement at my office, and all of you are welcome to attend. Even though I've given many openings, it's always good to practice and get some feedback."

"Maybe we can make it," Paul said. "Are you going to call any of us to testify?"

David shook his head. "It's never a good idea to put the defendant on the stand. As for you and Lorraine, the jury would probably dismiss your testimony as loving parents trying to protect your daughter. Sitting in the first row behind Amanda will convey the same message. Also, you can't confirm Amanda was in her apartment and in bed at the time of the murder."

David withheld additional reasons he did not want the Morelli family as witnesses. He genuinely believed in most circumstances, putting a defendant on the stand was a misguided and potentially damaging move. Amanda's case did not present an exception to the rule, and she did not need her past statements thrown in her face.

While David liked Amanda's father, he did not trust him because he had lied to him about an indirect connection to Marc and about his health. Paul could commit perjury on the witness stand, and no ethical attorney would risk it. David also knew the DA's office could possess more information on him. Perhaps Paul really had mafia ties, and if so, Jacqueline could use it for impeachment purposes, which created another unacceptable risk.

As for Lorraine, David suspected testifying in open court would be too stressful for her. The combination of her nerves and her tendency to be scatterbrained could cause her to forget certain facts or not present them in an organized fashion. He feared the jury could confuse forgetfulness with evasiveness and deception, which could reflect negatively on Amanda. Thus, the potential downside of Lorraine's testimony outweighed any upside.

On his way back to the office, David reviewed the DA's case and his defense in his mind. He knew he and Bev would make good points through the cross-examination of Jacqueline's witnesses, which would dictate the number of witnesses the defense would call. Fortunately, Valerie's testimony would make a significant difference, and David intended to call her last so the defense's presentation could end on a high note.

CHAPTER 26

Wednesday, January 6

THE START OF the Morelli trial was only five days away. David thought
his long hours in the office prepared him for virtually any contingency
and had no doubt Bev would be more than ready. Nevertheless, he felt under
more pressure than any other time in his legal career as both his client's freedom for decades and his law firm's reputation were on the line. In an effort
to reduce his stress level, David avoided Irene as much as possible and was
not entirely successful.

While David was working in his office and deep in thought, he noticed
a shadow fall upon his desk. He looked up and saw Irene standing two feet
in front of it.

With her hands on her hips, she demanded, "When are you going to
give me the filings for trial?"

David did not appreciate Irene's body language and attitude, but instead of letting his disapproval show, he said, "It's fine. We have plenty of time. You'll have the filings as soon as I'm finished, all right?"

"When will that be?" she asked in a condescending tone.

"Well, I don't know right now, and I'm fully aware of the court's deadlines. It's all under control. Don't stress over it."

Irene scoffed. "I need to know. I have a lot to do, and we have a deadline. I'm under a lot of pressure and –"

"What the hell! You're under a lot of pressure?" A deep well of anger rose to the surface. "Give me a break! You're not trying a murder case, a case for all the world to see. My client's looking at twenty-five to life, and you're the one who's under pressure. Get out of my office, right now!"

Irene leaned forward and slammed her hands down on his desk. "I don't like your attitude! You don't have any respect for me!"

David jumped to his feet and was about to curse her out. Before he could speak another word, Bev and Marc rushed into his office and got between him and Irene. Bev escorted Irene back to her desk, and Marc closed the door.

Marc then held up his hands. "Yeah, I know. I get it. She's a real pain, but now's not the time to deal with her. We still need her for trial preparation."

"No, we don't! I'm not an idiot!" David barked with his anger boiling over. "I know how to file documents with the court. Get her out of my sight, now!"

Marc's eyes bugged out.

"You heard me! Send her home for the rest of the day and keep her away from me until the trial is over. I already have too many things to do without dealing with her crap." David waived his right arm. "It's not just Irene being a pain in the rear. Despite the gag order, reporters keep calling me and asking for off-the-record comments. I don't need them chewing up my time."

Marc nodded. "I know. They've been calling me too. One gossip columnist offered a sizeable reward for an exclusive story, and she wouldn't shut up. I had to threaten her with Judge Perkins to make her go away."

"At least she went away." David tilted his head and was still irate. "You know what? Let's make Irene go away permanently." He took a step towards the door.

Marc gently placed his right hand on David's chest. "Wait a minute. I understand where you're coming from, but we'll need her during trial. You know how things can pop up, and if they do, Irene and I'll have to bust our tails while you and Bev are in court. Let's just get through the trial. Okay?"

David glanced at Marc and then stared at the floor, as he needed a couple of moments to process what he had heard. While he was still boiling, he could also engage in rational thought.

"Alright, fine. She stays, for now." He glared at Marc. "You're a great friend and law partner, but I swear, really soon, either she goes, or I go. Got it?"

Marc sighed. "Yeah, I guess I do. I'll keep Irene away from you. Can we just table the status of her employment until after the trial?"

"Fine. Maybe you should keep her out of the office as much as possible until it starts. If we still pay her, I don't think she'll care. Just keep in mind, if she gets on my nerves before the trial's over, I'm going to fire her right on the spot."

THAT EVENING, DAVID was ready to give his mock opening statement. Earlier in the week, David, Marc, and Bev had agreed that a few non-attorneys should listen to his opening so they could provide input from the perspective jurors' viewpoint. Thus, Marc had asked his wife Stephanie to invite her fellow airline employees.

Shortly before eight, Amanda, David, Bev, and Marc were waiting in the conference room, when Steph and three of her co-workers arrived with pizza. When Steph introduced them, David took particular note of Melinda, a statuesque Korean American. Everyone enjoyed the pizza, except for Bev, who had brought chicken salad. After Steph finished eating, she guided David to his office and closed the door.

Steph tucked several strands of her long strawberry blonde hair behind her ear. "So, what do you think of Melinda?"

"Well … she seems nice."

Steph gave a thin smile. "You can't hide your feelings from me. I've known you too long and can spot all of your tells." She took a small step closer and gazed into his eyes. "I saw the way you looked at her when we walked into the office. She broke up with her boyfriend last month, and she's now single."

David smirked. "And I'm a little too busy right now."

"The trial will be over soon enough, and afterwards maybe you can give her a call. Why not? Then again, over the past several weeks, you've given some hints that you're attracted to Amanda. Now I can see why."

"It doesn't matter because I don't date clients."

"What about after the trial?"

David scoffed. "Yeah right. Assuming we win, do you really think she'll want to see me again? I'd remind her of the nightmare she went through."

Steph raised her eyebrows and help up her hands. "You never know. Stranger things have happened."

"I'll give it some thought," he said to end the conversation even though he had little intention of doing so.

David returned to the conference room, where he announced the mock opening statements would begin. Marc played Jacqueline's part and went first, so the audience had a better understanding of the case. David then presented his opening. He engaged with his audience, was professional, and perhaps most importantly, was not long winded. Overall, Bev approved of the speech and had a couple of minor suggestions. All others in attendance praised his performance except for Steph.

"Your opening was impressive, but there was one little issue. May I?"

David waved his right hand toward her. "Please go ahead."

"You used the term 'circumstantial evidence' and didn't explain its meaning. I know what it means, but a juror or two might not. If they don't, they could get lost and not pay attention to everything you have to say. Drop the term, and your position will still be clear. The DA's whole case contains nothing directly linking Amanda to the murder."

David noticed a thin smile on Bev's face, her version of high approval, a truly rare event. He also appreciated Steph's comments. "Thanks. I'll keep that in mind."

ONCE EVERYONE ELSE had departed for the evening, David and Marc asked Amanda to return to the conference room.

"Amanda, please have a seat," David said. "Have you ever taken part in a trial?"

"No. I was occasionally present for a hearing and sat in the back."

"A trial is much different from a routine hearing, and we must consider the juror's perceptions. With that in mind ..." David rubbed the back of his neck. "Well ... we need to address your appearance."

Amanda's nose and forehead wrinkled. "What? What's wrong with the way I look?"

"Well, uh, nothing," he sheepishly said. "It's just ..."

Marc interrupted. "My learned colleague can't get to the point. There's nothing wrong with the way you look. You're attractive, really attractive."

Amanda briefly smiled. "Thanks. So, what's the issue?"

"Since you make a nice appearance, many potential jurors will have a favorable first impression of you, and let's keep it that way. Don't change your appearance during the trial. If you do, you might unintentionally create the impression you're trying to call attention to yourself, which won't go over well with some people." Marc paused and held up his right hand. "Come to think of it, many potential jurors have already seen you on TV or seen your picture in a newspaper or an internet article. Don't change your hair color or its length until the end of the trial. You also need to dress professionally. Wear only a modest amount of makeup and jewelry, and don't wear anything distracting."

Amanda nodded. "Okay. Can David and Beverly try to seat a jury full of single men who want to date me?"

David chuckled. "That'd be nice, but we can't discriminate based on gender. As for your clothing, your business suits are fine. Perhaps you should wear your hair up the first day, maybe in a French twist?"

"Sure. I can do that."

"Another important matter," Marc said. "You should assume at least one juror will be watching you at all times. Same goes for the media. Judge Perkins will tell the jurors to ignore the news, but some won't listen, and they'll blab to the other jurors. So, you must always make a good impression in court, and it's not as easy as it sounds. Trials can get dull and tiresome, and you can never look bored. If you have a tough time staying focused, take notes. Sometimes I take notes no matter what's happening to keep me alert and engaged with the case."

Amanda nodded. "Okay. Got it."

"You might've noticed Marc and I joke around a lot," David said. "However, there's nothing funny about a murder trial. Don't whisper jokes in my ear, and don't pass me a note with a joke or sarcastic comment. Passing other kinds of notes is perfectly fine, and –"

"It's okay to laugh if someone says something funny," Marc said.

"Not in front of Judge Perkins," David said with a scolding expression. "We also need to be careful about what we say in front of others because they'll try to eavesdrop. You may think one ordinary person overhearing a crack comment isn't a big deal. However, that same person could repeat the comment to a reporter or to someone else in a juror's presence, and both scenarios would be pretty bad."

Amanda sighed. "Okay, I added it to the list. It almost sounds like I'll be an animal on display at the zoo."

"No," Marc said. "It'll be *exactly* like that."

Amanda groaned. "That's just great."

David tapped his right index finger on the conference room table. "I almost forgot something. Remember the maroon outfit you wore to court last November? Do you still have it?"

"The maroon one? Yeah. It's in my closet."

"Don't wear it on the first day of trial. Wear it another day, and I'll let you know when."

"Okay … What's the big deal?"

"It'll take a while to explain. For now, just trust me."

CHAPTER 27

Monday, January 11

D AVID GRUMBLED BECAUSE another Monday came with below freezing temperatures. However, the frigid weather was the least of his concerns as January 11, 2010, was the first day of trial. In the last few days, the media had re-focused its attention on the Bensonhurst Babe. Many commentators speculated what would happen, and David surmised these talking heads were clueless. In addition, a local news channel had mentioned someone was selling Free Amanda T-shirts. Anything for a buck.

About 7:30 in the morning, David arrived at the Morelli residence, and as expected, Paul, Lorraine, and Amanda were dressed and waiting for him. Paul looked uncomfortable in a suit and tie, but his mood was still bright, while Lorraine seemed in a daze. Amanda appeared stressed, and the twitch in her left leg had returned. David requested they sit for a quick meeting at the kitchen table.

"David, how do I look?" Amanda asked.

"You look good."

"Really? I don't think I slept much last night. I used more makeup than normal to cover the dark circles around my eyes."

David gave his honest opinion. "If you didn't tell me, I wouldn't have known. You look great. Lorraine, how are you doing?"

"Oh ... I'm okay, I guess," she replied nervously. "My doctor gave me a prescription for ... for ..."

"Xanax," Paul said.

Lorraine grabbed her husband's arm, apparently leaning on him for strength. "Yeah, that's it. I took a pill this morning."

David nodded and knew the Morellis were under a great strain. "I understand. In the days ahead, you'll get used to sitting in court and won't need the pills anymore. Not much will happen right away. Today, we'll begin jury selection, and Beverly will meet us at the courthouse. Both Marc and our private detective, Frederick Ferguson, are standing by to assist, if necessary."

Lorraine gave a weak smile. "Aren't you nervous?"

"Nope."

David lied as he did not want to increase Lorraine's stress level. Besides, he would feel much better as soon as Judge Perkins took the bench. Once a trial started, a switch flipped in his head, which caused his anxiety to disappear and his drive and focus to assert themselves.

"Okay folks, here's some last-minute advice," David said. "When we arrive at the courthouse, reporters and camera crews will be outside. Please don't smile or engage with them at all, which includes waving to anybody or shaking hands. Just walk past them. When we're out in public, both inside the courthouse and outside, please don't talk about the case. We can discuss anything in private during a break, during lunch, and after court adjourns for the day. Okay?"

No one raised an objection, and only Paul nodded in agreement.

"Alright. Time to go, and I have a little surprise waiting for you."

Once David and the Morelli family stepped outside, they saw a black limousine parked by the curb. The driver, dressed in black, stood next to the right front bumper.

David gave a wide smile. "So, I thought for the first day, why don't we ride in style? I'm not billing you for this. It's on me."

THE DRIVE TO lower Manhattan was typical for a weekday morning: a slog through heavy traffic. Despite the limousine's comfort, David was anxious. Every minute he spent in the limo gave him more time to worry about what could go wrong during the trial. Despite leaving the Morelli home extra early, he also worried about arriving at the courthouse on time.

Shortly before reaching their destination, David ordered the driver to drop them off around the corner from the front entrance. He feared if the media saw the limousine, they would assume the Morelli family was wealthy or pretentious, and many potential jurors would not appreciate such reporting. Besides, he assumed news vans would be parked in front, which would leave no place to pull over.

Despite the frigid air making every moment outside an ordeal, David heard no complaints during their short hike to the courthouse steps. When he turned the corner, he noticed a group of reporters huddled together, trying to stay warm. Others trained their cameras on the approaching group. As instructed, Paul, Lorraine, and Amanda walked past them without acknowledgement. David imagined Paul had to make an enormous mental effort to restrain himself.

ONCE DAVID PASSED through the courtroom doors, he observed spectators throughout most of the gallery. He also heard a muted buzz, as no one spoke above a whisper due to Judge Perkins' ridiculous quiet rule. Bev arrived moments later, and at the defense counsel's table, David sat down in the middle with Amanda to his left and Bev to his right. Paul and Lorraine took their places in the first row behind them and next to their son, Daniel, and his wife, Trudy. Pete, Debra, and other family friends sat in the second row.

Jacqueline Marshall arrived without a trial partner, which surprised David because flying solo was extraordinary for a high-profile murder trial. Before taking her seat, Jacqueline coldly glanced toward the defense table, and pursuant to the judge's standing orders, she provided a copy of her witness list with the names in the order she would call them. David and Bev studied it for about a minute and then heard a familiar refrain.

"All rise! The Supreme Court of the State of New York is now in session! The Honorable Sherman Matthias Perkins presiding!"

While the judge never had a pleasant disposition, he appeared more disappointed than normal and failed to greet others. David suspected he was having a rotten morning, had grown tired of jury trials, or was ready for retirement.

Judge Perkins cleared his throat, and in his raspy voice, he asked, "Do the parties have any last-minute motions?"

"No, Your Honor," Jacqueline said.

"None for the defendant," David answered. In fact, he knew "none" was the only reasonable response. The judge considered last-minute motions ambush tactics and did not look favorably upon attorneys who made them.

Judge Perkins ordered the bailiff to bring in the first portion of the jury pool. Early in his legal career, David had enjoyed jury selection. He had met people from all walks of life who had their own stories, some of which were vastly differed from his own. However, after several trials, he had found the process tedious and had heard every excuse why someone could not serve as a juror. Despite his boredom, he remained focused and knew besides his legal skills, Bev was the master of jury selection. By noon, Judge Perkins had dismissed many potential jurors for several reasons, including self-employed, caregiver for a family member, and medical reasons.

Once court recessed for lunch, David announced to Bev and all five members of the Morelli family, "I know the perfect place to relax and eat in private. Shall we go?"

"Sorry, Trudy and I can't," Daniel said. "I need to take her to the train station. I'll be back for the afternoon session, and I'll try to attend the trial as much as possible."

After Daniel and Trudy departed, Amanda grabbed David's arm and whispered, "As I said before, Daniel and I are on much better terms, but Trudy's another matter. She's still a complete bitch to me. Daniel probably begged her to come to the city for one half-day."

David stepped in front of his client to block most spectators' view of her and made certain anyone remaining in the gallery only saw the back of his head. He then whispered, "Don't you remember what I told you about talking in public? I meant any talking. Some people don't need to hear you since they can read lips. Please don't screw up again."

Amanda's eyes got wide. "Okay, okay. I'm sorry."

In a softer tone, David said, "Apology accepted. Hopefully, no one was paying close enough attention. Now, let's go to lunch."

DAVID TOOK BEV, Amanda, and her parents to the Red Chili House, the same Chinese restaurant where the Morellis had previously eaten with him. When they arrived, patrons filled all the tables, and various loud conversations overlapped each other.

Paul appeared bewildered, as if someone asked him to teach a class on astrophysics. "We're going to talk and eat in private here?"

David gave a wry smile. "Just wait."

Less than one minute later, Mr. Chen, the diminutive owner with wire-rim glasses and a bad comb-over, approached David and shook his hand. "Follow me, please," he said.

A QUESTION OF MURDER

Mr. Chen escorted the Morelli party past a score of tables and into the kitchen, where the staff worked at a frantic pace. Between shouting in Cantonese and the banging of pots, pans, and woks, the back of the house was noisier than the front. Once Mr. Chen reached the end, he opened a door, revealing a tastefully furnished private dining room, which included eight armchairs draped in red leather surrounding a round table covered with a white tablecloth. A gold double happiness Chinese character hung from a red wall. Mr. Chen swung out his arm, inviting them to enter. "Always available for special guests. Enjoy your lunch."

After a waiter took their orders, David turned his attention to the witness list. "Interesting. Jacqueline's calling Bill Saxer first."

Bev gave a subtle nod.

"Why's that interesting?" Paul asked.

David looked at Bev. "Would you like to answer, or shall I?"

She motioned for him to proceed while maintaining her usual stoic appearance.

"During most murder trials, the district attorney's office first lays out the crime scene for the jury. They parade photos of the deceased and present their scientific evidence, which can be very compelling."

"Okay," Paul said. "What's their strategy this time?"

"Jacqueline wants to begin by explaining why someone would want to kill Big Bobby and inoculate the jury as to his highly inappropriate behavior. Better to hear it from her witnesses than wait for us to engage in character assassination. Unfortunately for her, her trial strategy is flawed."

"Why is that?" Lorraine asked.

This time David motioned to Bev, who said, "We can litigate our theory of the case starting with the prosecution's first witness."

CHAPTER 28

Wednesday, January 13

J URY SELECTION HAD continued Monday afternoon and throughout
Tuesday. During this process, Paul Morelli had scribbled notes regarding who should be kept on the jury and who should be excluded. David had
found his thoughts insightful and speculated he had read *Jury Selection* by
Beverly Cohen a little too well. By the end of Tuesday, a twelve-member jury
was in place, consisting of five women and seven men, plus four alternate
jurors, two men and two women. All sixteen individuals came from various
backgrounds, races, and religions, and none were young, single men who
wanted to date Amanda, as she had jokingly hoped.

Prior to the start of Day 3, David, Amanda, Paul, and Lorraine sat in
a booth at a coffee shop two blocks from the courthouse. David detected the
scent of black coffee coming from the mugs in Paul and Lorraine's hands,
which mixed with the aroma of the onions and bell peppers from a Denver
omelet at the next table.

Paul took a sip of coffee. "So far so good."

David nodded. "Pretty much. We have a decent jury but not a great one. I'm a little concerned with Juror Number 7. His body language and the tone of his answers tell me he favors law enforcement. However, if we started over and picked the jury again, I don't think the result would be more favorable."

Lorraine asked, "Who's Juror Number 7?"

"The white guy with the big stomach and goatee. On another note, how are you feeling?"

Lorraine gave a weak smile. "Fine, I guess."

David looked at Amanda. "And you?"

"Nervous."

"That's understandable. And Paul, I take it you're doing well?"

The big man smiled. "Hey, I'm doing great. When's that not the case?"

David chuckled. "Hard to argue with that."

BACK AT THE courthouse, the morning session began with Jacqueline's opening statement. As expected, she told the jury she intended to prove Amanda had conspired with a mysterious, tall blonde woman who had led J. Robert Simpson to his death. She also alleged during the evening in question, Amanda had communicated with the blonde woman by cell phone and had a motive, means, and opportunity to murder Big Bobby.

Jacqueline was long winded, and David believed she did not adequately connect with the jury. About forty minutes into her opening, he noticed half the jurors looked bored, and she did not appear close to being finished. David and Bev had a Plan B if Jacqueline droned on and on. He would give a much shorter opening statement, even shorter than last week's mock opening. They had theorized the less he spoke, the more likely the jury would pay attention.

Once Jacqueline had finished, Judge Perkins turned his gaze to the defense table. "Mr. Lee?"

David stood, buttoned his suit jacket, and with an air of confidence stepped into the well, the area between the attorney tables and the judge's bench.

"Ladies and gentlemen of the jury, the evidence will demonstrate much of which Ms. Marshall asserted this morning is absolutely true. The deceased was a sexual harasser on steroids, and my client, Amanda Morelli, hated him. So did almost everyone else who encountered him."

He paused for dramatic effect.

"Yes, it's true Ms. Morelli knew how to fire a gun, but how much training does someone need to fire one at point-blank range? It's true Ms. Morelli worked for years in the building where the murder occurred, which meant she was familiar with security measures. Many others also worked there and had the same knowledge. So did frequent visitors."

David scanned the face of each juror and noticed a couple were already losing interest.

"However, there are serious flaws in the prosecution's case. They do not have the gun used to shoot J. Robert Simpson, and they cannot put it in Ms. Morelli's hand. They also cannot show she was in the building during the murder, and they cannot connect her to the tall blonde woman who led Simpson to his death. So, why did they charge my client?" He held out his hands and raised his eyebrows. "Well, they needed to pin the murder on someone."

David nodded to the jury, took a couple of steps towards the defense table, and stopped when he heard Judge Perkins clear his throat.

"That's it?" the judge asked.

"Yes, Your Honor," David said. "The lack of evidence will speak for itself."

The prosecution's first witness was Bill Saxer, who came to court in a brown sports coat and bland yellow tie, the same outfit he had worn when he first came to David's law firm. David wondered if Saxer always tried to dress as boring as possible.

At a slow and deliberate pace and between sips of water, Saxer testified about his prior law firm's history and its financial difficulties after the mortgage meltdown. He explained why his firm brought in Simpson and why the senior partners had kept him on board despite his constant sexual harassment. Saxer acknowledged everyone had hated Big Bobby, which Simpson had called himself. He also noted the women had referred to him as Big Bastard.

Saxer also testified about Amanda and her work product. While he had liked her as a person, he and the other senior partners had denied her a junior partnership. He attempted to gloss over his reasons, but Jacqueline made him discuss them in detail. At that point, David glanced at Amanda, who appeared hurt, even though this testimony came as no surprise. He wrote to her:

> Sorry about that. By tomorrow, no one
> will remember this part.

After a few more questions from Jacqueline, David began his cross-examination.

"Mr. Saxer, I believe you testified about two weeks before the murder, Simpson left a meeting to chase after a tall, blonde, female messenger. Is that correct?"

"Yes," he said while staring straight ahead.

"Did you ever hear Ms. Morelli threaten to commit any acts of violence towards anyone?"

"No, never."

David took two steps closer to the witness. "Do you remember Donna Conway?"

Saxer casted his eyes toward the floor. "Yes, I do."

"Did she work as a paralegal at your old law firm?"

"Yes, she did," he said without raising his head.

David edged closer to the witness stand. "Was she working at the firm when the murder occurred?"

"No, she wasn't. She'd been let go."

"Did she ever make any inappropriate comments?"

Jacqueline jumped to her feet. "Objection hearsay."

"Sustained."

David glanced at Judge Perkins. "I'll rephrase, Your Honor." He then returned his attention to Saxer. "Did you take part in the decision to fire Ms. Conway?"

"Yes, I did."

"What was the basis of the decision?"

"Objection hearsay," Jacqueline barked.

Judge Perkins shifted his gaze toward David.

"Goes to the witness' state of mind, Your Honor."

"Overruled."

Out of the corner of his eye, David observed four jurors lean forward. "Why was Conway fired?"

Saxer swallowed and raised his head. "She had threatened to slit Simpson's throat."

David heard gasps throughout the courtroom, and at least three jurors appeared startled. He strolled back to the defense table. "No further questions, Your Honor."

"Any redirect, Ms. Marshall?"

"No, Your Honor."

Judge Perkins remained expressionless, raised his right hand to the level of his head, and swiveled in his chair a quarter turn to the right. After about ten seconds, he turned his head to the left to face the attorneys. In a raspier than normal voice, he said, "It's getting close to the lunch hour. We'll take a recess a little early."

Once the jurors had filed out of the courtroom, the judge's expression became more severe, and a vein in his neck bulged. "Counsels, in my chambers right now."

Jacqueline, Bev, and David followed His Honor and barely made it through the door to his personal office when he slammed it.

"What the hell is going on? Are you wasting this Court's time because the actual murderer isn't on trial?" he demanded as he waved his right arm.

"No, Your Honor," Jacqueline said in a matter-of-fact way.

"May I?" David asked while attempting to sound as deferential as possible.

The judge stared at him. "Go ahead."

"Last June, Donna Conway was in Philadelphia recovering from back surgery."

"Are you certain?"

"For the most part, yes."

"Uh-huh. For the most part," the judge said as he again threw his right arm into the air. "That's not reassuring. Ms. Marshall?"

"Your Honor, NYPD investigated Conway's whereabouts, and we're certain she was out of town on the night in question."

The judge glared at Jacqueline and then David, while the bulge in his neck continued to throb. "This Court won't allow the jury to be misled, intentionally or otherwise, for even a brief period. The parties shall immediately draft a factual stipulation concerning Ms. Conway's whereabouts at the time of the murder, and we *will* read it to the jury after lunch. Is that clear?"

"Crystal clear," David said.

Jacqueline nodded.

"Now get out!" Judge Perkins ordered as his outstretched arm pointed towards the door.

JACQUELINE MARSHALL'S NEXT witness was Kelly Holcomb, a thin woman in her early thirties with intense, mahogany brown eyes. Holcomb testified she had organized the women at the firm against Simpson, and she discussed various complaints of sexual harassment. Shortly before the murder, Holcomb had decided if the senior partners did not reign in Big Bobby in the immediate future, she would have sued on behalf of all the women who worked at their law firm. Bev asked no questions on cross-examination.

Leslie Van Martin, the EEOC employee, then took the stand. She was a heavy-set woman whose eyes darted back and forth as she entered the courtroom, which caused David to suspect she was uncomfortable speaking in public. Nevertheless, she testified Amanda came to her office to file a complaint against Simpson.

About five minutes into her direct examination, Jacqueline asked, "After you explained the EEOC process, did the defendant react in any way?"

"Uh, yes. She seemed upset because it'd take too long."

"Did she appear to be angry?"

Van Martin twisted her mouth. "Maybe."

"Did the defendant make any comments about Simpson's physical condition?"

"Yes, she said he'd be better off dead."

"Were those her exact words?"

Van Martin nodded. "Yes."

Once again, the defense waived cross-examination. David expected another witness would testify given one hour remained for the normal court hours. However, Judge Perkins announced they were finished for the afternoon and provided no explanation.

CHAPTER 29

Thursday, January 14

PURSUANT TO DAVID'S request, Amanda arrived in court wearing her maroon business suit with a knee-high skirt and matching two-inch heels, looking nothing less than stunning. David planned for the jury to get a closer view of her without her taking the stand.

The fourth day of trial commenced with Judge Perkins taking the bench in another irate mood and refusing to allow the bailiff to seat the jury. He instead ordered the attorneys and Amanda into his chambers. David did not know who or what had lit the judge's fuse. He and Bev never crossed an ethical line, and Jacqueline was not foolish enough to get herself in trouble. Thus, David suspected a juror had an agenda, or someone had caught one conducting independent research. A juror could have inspected the O'Connell building, the site of the murder, and had blabbed to another juror, who then informed a bailiff.

Judge Perkins closed the door to his personal office and ordered, "Counsels and Ms. Morelli, remain standing."

David had been in court for several of the judge's less pleasant moments but had never seen him so upset. The bulging vein in his neck had returned, his facial muscles were tense, and his eyes almost popped out of their sockets. David glanced at Bev, who seemed unmoved and had her hands clasped in front of her. Her ability to keep her composure even in the most trying of circumstances amazed him.

Judge Perkins moved within inches of David, which made him uncomfortable and allowed him to smell the judge's bad breath.

"Mr. Lee, have you read this morning's edition of the *New York Times*?"

"No, Your Honor."

He took a step back, twisted his body, and reached for the newspaper on his desk. He twisted back and smacked the paper onto David's chest.

"Here's my copy of the front section, folded to the correct page," he said as David grabbed it with his right hand. "The article in the upper left-hand corner has several quotes from an unnamed source who discussed the defense's strategy in detail. Did you speak to a reporter in violation of the gag order?"

David was taken aback and offended. Attacking his character was the third rail, and normally, he would give a swift and angry reply. This time, he held his fire to avoid a fine or a night in jail.

He calmly said, "Of course not, Your Honor."

"Uh-huh. Prior to the final pre-trial hearing, an unnamed source told reporters the defense was ready for trial. That was you, wasn't it?"

"Yes, it was, and at the time, there was no gag order."

Judge Perkins glared at him. "And I'm supposed to believe you now?"

David no longer cared if he was speaking to a judge. He was about to bark back when he noticed Bev giving him a subtle look, encouraging him to contain himself. Bev also took the judge's copy of *The Times* from his hand.

"Your Honor," David said deferentially, "as opposed to many other attorneys, I don't lie to the court. I'm also not stupid enough to violate the gag order and risk getting sanctioned."

While Judge Perkins still appeared upset, his eyes returned in their normal positions, and his neck vein stopped throbbing. David also noticed Bev reading the article in question.

Bev then raised her head and said, "Your Honor, I know for a fact my colleague did not recently speak with a reporter from *The New York Times.*"

Judge Perkins scoffed. "Oh really! How do you know, magic?"

Bev made a slight frown. "No, I recognize my own words in the article."

"What!" the judge exclaimed as his eyes bugged out again.

"I gave an interview to a reporter three days before you imposed the gag order. The article was published the next day and included some of the same quotes in here," Bev said as she pointed at the paper in her left hand. "Someone recycled the piece and made it seem more current."

"Are you certain?" Judge Perkins asked.

"Absolutely. I recognize my own words."

Judge Perkins crossed his arms and stepped toward his desk and then toward the attorneys. He stared at David for a couple of seconds and then turned his attention to Bev. After about five more seconds, he commanded, "Counsels get out! Ms. Marshall, call your next witness."

As David and Bev left the judge's chambers, he gestured for Bev to follow him into a hallway outside the courtroom and away from the spectators in the gallery.

When he was certain no one was nearby, he whispered to Bev, "Do you think Judge Perkins will sanction us?"

"I sincerely doubt it."

"What if he does? I can handle a fine, but I don't want it going on my record."

Bev raised an eyebrow. "If it happens, I'll contact a friend on the judicial disciplinary committee. We'll request a hearing, and she'll haul in the judge. We'll show her a copy of today's article and the one printed last month." She raised the paper in her left hand. "Why do you think I kept his copy?"

David released a light chuckle.

Bev added, "During the next break, I'll call Marc and ask him to order a copy of the December 12th edition, which has my quotes. Will that put your mind more at ease so you can focus on the trial?"

David nodded. "Yeah, it will. Thanks."

THE PROSECUTION'S FIRST witness of the day was Jonathan Ellrod, a nondescript, middle-aged attorney who had reviewed Thorton's emails. He had found the "Let's kill him" email, which Amanda had sent to Valerie three days before the murder. On cross, Bev used this witness to admit into evidence five other emails containing negative comments about Simpson, although none of them suggested injuring or killing him.

Jacqueline's next witness was Evan Huang, the bartender from the restaurant near Amanda's former place of employment. With his goatee, spikey hair, and tattoos peeking out from the long sleeves of his white dress shirt, he stood out in the crowded courtroom. Huang testified Amanda and her friend (Valerie Fernandez) sat near the bar the Monday before the murder. Both were drinking, but neither appeared intoxicated. Since the restaurant was not busy, he overheard them discuss how to kill someone called Big Bastard, and they settled upon shooting him twice in the head.

On cross, Bev asked, "Were Ms. Morelli and her friend whispering?"

"No. They were talking normally."

"Did they use any code words or euphemisms?"

"Uh ... I don't think so," Huang said as he rubbed his left arm.

Bev walked into the well and toward the jury. "Based upon what you saw and heard, do you believe the two women tried to keep their conversation confidential?"

"No, I don't believe so."

Bev stopped in front of the witness stand. "Did they know you were listening?"

"Yeah. One of them, the defendant sitting over there," Huang said and pointed at Amanda, "she asked her friend if I was listening. Her friend said she didn't care."

"So, they were serious about plotting a murder and didn't care if you heard them, even though you could call the police or testify against them?"

"Objection, speculation," Jacqueline said.

"Sustained."

"Did my client, Ms. Morelli, and her friend appear so stupid or foolish that they would openly discuss a murder plot?"

"Objection, speculation."

"Sustained," Judge Perkins barked. "Move on Ms. Cohen."

"Did the women ever smile or laugh?" Bev asked.

"Maybe."

Bev raised an eyebrow. "Maybe, you're not sure? Didn't you tell the police they were smiling and laughing?"

"I guess so."

"Do you think they were serious about killing someone?"

Huang shrugged. "Maybe, it's a tough town. I've heard people say a lot of things."

"Did you call the police?"

"No."

"No?" Bev removed her glasses. "Mr. Huang, if you thought Ms. Morelli and her friend were serious about killing someone, why didn't you call the police? Are you that callous?"

Huang shifted his gaze from Bev to his hands in his lap.

"Do you have an answer? Why didn't you call the police?"

"Uh ... I don't know," he said while still looking away from Bev. "Maybe I didn't take them seriously. It's a nice place, and our clientele doesn't commit crimes."

Bev put on her glasses. "No further questions, Your Honor."

AFTER THE MORNING break, Jacqueline summoned Jason Hill, the crime scene investigator, who had a pear-shaped body and a pock-marked face. Based upon Hill's manner of speech and quick responses to questions, David concluded he was intelligent, too intelligent to be a government employee and could earn far more money working in the private sector.

Through Hill's testimony, the photos of the deceased and his office were admitted into evidence. Hill testified he had found fingerprints on Simpson's desk, including Amanda's thumbprint. He also found smudged prints on the glass door to Simpson's office, which he could not identify. Hill further stated the office's door handles had been wiped down, which erased any fingerprints.

Based upon the position of the body, the location of the entry and exit wounds, the bullet holes in the throw pillow, and the two holes in the wall, Hill reasoned the bullets traveled on a slightly downward trajectory, about five degrees from horizontal. He determined the locations of Simpson and his killer at the time of the first shot, and to assist the jury, he presented a detailed drawing of the scene. Two mannequins represented Simpson and the killer. One mannequin sat on the couch and, with both hands, held a pillow in front of its face. The second mannequin stood with its knees bent and a handgun in both hands. The second mannequin's arms stretched out and the gun's muzzle contacted the pillow. Hill also concluded the mannequin with the gun was the same height as the defendant.

On cross-examination, David asked, "As part of the police's investigation, someone spoke with the cleaning crew, correct?"

"Correct."

"Isn't it true they made their rounds during the early morning hours the same day as the murder?"

"Correct. After the murder, I believe they reached the tenth floor around three in the morning, and that's when they found the body."

David cocked his head. "However, the cleaning crew was not certain the last time they had wiped down Simpson's desk."

"I believe so."

"So, isn't it true Ms. Morelli could've placed her thumbprint on the desk earlier the same day as the murder, the day beforehand, or earlier in the week?"

"Sure," Hill said in a blasé manner.

"Alright. Did you conduct a thorough examination of the crime scene?"

"Yes, of course."

"And no shell casings were left at the scene?"

Hill nodded. "Correct."

"And there were no shoe prints in the carpet inside Mr. Simpson's office?"

"Correct again."

David was pleased and not finished. He was about to use Hill's expertise to his advantage.

"Let's next address the height and position of the shooter," David said. "As part of your analysis, you assumed the killer took a proper shooting stance with his knees slightly bent and arms stretched out."

"Yes, I did."

"If a slightly shorter person, say someone five-foot-three, stood straight and fired, the bullets would have traveled on the same trajectory?"

Hill took a breath and stared into space. A moment later, he said, "That's a fair assumption."

"Suppose the shooter was a taller person, about five-six or five-seven, and his knees were bent a little more. Would the bullets have travelled along the same trajectory?"

"There's a problem with your theory. If the shooter crouched more, she would've lacked balance, and the shots would've been less accurate."

David feigned surprise. "Well, how accurate does someone need to be at point-blank range?"

He heard two jurors chuckle and noticed Judge Perkins was not amused.

"Mr. Hill, based upon my hypothetical, could a slightly taller person have fired the fatal shots?"

With a half-frown, the witness said, "I suppose so."

AFTER THE LUNCH break, David watched the jurors as they re-entered the courtroom. Most appeared refreshed and ready for more testimony, but Juror 7, the Caucasian man with the large stomach and goatee, was the notable exception. He plodded towards his seat with his hands in his pockets and casted a dirty look towards him. David had suspected he would be the wild card during deliberations and now feared he would be an advocate for the prosecution.

JACQUELINE MARSHALL THEN called the waiter from the restaurant where Simpson ate shortly before his death. During his brief testimony, he said he had seen Simpson having dinner with a tall blonde woman. The defense had no questions.

The next witness was Eric Stonewall, one of the O'Connell building's security guards. As he walked toward the witness stand, David noticed his pale, round face displayed a look of resignation, as if he were dragged to the principal's office due to his misbehavior in class. In addition, instead of showing respect to the court by wearing a suit and tie, he was dressed in a short-sleeve shirt with a collar.

Jacqueline asked him, "On the evening of June 18, 2009, did you see J. Robert Simpson?"

"Yeah."

"Was he with anyone else?"

"Yeah. A tall woman."

"What was the color of her hair?"

Stonewall sighed and crossed his arms. "Blonde."

"Where did you see her and Mr. Simpson?"

"In the lobby."

David was unimpressed with Stonewall given his rotten attitude and his short, blunt answers. Two security guards had been on duty during the evening of the murder. David asked himself whether the other one would have been a worse witness, which would be the case only if the other guard had a lobotomy or was comatose.

"While in the lobby, did the tall blonde woman say anything?" Jaqueline asked.

"Yeah," Stonewall said. "She said she needed to make a phone call. She told Simpson to go upstairs, and she'd join him in a few."

"Did Simpson go upstairs?"

He snickered. "What do you think?"

Judge Perkins growled, "Answer the question."

"Yeah. He used the elevator."

"What did the blonde woman do?" Jacqueline asked.

"She stepped outside."

"Did she ever return?"

"No."

Jacqueline played the video from a security camera in the lobby, which depicted what Stonewall had described. "Is that what happened?"

"Yeah."

AN EMPLOYEE OF a cell phone company told the jury a woman named Bonnie Parker bought two cell phones sixteen days before the murder, and their numbers ended in 7881 and 7882. For two weeks, the 7881-phone communicated with Simpson's cell phone and no others. The 7882-phone only had call activity during the evening of the murder. It received a brief call from the 7881-phone, and several minutes later, 7882 communicated with 7881 for a few seconds. For both calls, the cell tower closest to the O'Connell building made the connection.

During her questions, Jacqueline indicated the tall blonde woman and Bonnie Parker were one in the same, and the tall woman had called the shooter, who made the return call. Normally, David would object to leading questions, but he wanted the jury to reach the same conclusion. Once Jacqueline finished with the witness, he asked no questions.

Judge Perkins reacted by opening his mouth and swiveling his chair to the right. David recognized this behavior as the judge unintentionally signaling he did not understand what the defense was doing. If it dawned on him, he would spin back to face the attorneys. However, he instead ordered, "I'll see the attorneys and Ms. Morelli in chambers."

THIS TIME, THE judge did not slam the door, but given the look on his face, David suspected the judge's blood pressure rose without a good reason.

"Mr. Lee and Ms. Cohen, there was almost no pre-trial litigation, and you gave an abbreviated opening statement. You've objected to none of the prosecution's questions, and you made no objections to any exhibits. For most witnesses, you asked no questions on cross. I don't want this case coming back to me based on ineffective assistance of counsel. Mr. Lee, do you know what you're doing?"

"Yes, Your Honor," he said confidently.

Judge Perkins scoffed. "Really? Ms. Cohen, do you know what you're doing?"

"Absolutely."

"And I'm supposed to believe it?" The judge waved his right arm in the air, stomped toward shelves filled with legal books, and stomped back. "Ms. Morelli, do you approve of your attorneys' performance?"

"Yes, Your Honor."

Judge Perkins scoffed again. "Unbelievable!"

Bev took one step forward and stared at the judge. "Permission to speak freely?"

"Go ahead."

"I've been a defense attorney for a long time, and you should know better," she said as she shook her right index finger. "When you were a pros-ecutor, you had an outstanding record filled with trial victories, except when you lost three times to me. In this case, the defense hasn't engaged in scorched earth litigation as it would've been unnecessary and pointless. We're putting on a defense, and don't forget, the trial's far from over. Just wait. Soon enough, you'll have a very different opinion about the defense."

Judge Perkins raised his eyebrows, and his eyes bugged out. David tried to look away and waited for him to explode.

The judge instead stated, "Fine, but I'll be watching you. We're in recess for fifteen minutes."

As David and Bev returned to the courtroom, he whispered, "Perkins lost to you three times?"

"Yes. One defendant had two mistrials, and the judge dismissed the case after the second one. Another case was dismissed due the property room mishandling the evidence. That's three wins in my book."

FOLLOWING THE AFTERNOON break, Jacqueline called Derek Collins, a video and computer expert with NYPD. His pinstriped blue suit, white dress shirt, and red and blue striped silk tie covered his lanky frame. Collins' dark brown hair was perfectly coifed, and David suspected he used a daily facial cleanser. In addition, his purposeful stride and raised chin reflected confidence to the point of arrogance.

Collins testified he had reviewed video footage from the O'Connell building's lobby, from the camera in front of the parking garage entrance, and from the camera down the street. Jacqueline played the relevant portions of the original and enhanced videos concerning the view of the street. During one portion, Collins pointed out a woman in a gray wig and a cane emerging from the north side of the O'Connell building several minutes after Simpson had entered the lobby. Collins also explained why he believed the cane was only a prop.

As David stood to begin his cross, he knew Judge Perkins would not appreciate his upcoming courtroom theatrics. While he wanted to stay on the judge's good side, he was more concerned with making a substantial impression upon the jury, who would ultimately decide his client's fate.

"Mr. Collins, does the video footage confirm Ms. Morelli left the building mid-afternoon on the day of the murder?"

He leaned back in his chair and crossed his legs. "Yes, it does."

"Did she ever re-enter the building later the same day?"

"None of the cameras captured her image again."

"Did you see any footage of the woman in the gray wig entering the building?"

"No."

"And you believe the woman in the gray wig is the same height as my client, correct?"

"Yes, that's correct," Collins said with his chin thrust in the air.

"Well, the woman in the gray wig was hunched over. Doesn't that make it difficult to determine her exact height?"

Collins smirked. "No, I don't think so."

"Have you ever seen my client standing right in front of you?"

"No."

David turned to the bench. "With the Court's permission, I'd like Ms. Morelli to stand before the witness."

Judge Perkins flicked his right hand.

Amanda rose and walked until she was five feet in front of the witness stand. Not coincidentally, she stood closer to the jurors, most of whom stared at her.

Collins uncrossed his legs and sat upright.

David remained in the well and behind Amanda so the jurors could still see him. "Now, can you say Ms. Morelli is the same height as the woman in the video?"

In a condescending tone, he replied, "Your client's wearing high heels, and the woman in the video wore more practical shoes."

David smiled. "My apologies." He strode toward the defense table and reached into Amanda's purse. He retrieved a pair of tennis shoes, walked back, and gave them to her. David then stood between his client and the judge.

Amanda took off her heels and put on the tennis shoes. While doing so, David noticed four male jurors examining her legs, including Juror Number 7. David grabbed the heels and placed them on the defense table.

David knew Amanda changing her shoes to attract the male jurors' attention was a sexist move, and he did not care. Her freedom was on the line, and he would exploit any advantage so long as he would not upset the state bar. Some of the female jurors could have been offended by the men staring at Amanda's legs, and if so, David assumed they would release their scorn on their male colleagues, not him.

David returned to his prior spot in the well and asked, "Mr. Collins, is my client the same height as the woman with the gray wig?"

"Yes, she is."

Amanda remained calm, clasped her hands behind her back, and knew what would happen next.

"Is it possible Ms. Morelli is slightly taller or shorter by an inch or less?"

"No," Collins said bluntly.

"Uh-huh." David cocked his head. "So, despite the woman in the video hunching over, you can determine her height to the smallest fraction of an inch and know it is exactly the same as my client?"

Collins looked away and shifted in his chair.

David glared at him. "You don't have to answer the last question. Aren't there many women in New York the same height as Ms. Morelli, an inch shorter, or an inch taller?"

"Of course."

"Aren't some *men* the same height?"

Collins smirked with his chin once again in the air. "Yes, but do they have the same build? I don't think so."

David again turned towards the bench. "Your Honor, I respectfully request another person stand next to my client."

Judge Perkins gave another permissive wave.

David turned his head toward the back of the courtroom. Marc opened the door, and a short, slender man entered, whose fair skin matched his blonde hair, which had a permanent windswept appearance. The slender man wore a dress shirt, tie, and slacks but no jacket or sports coat so that the jurors could observe his build. The man walked into the well and stood between Amanda and the jury box.

David pointed at him. "Doesn't this man's height and build match my client?"

"Roughly, yes," Collins said. "You probably found the one man in New York who does."

"Isn't it possible this man could have been the *person* with the gray wig and cane?"

Collins chuckled. "What? Not a chance. What man would dress like that?"

"Oh really?" David said as he cocked his head again. "What man would dress like a woman? Perhaps a drag queen?"

The slender man dramatically reared his head and raised his right hand to his chest, which caused about half the jurors and a large portion of the gallery to laugh. On the other hand, the vein in Judge Perkins' neck made another appearance.

"Counsels, approach," he ordered.

David, Bev, and Jacqueline came within inches of the bench.

Judge Perkins fumed and put his left hand on his microphone. "Mr. Lee, that's the last stunt you'll pull in this courtroom. Now stand back." Once the attorneys returned to their original positions, the judge commanded, "Ms. Morelli, go sit down." He then pointed at the drag queen. "You sir, leave my courtroom now."

The slender man acknowledged with a nod and made a swift exit.

David then said, "No more questions, Your Honor."

As he strolled to the defense table, he noticed Bev twice tap her right index finger on the table, which indicated her approval. He also saw a wide smile on Paul's face.

Paul then mouthed, "That was fun."

David thought to himself, *Yes it was. Yes indeed.*

CHAPTER 30

Friday, January 15

JACQUELINE'S NEXT WITNESS was Nathan Flynn, the lead detective for the Morelli case. His cheap suit matched his unruly gray hair, and his deep facial wrinkles and bad skin reflected decades of drinking and smoking. In fact, as the detective passed by the prosecution and defense tables, David noticed the stale scent of cigarette smoke.

With a voice as refined as coarse sandpaper and between coughing spells, Detective Flynn testified about the investigation's various stages, beginning with the initial interviews of all those who worked for Thorton, Saxer & Caldwell at the time of the murder. He also described how his team eliminated individuals as suspects and then addressed the evidence against Amanda.

Jacqueline questioned her witness for an extended period without a script or notes. David believed if most attorneys tried it, they would stumble and bumble before the jury. However, Jacqueline's performance was an impressive feat, and she had not yet finished.

"Detective Flynn, did you ever speak with the defendant?"

"Yes. Monday after the murder."

"Did you ask the defendant her opinion of J. Robert Simpson?"

"Yes." Flynn coughed into his sleeve. "She said, 'He wasn't so bad.'"

"Based upon your investigation, did you ever come to any conclusion regarding this statement?"

"Yes. It was wildly inconsistent with the 'Let's kill him' email."

Jacqueline paused for a few seconds, presumably to let the prior answer soak into the jurors. "Did you ask the defendant whether she ever owned or handled any firearms?"

"Yes, I did. She admitted –" The detective pulled out his handkerchief and twice coughed into it. "Excuse me. She admitted a family friend taught her how to fire a variety of weapons."

"Including a .38?"

"Yes."

Jacqueline paused again, and this time David knew it was intentional.

"Did the defendant own any guns?"

"She said she didn't."

"Did you ask her if her parents owned any firearms?"

"She said her parents used to own a .38 handgun, the same caliber as the murder weapon. I oversaw the search of their residence, and no firearms were located."

"No further questions, Your Honor."

Judge Perkins glanced at David, who rose and moved to stand in the middle of the well.

"Detective Flynn, let's address the search of the Morelli home in Bensonhurst. You were looking for a gray wig, a cane, certain articles of clothing, a .38-caliber handgun, and two cell phones, correct?"

"That's right."

"And you found none of these items?"

"That's right."

"Okay. Let's focus on Ms. Morelli's interviews. Was she always cooperative with the police?"

The detective again coughed twice into his handkerchief and then said, "Yes, she was."

"Did she ever invoke her right to remain silent?"

"No."

"Did Ms. Morelli ever lead you to believe she was trying to hide something?"

"You could say that."

"Are you referring to her saying the deceased wasn't so bad?"

"Yes." Detective Flynn coughed again. "I later concluded she wanted to deflect attention from herself. She tried to create the appearance she didn't hate Simpson and didn't have a motive to kill him."

"Uh-huh," David said and cocked his head. "Well, isn't it possible she meant Simpson wasn't so bad that someone should've killed him?"

"No, I don't believe so."

"Isn't it true neither you nor anyone else ever asked any follow-up questions regarding my client's opinion of the deceased?'"

"That's correct."

"Could you explain why?"

The witness coughed three times and stretched his arm towards the bailiff, who brought him a bottle of water. After drinking half of it, he seemed ready to continue.

"Detective Flynn, do you have an answer?"

"What was the question?"

"Why didn't you or anyone else ask follow-up questions to determine what Ms. Morelli actually meant?"

"There was no need."

David scoffed. "Oh really? So, you believe your investigation was very thorough?"

"That's right."

David smiled to himself because Flynn had stepped into a little trap. "Prior to my client being arrested, you and your team didn't talk to any of the law firm's former employees, more specifically, any former employee who hated the deceased. Is that right?"

The detective gave him an icy stare.

David cocked his head again. "Let's try it another way. Isn't it true Donna Conway used to work for the same firm as Simpson?"

"Yes."

"Isn't it also true she was fired for threatening to slit Simpson's throat?"

"Yes, but so what?" Flynn said while flashing a glowering expression. "We investigated, and she was in Philadelphia when Simpson was shot."

"Uh-huh. Isn't it also true NYPD never knew Ms. Conway existed prior to my client's arrest and indictment?"

"Yes, but so what?"

"You first heard about Ms. Conway from the Assistant District Attorney, correct?"

"Yes."

"And the ADA heard about her from the defense?"

"Yes."

"Detective, perhaps you weren't so thorough. Anything else you forgot to investigate?"

"Objection, argumentative," Jacqueline said as she jumped to her feet.

"Sustained."

"Detective, did you ever determine the identity of the tall, blonde, female messenger who came to the law firm sixteen days before the murder?"

"No," Flynn said while he drew his brows together. "We never had any good leads."

"Were you able to identify the tall, blonde woman with Simpson minutes before his murder?"

"No. The security guards on duty only gave a general description."

"Could they have been the same person?" David asked.

"It's possible."

"And you discovered during the last two weeks before his death, Simpson was communicating with a woman who bought cell phones under the name Bonnie Parker?"

Flynn coughed again. "Yes. Someone bought cell phones using that name."

"Do you believe the name Bonnie Parker was an alias?"

"Yes. She provided the cell phone company with a driver's license number, address, and credit card number, and all of them were bogus."

"Do you believe Bonnie Parker and the tall blonde woman were the same person?"

"It's possible."

David feigned surprise. "It's only possible? The security guards and a waiter saw the tall blonde woman with Simpson right before his death. The last two calls on the Bonnie Parker cell phones occurred within minutes of the murder, and they connected through the cell tower closest to the building where the murder took place. Yet, it's only *possible* the tall woman and Bonnie Parker are the same person?"

"That's right," Detective Flynn said.

"One last thing. Do you believe many people disliked and even hated J. Robert Simpson?"

"That's a reasonable conclusion."

"Are you certain you found all of his enemies?"

Flynn stared ahead while the muscles in his jaw tightened.

David waved his right hand. "That's fine, Your Honor. The witness doesn't have to answer. No further questions."

Judge Perkins turned his gaze towards Jacqueline.

She rose and said, "No redirect, Your Honor."

As he stepped down from the witness stand, Detective Flynn casted a sneer towards David, who imagined they had equally low levels of respect for each other.

The prosecution's next witness was Detective Katherine Brown, a thin, stern woman with a tight face and red hair coiled in an equally tight bun. Brown testified she had overseen the execution of the search warrant at Amanda's apartment, where no items listed in the warrant had been found, including a .38-caliber handgun. She instead located a .22-caliber pistol in the bedroom closet. Photographs of the closet, the gun case, and pistol were admitted into evidence. Detective Brown also noted she found the pistol after Amanda said she did not own a firearm.

On cross, David asked, "Who was the registered owner of the pistol?"

"Ms. Morelli's ex-husband," Brown said with all the emotion of a soulless robot.

"So, at some point, he gave her the gun?"

"That's a fair assumption."

"Detective Brown, you found the pistol in a back corner of the bedroom closet, correct?"

"Correct."

"On the top shelf?"

"Correct."

"And the pistol was inside a small black case?"

"Yes," she said without a hint of emotion.

David wondered if she possessed the ability to interact with others in a social setting. "Isn't it true no one could easily see the case containing the pistol? Someone had to remove a few items first?"

"That's right."

"Okay. Please turn to the first photo depicting the gun case." David waited while she did so. "There's a layer of some gray substance on top. Isn't that dust?"

"I believe so."

"Which shows no one moved the case for a long time, correct?"

Brown scoffed. "Yes, of course."

"Had the gun ever been fired?"

"No, it looked brand new," she said as she returned to answering questions without emotion.

"Detective Brown, you found two ammunition clips inside the case. Were any bullets in either clip?"

"No."

"Was there a round in the gun?"

"No."

David nodded. "Did you find any ammunition in Ms. Morelli's apartment of any caliber?"

"No, we didn't."

"Detective Brown, isn't it true a .38 has a lot more firepower than a .22?"

"Yes, of course."

"Your service weapon is a nine-millimeter handgun, correct?"

"Objection, relevance," Jacqueline said.

Judge Perkins stared at David.

"Your Honor, if you'd allow the defense to ask a few more questions, the Court will see the connection momentarily."

Judge Perkins did not react.

David interpreted his lack of response as permission to proceed. "Your service weapon is a nine-millimeter handgun, correct?"

"Correct."

"It's fairly comparable to a .38 in terms of firepower, isn't it?"

"That's right."

"Detective Brown, do you know of any police department issuing .22-caliber handguns as a standard service weapon?"

"I'm not aware of any."

"Because a .22 lacks sufficient firepower?"

"Most likely."

"Alright. Please consider the following scenario."

Brown remained stone-faced and motionless.

David walked at a slow pace towards the jurors. "We know Ms. Morelli was familiar with firearms, and a .22 doesn't have much firepower. We also know the .22 in question was in the back of her closet." He stopped just before he blocked the jury's view of Detective Brown. "Dust covered the case, no one had ever fired the gun, and my client didn't buy it." David held out his hands. "Ms. Morelli thought little of it, because in her mind, it wasn't a real gun. She just threw it in the closet," he said as he made an underhand tossing motion, "and forgot about it. Therefore, when asked about owning any firearms, she made an honest mistake by stating she didn't own a gun. Does this scenario sound plausible to you?"

Detective Brown scoffed. "No. How can someone forget about owning a lethal weapon?"

"Oh really? Your Honor, no more questions for this witness."

Jacqueline's next witness was Detective Joseph Blackwood, a white male in his late thirties with short brown hair and an athletic build. Blackwood had conducted a follow-up interview with Amanda after the police had found her fingerprint on Simpson's desk. According to Blackwood, Amanda had said she never went into Simpson's office.

Moments before Bev launched into her questions, David passed a note to Amanda:

Time for some more fun!

"Detective Blackwood, according to your testimony, Ms. Morelli told you, 'I never went into Simpson's office.' Are you sure those were her exact words?"

"Yes, I am," he said confidently.

"Isn't it possible she said she tried to stay out of Simpson's office as much as possible?"

"No."

"By the time you spoke with my client, did you consider her a suspect?"

"Yes, we did."

"Didn't your interview provide a partial basis for Ms. Morelli's arrest and indictment?"

"I don't know. Ask the DA."

Bev raised her eyebrow. "Are you serious? You don't know?"

"It wasn't my call."

"Detective Blackwood, have you ever committed perjury on the stand?"

"Never."

Bev took two steps closer to the witness and stared at him. "Oh, are you certain?"

He paused and then said, "Of course."

"Isn't it true you've been with NYPD the past seven years?"

"Yes."

"Weren't you previously a police officer in Newark?"

Blackwood turned pale. "Yes, I was."

Bev continued to stare at him. "Isn't it true while you were with the Newark Police Department, you worked on the Leon Washington case?"

"Uh, yes," he said as he shifted in his chair and glanced at Jacqueline, as if he were pleading with her to rescue him.

"The appellate court threw out Leon Washington's conviction over your false police report and lying on the witness stand, correct?"

"No, I never lied!"

Bev walked to the defense table, grabbed a quarter-inch stack of papers, and held them high in the air. "Your Honor, this is the relevant decision from the New Jersey appellate court. I'd like it marked and admitted into evidence." She dropped the papers on the table. "I'm done with this witness."

On redirect examination, Jacqueline asked, "Do you remember earlier today you took an oath to tell the truth?"

"Yes."

"When you testified about your interview with the defendant, were you telling the truth?"

"Absolutely," Detective Blackwood said a little louder.

"Did you take notes when you interviewed the defendant?"

"Yes, of course. I always take copious notes."

"Were your notes an accurate reflection of what the defendant said?"

He nodded. "Yes."

"When did you incorporate those notes into your report?"

"I'm not certain as to the exact time, but I always type up my reports within twenty-four hours of an interview."

"Did the report accurately reflect the defendant's statements and what was in your notes?"

"Yes."

"No further questions."

As she sat down, Jacqueline kept a stoic appearance, but David knew she was angry because no one had told her about Blackwood's termination for misconduct. David also surmised she was frustrated as he was the last witness for her case-in-chief and the last witness of the day. Thus, his damaged testimony would stick with the jury over the weekend.

CHAPTER 31

Monday, January 18

A BOUT THIRTY MINUTES before the trial resumed, David isolated himself in a quiet corner of the courthouse and panicked. He also called Marc on his cell phone. "We've got a serious problem. Valerie's a no-show, and I can't reach her on her cell and home numbers."

"Ah crap!"

"Where are you? I need you to find her ASAP."

"I'm at home and was about to leave for the office. Valerie lives close by. I'll get over there right now."

"Fine. Call me back." David ran his hand through his hair. Despite his present mood, he did his best to project a calm appearance. He turned the corner and found Bev and Amanda standing side-by-side, waiting for the bailiff to unlock the doors to Judge Perkins' courtroom.

David smiled at Amanda. "Excuse me." He turned to Bev, and with his false expression still in place, said, "Could I speak to you for a couple of moments?"

Bev nodded to Amanda, and David escorted her to the secluded location around the corner. He then dropped his façade and felt his chest tighten.

"We've got a big problem," he said. "Valerie's not here, and I can't reach her by phone. Marc's trying to track her down."

Bev remained calm. "Let's not get carried away. She could be running a few minutes late, or she could be in the subway and can't get a signal."

David ran his hand through his hair again. "Yeah, I know, but …"

"Let's not assume the worst or jump to conclusions. She's also not our first witness, and we can buy some time." Bev raised her eyebrow. "However, it wouldn't hurt to run through our options."

"Good idea," David said while trying to control his anxiety. "If Valerie is a little late, we're … uh … In another trial, Judge Perkins didn't allow a short continuance for a witness to appear. So, he probably won't this time, regardless of the reason." He exhaled. "Last weekend, we discussed calling no witnesses and during closing, we'd argue we didn't need any since the prosecution failed to prove its case. I think that scenario is still off the table."

"Agreed," Bev said in a matter-of-fact way. "Even if Valerie doesn't testify, we should call our first two witnesses. They'll make some good points."

David nodded and looked at the floor. "Yeah, but I'd rather not stop after them."

"We have other witnesses on our list, and I strongly suspect Judge Perkins won't allow us to call a multitude to bash Simpson's character. He'd consider it cumulative testimony and a waste of time."

David had a sudden revelation and picked up his head. "Yeah, unless Simpson's depicted from another perspective."

Bev again raised an eyebrow. "Charles Thorton?"

"Right. The Old Man can testify about Amanda's character and discuss his interactions with Simpson."

Bev pursed her lips. "I thought you said he was doing poorly."

"He is. I'd rather finish with Valerie, but if she's a no-show, end with the Old Man."

Bev removed her glasses and tapped the end of an earpiece on her right cheek. "Hmm. Under the circumstances, calling three witnesses might be better than two …" After a few seconds, she donned her glasses. "Fine. Fernandez is Plan A, and Thorton is Plan B. Why don't you remain out of sight, and I'll keep my eye out for Fernandez?"

David nodded. "Sounds good. Could you also explain to Amanda what's happening without freaking her out?"

"Of course."

For the next twenty minutes, David paced back and forth and kept checking his phone, making certain he still had a signal.

Marc finally called back. "Hey, Valerie's really sick. I think she's got the flu."

David's anger flared. "Damn it, Marc! Stop messing with me!"

"Whoa! Hang on. I'm not messing with you. I'm at Valerie's place right now, and she looks terrible. She couldn't answer the front door, and one of her kids let me in. There's no way she can take the stand. Her mother's coming over, and she'll take Valerie to the ER."

"Terrific," David said sarcastically. "Sorry about the outburst. Looks like the Old Man will be our last witness."

"Uh, I guess so. That was a fast decision. Don't you want to run it past Bev first?"

"We already discussed our options. Please get Thorton, bring him here, and run through his testimony again. Do you know where to find his Q&A?"

"Yup. I'll take care of it. Everything's under control."

"Yeah, right."

ONCE THE TRIAL resumed, Beverly Cohen questioned Theresa Quintero, an average-sized Latina in her mid-thirties. Except for her blonde hair showing its darker roots, Quintero had no distinguishing characteristics and could blend into any crowd. As she sat in the witness chair, she tugged at her purse strap.

"Ms. Quintero, where were you employed in early 2009?"

"I was a paralegal at the Law Offices of Thorton, Saxer & Caldwell."

"Where was your cubicle?"

"Close to Mr. Simpson's corner office."

"How'd he treat you?"

"Not very well," Quintero said and tugged the strap again.

"Could you please elaborate?"

"Okay … He was a … horrible person and constantly harassed me. One time, he slapped me on the behind, and a couple of times, he asked if I had been a prostitute in Mexico. Excuse me." She took a tissue from her purse and wiped away a tear below her left eye.

"Did Mr. Simpson make other comments you found inappropriate?"

"Do I have to tell you all of them?"

"No, it's not necessary," Bev said. "How often did he make inappropriate comments?"

"Almost every day."

"Ms. Quintero, did you respond to the comments in any manner?"

"I, I don't know. A few times, I called in sick. Eventually, I spoke with Mr. Thorton, and he let me move to another cubicle away from Mr. Simpson's office."

"Did the move improve your situation?"

Quintero wiped her left eye again. "No, not really … He still bothered me from time to time. I started looking for another job, and I was still working there when he was killed."

"What was your reaction to Mr. Simpson's death?"

"I, I know it's not a nice thing to say, but a great weight had been lifted from me."

Bev gave the witness a couple of moments to collect herself before moving onto the next topic. "While working at the Thorton firm, did you ever lose your key card during the last year prior to Mr. Simpson's death?"

"Yes. It happened two times."

"Did you get them replaced?"

"Yes. I went down to the security office and told them I lost my card. I showed my ID and got a new one. That was it."

"Did they ask you how or when you lost your key card?"

"No."

"No further questions."

Jacqueline began her cross-examination with one mundane question after another, and David did not know where she was going. He glanced toward the jurors and saw three with looks of bewilderment, while the others appeared disinterested. Juror Number 7, the man with the large stomach and goatee, crossed his arms and frowned.

Jacqueline then addressed one topic too many. "Are you a violent person?"

Quintero gave a faint smile. "Oh, no."

"Was anyone else at the Thorton law firm a violent person?"

"I'm not sure. Give me a moment, please." Quintero closed her eyes. "I'm trying to remember …" She opened them, and her face brightened. "Oh yeah. Donna Conway threatened to slit Mr. Simpson's throat."

Jacqueline clenched her left hand behind her back, indicating she knew she had made a mistake.

Amanda showed David a quick note:

Oops?

Yup! No clue how she knew

David called the next defense witness, Michael Dobson, a young African American. While he was short in stature, his suit barely held his muscular frame.

David asked, "Mr. Dobson, where do you currently work?"

"I'm a manager at a warehouse in Queens."

"Where were you working in June 2009?"

"I was a security supervisor at the O'Connell building."

David nodded. "Why'd you change jobs?"

With a scowl on his face, Dobson said, "They fired me, made me the scapegoat for the murder so that they could keep the building's contract."

"Please describe the building's security last June."

He scoffed. "It was a joke, man. The owners were too cheap to pay for real security."

"Could you please elaborate?" David took two steps into the well.

"Last June, there were no cameras in the elevators, outside the building, or on the upper floors, and the emergency exit doors had no alarms. Shoot, anyone on the inside could have opened one and allowed someone on the outside to enter the building without security knowing about it." Dobson shook his head. "Man, we were just window dressing."

"Did building security issue key cards?"

"Yeah. You needed a key card to use the regular elevators during the off hours and the freight elevators 24/7."

"How'd the key cards work?"

"They were crap."

Judge Perkins turned his head toward the witness. "Watch your language, young man. Please answer the question in a more professional manner."

Dobson swung his head toward the judge. "Sorry." He then redirected his attention to David. "We programmed the cards by floor. The Thorton law firm was on the ninth and tenth floors, which meant during off hours, their cards only opened the elevator doors on those floors and the ground floor."

"Uh-huh. Did each card belong to a particular person?"

Dobson scoffed again. "No, it would've made too much sense. We didn't code the cards that way and didn't keep track of which ones were lost. Instead, we reprogrammed them every six months on a rotational basis, which deactivated lost cards."

"Prior to the murder last June, when was the last time security reprogrammed the cards for the ninth and tenth floors?"

"In April."

"During last June, did security guards patrol the upper floors?"

"No."

"Why was security so lax?"

Dobson rolled his eyes. "Do I really need to spell it out? The owners were too damn cheap to pay for it."

"Thank you," David said. "No further questions."

On cross-examination, Jacqueline asked, "Aren't you bitter because the security company fired you?"

"Yeah, sure," he replied hostilely. "No one likes to be fired, especially when he didn't deserve it."

"Do you think your bitterness tainted your testimony?"

Dobson furrowed his brow. "Give me a break, Lady."

"Have you read the security company's personnel file on you?"

"No."

"Would you be surprised to learn your superiors claimed you were difficult?"

"That's the way they put it?" Dobson asked as he shook his head. "I wanted to fire a couple of lazy guards, and the company wouldn't let me. Another time, I tried to explain to Mr. O'Connell why building security was inadequate. He didn't want to hear it, and he went behind my back to complain to corporate. If that makes me difficult, then yeah, I am."

"Nothing further, Your Honor."

Judge Perkins cleared his throat. "We're in recess for the morning break."

WHEN DAVID AND Amanda stepped into the hallway, Marc stood next to Charles W. Thorton, who looked like a sad and broken man. His remaining hair was white, and the wrinkles in his face were deep and prominent. His shoulders hunched over, and his skin was pasty and too pale.

When Thorton saw Amanda, he forced a weak smile. "Good morning. I wish I were seeing you again under better circumstances."

Amanda's lip quivered. "So do I. Excuse me." She dashed down the hallway toward the women's bathroom.

David knew The Old Man's appearance shocked her, and he regretted not preparing her in advance. He also concealed the truth and told him, "The trial's been hard on her."

Thorton nodded. "Of course. I'll try to do my best."

AFTER THORTON TOOK the stand, David guided him through a brief history of his law firm. The Old Man also discussed the firm's financial struggles and bringing J. Robert Simpson on board. David suspected Thorton's memories were painful as he spoke in a slow and halting manner and had difficulty maintaining eye contact.

Thorton testified he wanted to get rid of Simpson due to his atrocious behavior, but the other partners prevailed. He almost broke down when he addressed his firm's demise. Upon David's request, Judge Perkins ordered a ten-minute recess to allow Thorton to compose himself. After the break, David continued with his questions.

"What's your opinion of Amanda Morelli?" David thought he saw a sparkle in Thorton's eyes.

"I was very fond of her, and she was like a daughter to me." He looked at her. "I wish I would've told you that sooner."

David wanted to turn around to see Amanda's reaction, but he feared her expression would break his concentration.

"Why didn't Amanda make junior partner?"

Thorton's sparkle disappeared. "It was a tough decision, but she wasn't partner material. Even before she applied, I suspected she wasn't happy at the firm. I gently broke the news to her and told her she was more than welcome to stay on board. I also told her if she wanted to leave, I'd write a letter of recommendation."

"Do you believe Ms. Morelli has a pleasant personality?"

He showed a faint smile. "Oh yes."

"Based upon your interactions with her, do you believe she's a violent person?"

"No, far from it."

"Do you believe she was capable of killing J. Robert Simpson?"

Thorton straightened his back and in a louder voice said, "She's not, and I know she didn't do it."

"Why is that?"

"Because I did."

David froze and heard gasps throughout the courtroom. He imagined the news stunned Amanda but could not turn around to look at her or anyone else besides the man on the witness stand.

Once David regained his composure, he asked, "Why'd you kill Simpson?"

Thorton looked at the floor. "I really didn't want to kill him, but it happened."

"Why?"

The Old Man tugged his collar and turned his head towards the jury. "I knew Simpson was sexually harassing the women. Twice during the week before his death, a paralegal came to my office in tears. Something had to be done."

"What happened on the evening of the murder?"

"I took the chance Simpson would be in his office, and I wasn't certain what I'd do. I searched for a way to force him out, and nothing I said had an effect on him." The Old Man frowned. "Simpson laughed and berated me. I don't know why I had a gun with me, but I did. In a fit of anger, I reached for it and shot him." He redirected his eyes from the jury to the floor.

"Do you regret what you did?"

Thorton exhaled while continuing to look at the floor. "Oh ... to some extent, I suppose. I'm sorry the police arrested Amanda, and now she's on trial. I should've come forward much sooner. I'm sorry. I really am."

"No further questions."

As David returned to his seat, he noticed Jacqueline twirling a pen in her left hand. From his past experiences, he knew she was confident and ready to attack. He also dreaded what was about to happen.

"What kind of firearm did you use to shoot Mr. Simpson?"

The Old Man mumbled incoherently.

"Please speak up. What kind of firearm did you use?"

"A nine-millimeter semi-automatic pistol."

"Do you own a .38-caliber handgun?"

"No."

"Are you aware the police recovered two .38 slugs from the crime scene?"

Thorton shook his head. "Two bullets might've been recovered, but they were nine-millimeter rounds. A nine-millimeter and a .38 are remarkably similar. Someone must've made a mistake."

Amanda wrote to David:

He's lying, isn't he?

Afraid so

How badly does it hurt me?

Discuss later

"Uh-huh," Jacqueline said. "That was the one time you went to the office late in the evening?"

"Yes, that's right."

"Why didn't a security camera see you enter the building on June 18?"

Thorton shrugged. "I evaded them."

"How'd you do it?"

"I just did."

Jacqueline stared at Thorton, who broke eye contact.

"Just one more question. Did you know the woman with Simpson just prior to the murder?"

"What woman?"

"That's what I thought. No further questions."

David's morale plummeted as he concluded any shred of Thorton's credibility had disappeared.

Judge Perkins asked, "Mr. Lee, any redirect?"

"No, Your Honor," he said as he rose. "May we have a brief sidebar?"

Judge Perkins motioned for the attorneys to come forward and placed his left hand over his microphone.

As soon as he came with inches of the bench, David whispered, "Your Honor, the defense has one more witness, Valerie Fernandez. She's suffering from the flu and had to go to the ER."

"Too bad, Counsel. Does this mean the defense rests?"

"Your Honor, I'm not asking for much, and –"

"Yes, you are," Judge Perkins growled. "If the defense rests, we'll proceed with the rebuttal case for the prosecution, if any. If there's none, the jury can hear closing arguments and begin deliberations."

"I understand, Your Honor," David said, "but may we still adjourn early and give Ms. Fernandez one more opportunity to appear? She's a critical witness."

Judge Perkins appeared unimpressed. "Ms. Marshall?"

"The People take no position."

The judge paused for about ten seconds. "Alright. We'll adjourn, and if Ms. Fernandez isn't present first thing in the morning, the defense rests."

"Thank you, Your Honor."

A FEW MINUTES later, David and Marc conferred in an attorney conference room.

Marc held out his hands with his palms out. "I swear, when I prepped
the Old Man, he said nothing about shooting Big Bobby."

David rubbed his forehead while leaning against a table. "Yeah, I know.
No one saw it coming, and I'm sure the jury knows he lied. Not a terrific way
to end the day, is it? During her closing argument, Jacqueline will hit us over
the head with Thorton's testimony."

"Oh yeah. If I were still a prosecutor, I certainly would. I'd argue
the defense is desperate and maybe imply you instructed Thorton to
commit perjury."

"Terrific. At least Jacqueline didn't object to a continuance until tomorrow morning."

"I think you missed something," Marc said. "She didn't expect the Old
Man to lie and needed some time to round up witnesses for her rebuttal case.
Then she'll beat it into the jury that he lied."

David sighed. "Yeah, I know. Let's discuss with Bev. Perhaps we should
stipulate the killer used a .38 and not a nine mil. We'd essentially acknowledge
Thorton lied, which might lessen the damage to our credibility."

"Sure. What are our chances with the jury?"

David exhaled and gazed at the ceiling. "If Valerie doesn't appear, and
we have to rest our case tomorrow morning ... Well, we made some good
points, but thanks to Thorton ... I don't know." He looked at Marc. "Maybe
we get lucky and have a hung jury. It's better than a conviction, but second
trials usually favor the prosecution, and it will this time. What are the odds
Valerie makes a speedy recovery and testifies tomorrow?"

"Not good at all."

"Damn! I was afraid of that."

CHAPTER 32

Tuesday, January 19

THE MEDIA, THE Morelli family, and their friends packed the courtroom as everyone anticipated closing arguments and a jury verdict. But first, Judge Perkins began the morning session outside of the juror's presence.

"Does the defense rest?" he asked.

While he knew it was futile, David said, "Your Honor, Valerie Fernandez is still too ill to testify. Is there any possibility of continuing for one more day?"

"No," the judge said coldly. "The defense rests. Ms. Marshall, do the People have a rebuttal case?"

"Yes and no, Your Honor. We were prepared to recall a witness to prove two .38-caliber rounds, not nine-millimeter, killed Simpson, which is now unnecessary. The defendant stipulates the bullets were .38s."

Judge Perkins glanced toward the defense table.

"That's correct," David said.

"Very well. We'll bring in the jury, read the stipulation, and then have closing arguments."

In the state of New York, the defense presented its closing first, which did not make sense to David. Since the prosecution had the burden of proof, it should argue first. Perhaps more importantly, by providing the first closing, the defense could not respond to comments in the prosecutor's argument. This forced a defense attorney to make an educated guess regarding the prosecution's pitch and give a proactive rebuttal before the assistant district attorney spoke. Despite this obstacle, David and Bev were well prepared, and since this was her last trial, David gave her the honor of making her final closing argument.

Bev rose and stood next to the defense table. "Ladies and gentlemen of the jury, in one way, this is a simple case. You only need to answer one question: Do you believe beyond a reasonable doubt Amanda Morelli murdered J. Robert Simpson? I submit to you the answer is no. In fact, you should have more than a reasonable doubt in your collective mind."

Bev walked into the well and toward the jurors. The courtroom was so quiet that David could hear her footsteps.

"Simpson was a loathsome individual, and the women at Thorton, Saxer & Caldwell despised him. He made their lives miserable, and others hated the deceased as well. Despite a wide variety of potential suspects, the district attorney's office settled on my client. Why? She could not stand Simpson, and nobody can confirm she was sick and in bed during the evening of June 18, 2009." Bev removed her glasses and shook them. "That's certainly not enough to prove she's guilty."

David noticed Bev had the attention of all twelve jurors and the four alternates, but Juror Number 7 had folded his arms on top of his large stomach, which he interpreted as a terrible sign.

"According to the DA, Ms. Morelli knew how to enter and exit the building without being detected because she was familiar with its security measures or the lack thereof. The DA also believes she's the same height as the shooter, who was the person in the gray wig. Belief alone isn't enough, not even close."

Bev donned her glasses and walked to the juror's left side. "The police concluded the murder was an inside job, and the shooter worked at the law firm." She opened her arms. "Why? Only someone at Thorton would've known no one else would've been working there in the evening. That same someone would've known how to enter and exit the building without detection." Bev held up her right index finger. "Not so fast. The law firm wasn't a secret government agency, and its work habits were a matter of public knowledge. Furthermore, building security was porous at best and easy to circumvent, which widens the possibilities as to who could've committed the murder."

David thought all the jurors were paying close attention, except Juror Number 7, who continued to cross his arms and scanned the audience in the gallery.

Bev walked up to each juror member and made eye contact. "NYPD claims they conducted a thorough investigation. Do you think so? I don't. They never knew about Donna Conway until after they arrested my client. The police interviewed Ms. Morelli but asked no follow-up questions to clarify some of her comments. Why'd they fail to do so? Because they had already concluded she was guilty. However, you must reach a verdict based upon the facts and the law, not mere assumptions."

David thought he saw a female juror nod in agreement.

As she spoke, Bev strolled in front of the jurors again. "Let's not forget one detective previously lied on the stand. Did he lie to you? How many other detectives had an agenda? How does this affect your analysis?"

Juror Number 7 was looking down and picking at his fingers.

"Let's not forget Donna Conway threatened to slit Simpson's throat, but the police never knew about her until we told the district attorney's office. What else did the police miss? They failed to recognize the murder was a professional hit. Somebody wanted Simpson dead and paid a hit man to do it, and the evidence supports this conclusion."

Amanda scribbled to David:

She's really good.

"In early June 2009, someone sent the tall blonde woman to the law firm to attract Simpson's attention. Also, in early June, the same woman bought two cell phones under the name Bonnie Parker. Using one phone, she communicated with Simpson and strung him along, and on the evening of the murder, they had dinner. The blonde woman told Simpson she wanted a drink and maybe more in his office. Of course, Big Bobby was more than willing to oblige. Who was this woman?"

Bev waited as if she expected someone to answer.

"She was a skilled con artist. She was also aware of the security cameras in the building's lobby and made certain they did not record her face. This woman stepped outside and made a phone call to alert the killer Simpson was heading upstairs. After shooting him, the killer called the blonde woman to confirm Big Bobby was dead." Bev removed her glasses again.

David observed a male juror check his watch, which was disappointing.

"Please note I'm referring to the murderer as a person, not a woman, because the evidence presented to you doesn't reveal the shooter's gender. The DA claims the person in the gray wig who appeared on the street shortly after the second call was the shooter. Perhaps, but even the enhanced video of the scene failed to reveal this person's sex or facial features."

Bev returned her glasses to their proper place and paused while a spectator in the gallery sneezed three times.

"The lack of evidence at the crime scene shows the murderer was a professional. The killer didn't leave any shell casings and wiped off the handles to the office door. Those were the actions of a cold and methodical person. He didn't leave behind any DNA, which again is consistent with a professional contract killer. The prosecutor might tell you using a pillow as a silencer means an amateur committed the crime. Is that so? Nobody knows why the shots were fired through a pillow. If the shooter knew how to bypass security and was aware nobody else would be on the tenth floor, he probably was also aware of the throw pillows and used one to his advantage. Besides, since the killer and Simpson were only persons on the floor, he didn't need a silencer because no one else would've heard the shots."

Bev took three steps back.

"It's clear a professional hit man was responsible for Simpson's murder, not my client, who cooperated with the police. Isn't her full cooperation consistent with an innocent person's behavior? Suppose you believe the defense's theory is a decent one, but you aren't convinced. That's fine and not the point. The defense doesn't need to prove its alternate theory of the crime. Instead, the prosecutor needs to prove her theory beyond a reasonable doubt, and she falls far short of the mark. Therefore, you have no choice but to find Amanda Morelli not guilty. In fact, it's your only reasonable choice."

Jacqueline then gave her closing argument, and David was unable to focus on her words, as he felt adrenaline rushing out his body. He had experienced the same effect at the end of other trials, and it was more pronounced this time. He resorted to scribbling little drawings on a legal pad to remain alert. After Jacqueline finished her argument, Judge Perkins provided instructions on the applicable law, which took far too long and were essential for the jury to hear. The judge then dismissed them to deliberate.

David told the Morelli family he would meet them at the coffee shop down the street. He first had a conversation with Marc in a quiet corner of the courthouse.

David gave a wry smile. "The trial's basically over, and you know what that means? Time to fire Irene."

Marc sighed. "Yeah, I know. I'll take care of it. It won't be fun breaking the news to my family. Do you want to give Irene a severance package?"

"I hadn't thought about it. Sure, I guess, but let's not be too generous."

"Okay. We're going to need a receptionist/office manager and at least one paralegal. Got any ideas?"

David smiled again. "How about Valerie Fernandez? She's not happy at Harrison Day."

"But she's got the flu."

"She won't be sick all the time."

"But she has a potty mouth."

"I thought you'd like that."

Marc chuckled. "Okay, you got me. Got anyone else in mind?"

"As far as office staff, not yet. I strongly suspect that after the trial, win, lose, or draw, our little firm will have plenty of potential clients knocking on the door. We've talked about bringing on another partner, and now seems like a good time to do so."

"Any ideas?"

David nodded and grinned. "Oh, I have one."

"Amanda?"

"No." David waived his hand. "She's done with litigation, and let's face it, she's not out of the woods yet."

Marc gave a half-frown. "Yeah, no kidding. Who else do you have in mind?"

"We'll talk about it later, and when we do, brace yourself."

ONCE DAVID ARRIVED at the coffee shop, he noticed Amanda's brother had tucked himself away in a booth by himself and appeared to be in the middle of a business call. Pete sat in a corner with other men in their sixties. Lorraine and Debra shared a small booth, while Paul once again greeted others and worked the room. David concluded Paul and Lorraine's moods were about the same as when he first met them, as if they had no worries.

Someone mentioned the trial to Paul, who replied, "Hey, I know my Amanda didn't do it. Don't worry about it."

David imagined "don't worry about it" was the big man's attitude about life in general, and he could not afford the luxury of embracing such a philosophy.

David joined Amanda at a small booth and needed replenishment to regain his energy. As soon as the server arrived, he said, "I don't need to see the menu, thank you. I'll order a club sandwich, fries, and a Coke."

"Nothing for me, thanks," Amanda added. After the server left, she said, "I'm too nervous to eat. It feels as if my stomach is on the worst roller-coaster in the world."

David nodded. "I understand. Maybe you should distract yourself by thinking of something else. What's happening with the NHL hockey season?"

Amanda's mood somewhat brightened, and she talked about the Rangers and the Islanders. Even after his food arrived, she continued to talk about hockey. While David had no interest in the sport, the topic helped pass the time and relaxed Amanda to an extent.

David guessed the jury would be out for the rest of the day and into the next, but at 1:30, he received a text message from the court clerk, stating the jury had reached a verdict. David was shocked because they had probably deliberated for less than an hour after lunch.

ABOUT FIFTEEN MINUTES later, all parties and spectators were back in court. Tension filled the air as everyone held their collective breath, and the courtroom fell silent. When Judge Perkins entered, his footsteps sounded like thunder.

The jury then arrived, and David's heart pounded. He could not keep his eyes off them as he reached for Amanda's hand. He thought a short deliberation meant a not guilty verdict, but no juror made eye contact with him, which indicated otherwise. David noticed three jurors glancing in Jacqueline's direction, which increased his anxiety level. He feared he was about to hear the worst.

"Has the jury reached a verdict?" Judge Perkins asked.

"We have, Your Honor," said Juror Number 7.

Oh no! David thought. *They picked the worst possible foreperson!*

Juror Number 7 handed the verdict form to the court clerk, who turned it over to the judge. David could not determine the verdict from the foreperson's body language and facial expression, and his heart pounded harder.

Judge Perkins read the verdict form without any reaction. He then said, "On the sole count of the indictment, murder in the first degree, how do you find the defendant, Amanda Morelli?"

There was a long pause. David could not handle the suspense and almost screamed, "Say it, damn it! Say it!"

"We find the defendant not guilty."

A roar erupted from the defense side of the courtroom. David was elated, and the next several moments were a blur. Amanda could have hugged him, and maybe he received a slap or two on the back. Once he regained his focus, he turned to Bev.

"Thank you."

Bev nodded. "That was my job."

David wanted to hug her, but she was not that kind of a person. He also wanted to thank her for being his mentor and so much more, except he could not get the words out of his mouth. He instead uttered, "Ready for the press conference? Should be a good one."

"As of right now, I'm officially retired again, and I'll leave through the back entrance. Go enjoy the media circus." Bev grabbed her satchel.

David watched her leave the courtroom with her head held high. He then detected a tap on his shoulder and turned around.

"Remember me?" Amanda asked with a devilish grin.

"I think so," David said with a smile. He grabbed Amanda by the hand and guided her to a spot between the defense table and the judge's bench. He also turned his back to the remaining spectators.

Amanda looked puzzled. "What are you doing?"

"I don't want others to hear me or read my lips because I might make a fool out of myself."

"What?" she uttered with a nervous laugh.

"Will you go out to dinner with me?"

Amanda rolled her eyes. "The whole family's going out to celebrate, and you're obviously invited."

David cradled her hand and looked into her eyes. "That's not what I mean. I don't date clients, but the case is over, and you're no longer a client. Will you go on a date with me?"

Her eyes got wide. "Huh? I mean yes, but there's one problem. You made us both famous. How are we supposed to go out in public?"

He chuckled. "We'll figure something out. Now, are you ready for the press conference? Let's take the high road. We're glad it's over, and the jury made the right decision."

"Got it. Let's go."

CHAPTER 33

February to Early June 2010

THREE WEEKS AFTER the trial, David made a phone call to Jacqueline Marshall.

"Oh, it's you," she said with contempt in her voice. "Why'd you call? Rubbing it in?"

"No, not at all. I'm calling for a different reason, but I first need to mention something else. I hope you know I didn't tell Old Man Thorton to falsely confess to the murder."

"I know. It was obvious by the look on your face."

"Which was?"

"A deer in headlights. Should you be admitting Thorton lied?"

David chuckled. "Well, he wasn't my client, and I didn't need to spell it out for you. Besides, you probably won't prosecute him for perjury."

"No one is. The DA doesn't want the public to be reminded of what happened with Morelli."

David stood up to stretch his legs. "Makes sense. Anyway, here's why I called. Our law firm is getting busier, and Marc and I are looking for a third partner. How about it? Want to go into private practice?"

After a long pause, Jacqueline asked, "Are you serious?"

"Of course. You're a brilliant attorney, and we need one more. We're starting to represent individuals charged with white-collar crimes, and not all attorneys can handle the complexities they can present, but you certainly can. If you join us, we'll change the name of the firm to Marshall, D'Angelo, and Lee. Look, I know I'm making an offer right out of the blue. So, if you need some time to think about it, that's fine. Just get back to me when you can."

Following another long pause, Jacqueline said, "Huh. I never expected this call. I'm flattered by the offer, but I can't accept. To be perfectly candid, I already left the district attorney's office and joined Malik Watkins' firm."

David was stunned and put his left hand on his head. "*The* Malik Watkins, last year's African American attorney of the year?"

"That's him."

"Holy crap! I didn't even know a public servant ran in the same circles as him. How do you know him?"

"We've been married for the past three years."

David chuckled. "Really? I had no clue. That's great!"

"We didn't tell anyone because we wanted to keep our private lives private. Since we'll be working together, it's bound to come out, eventually. Please don't tell your reporter friends. We'd like to release the information when the time is right."

"Sure, not a problem. As long as you're sharing, I have a question. Why didn't you have a trial partner?"

"I guess it wouldn't hurt to tell you. Simpson had a friend at City Hall who pushed very hard for an indictment." Jacqueline scoffed. "Simpson having a friend in high places. Now there's a nauseating thought. Anyway, even though we could present a decent case, there were some problems, which you exploited. I expressed my concerns in an email to the DA and recommended we wait on an arrest pending further investigation. The DA rejected my opinion and ordered me to proceed. I could take the political hit if we lost, but a trial partner might not be so fortunate. So, I convinced the DA I could handle it by myself. Even though I loved being a prosecutor, I hated politics, and I decided Morelli would be my last defendant regardless of the outcome."

"Well, Jacqueline, I never heard about the DA blaming you."

"He didn't, and it would've been a very foolish idea. I sent a copy of the email with my comments about the case to Malik. If the DA had tried to throw me under the bus, Malik would've released the email and thrown him under a larger one, ran over him, put the bus in reverse, and ran him over again."

David chuckled. "That's awesome. Did the DA know Malik had a copy of the email?"

"Absolutely. I told him right after closing arguments and before the jury verdict."

He laughed hard. "Nice! Was he mad?"

"Of course, and I didn't care. Why should I?"

"Okay, thanks for the information, and good luck with your new career."

A FEW DAYS later, David and Marc offered a partnership to Angela Williams, a law school classmate and an Assistant U.S. Attorney in Brooklyn. In addition to her excellent legal skills, to David's amusement and Marc's chagrin, Angela routinely beat Marc at Nerf basketball.

IN EARLY JUNE, David proudly stood before a full church as a grooms-man for his sister's wedding. Escorted by their father, Courtney came down the aisle in an elegant, white mermaid-style dress with exposed shoulders. David glanced at his mother in the first row. Her frown showed she disapproved of Courtney wearing her hair down and not wearing the veil she had selected for her.

As the bride and groom took their respective places, David scanned for familiar faces in attendance. He spotted Bev and her husband Stanley, whom he finally met earlier in the day. David thought the adage of long-married couples looking like each other could be true. Stanley appeared remarkably similar to Bev, except his hair was gray and curly, while hers was white, layered, and straight. Marc and Stephanie sat next to them. Even though Marc could suffer a relapse of leukemia, he and Steph had decided to start a family, but they had not yet made a pregnancy announcement.

Valerie and her new boyfriend sat in the same row. While David had thought she would make an excellent addition to the firm, she had been a better fit than expected. Since she had a sharp and quick mind, David had recommended she apply to law school. After giving it some thought, she declined and stated she was happy in her present position.

David also noted Irene's absence. As promised, Marc had fired her, and to his surprise, his extended family had taken the news in stride. Marc had told him the worst comment he heard was, "So, she had to go, huh?"

David then directed his attention to the most amazing woman in the church: Amanda, his girlfriend of the past six months. She sat between his parents to the left and her parents to the right. David had introduced her at the rehearsal dinner last night, and his mother had been so impressed she insisted Amanda sit next to her during the wedding.

After Amanda's name had faded from the news, a commercial bank in Manhattan had hired her as part of their in-house counsel. She had accepted the position after confirming the bank had a zero-tolerance policy for sexual harassment, as the female CEO did not want the organization ran any other way.

DURING THE WEDDING reception, David and Amanda snuck up to her hotel room and stood on the twentieth-floor balcony. Since it was a warm evening, David left his tuxedo jacket and bow tie on the king-size bed. With glasses of champagne in their hands, the couple gazed at the city lights.

"This is just like a romantic movie," Amanda said. "A young and handsome couple fall in love. They get married in a beautiful church surrounded by family and friends, and the bride gets to wear an absolutely gorgeous gown. The last scene should be them standing here, not us."

Do it now, David urged himself and then turned to face her. "Perhaps the movie has a different ending."

"Oh?" Amanda said as she smiled and faced him.

"How about this one? The boyfriend gets down on one knee." David knelt and took her right hand. "He tells his girlfriend she's the most beautiful woman in the world, both inside and out. He can't imagine living the rest of his life without her, and he asks her to marry him."

Amanda laughed and pulled back her hand.

David dropped his head, and his heart sank even further. He then heard a gasp.

"What? You're serious?"

David felt Amanda's hands cusp his cheeks. She lifted his head and bent over to where they were face-to-face.

"You're serious?"

"Yeah."

Amanda gave David an intense, passionate kiss.

When she pulled away, he said, "So, what's your answer?"

Amanda chuckled, knelt, and lightly slapped him on the chest. "Very funny. You know, your proposal would've gone better if you would've bought a ring."

David threw up his head. "Crap. It's in my jacket." He stood and rushed to the bed with Amanda right behind him. He reached into the right pocket, retrieved a black ring box, and opened it.

Amanda's eyes lit up as she saw a one carat, center cut diamond, and for several moments, she could not stop staring at it.

David gave a wide smile. "Let's go back downstairs and show it off."

Amanda started to rise, sat back down, and closed the box. "No, it's Courtney's day, and I don't want to take the spotlight away from her. I'll tell my parents tonight and show them the ring." She gave a wry smile. "Perhaps emergency medical personnel should be standing by. Maybe you can quietly tell Courtney before brunch tomorrow, and we'll be more open about it on Monday." She gave a light chuckle. "By then, if you want to make a fool out of yourself and shout it from the rooftops, go right ahead."

CHAPTER 34

Friday, June 11

LATE AFTERNOON, DAVID once again arrived at the Morelli home in Bensonhurst. This time, he noticed pale blue and yellow flowers blooming within the brick enclosure in the front yard. He rang the doorbell, and Amanda answered in bare feet, jeans, and a T-shirt.

"Get down here, ya big ape."

David grinned and bent at the waist.

Amanda gave him a kiss on the lips and smiled when she saw the champagne bottle in his right hand. "Dom Perignon, very nice. You think it'll tip off Mom and Dad that we're engaged?"

"So, you don't think the ring on your finger gave them a clue?"

Amanda admired it. "Hmm, maybe. You got good taste, excellent color and clarity. How much did this set you back, at least ten grand?"

"Nice try. I'll take the Fifth."

She uttered a fake sigh. "Fine. Come inside."

Amanda's parents had not seen David since he proposed, and once he stepped into the living room, Paul was the first to greet him.

"Congratulations!" he said as he gave David a firm handshake and a slap on the back.

Lorraine hugged him and then asked, "Have you set a date for the wedding?"

David smirked. "Didn't Amanda tell you? We haven't decided, maybe by the end of the year."

David noticed the prominent scars on Lorraine's left wrist. If he had not known any better, the scars were consistent with her slashing her wrist, and she was the complete opposite of suicidal. In fact, David had known no one more upbeat and optimistic than her, except for Paul.

SINCE THE EVENING was an engagement celebration, Lorraine insisted serving dinner at the dining room table instead of the horrible one next to the kitchen. As for the meal, she almost outdid herself by creating a rustic Italian feast and panna cotta for dessert. David ate so much that his stomach begged him to stop.

After they finished dessert, Lorraine beamed at the sight of her daughter and future son-in-law. "Oh, I'm so glad the two of you found each other. It's so wonderful. It's too bad Amanda had to get arrested and put on trial for it to happen."

"Me too, Mom. However, spending my life with David almost made all of it worthwhile." She leaned to her right and gave him another kiss.

Lorraine and Paul took a few dishes to the kitchen, and when they returned, Lorraine said, "We should've gone to the police and told them I did it. It would've gotten Amanda off the hook."

David held up his right index finger. "It wouldn't have made a difference. The police would've concluded you were only trying to protect your daughter. Remember, we had a similar conversation right before the trial."

Lorraine smiled. "Oh yeah. I remember now." She then turned her head toward Paul. "Honey, why don't you sit, and I'll finish cleaning up in here and in the kitchen."

"Are you sure?"

"Of course, and the kids can get the ... you know."

Paul sat down while Lorraine gathered four dishes and silverware.

The big man then addressed Amanda and David. "We have an early wedding present for you. It's in the trunk in the attic."

"What is it?" Amanda asked.

"Oh, you'll see," Lorraine said. "Just go upstairs." She then stepped into the kitchen with the dirty dishes and silverware on top.

"Okay," David said while a bit bewildered.

As Amanda and David walked up the stairs to the second floor, David noticed a squeak halfway up.

"It's been like that for years," she said.

David wanted to get a quick look at Amanda's bedroom simply out of curiosity, but the door at the end of the upstairs hallway was closed. He instead saw another bedroom with two exercise bikes and a small bathroom next to it. He also caught a glimpse of the master bedroom.

While standing in the hallway, Amanda grabbed a short drawstring above her head and pulled it down, revealing a folding ladder. She unfolded it and stepped up to the attic. Once at the top, she flicked a light switch and then said, "Come on up."

David expected to see a drafty and creepy room. However, as he reached the top step, he noticed a room well-lit by three bare bulbs and the absence of spiderwebs and dust. The room was as clean as the rest of the home. He spotted two trunks about four feet behind three boxes marked "X-mas."

"Which one?" he asked.

Amanda shrugged. "Let's start with the one on the left."

Both knelt in front of it, and Amanda opened the lid. Inside were thick and worn blankets for the winter.

"This can't be the present," David said.

"Yeah, I don't think so. Maybe Dad's messing with us a little, and it's underneath." She removed the blankets and placed them on the wood floor until there was nothing in the trunk except for air.

"Must be in the other one," David said as he picked up two blankets and was about to return them to their former place.

Amanda grabbed his arm. "Wait, this trunk has a false bottom."

David put the blankets on the floor. "Are you sure?"

"Yeah. When Daniel and I were growing up, Mom and Dad bought us magic kits, and we had a wooden box with a hidden compartment. Look at the bottom. It's stained the same color as everything else, but the grain is different. I think it's plywood, and the rest of the trunk is probably oak … and look over there," she said while pointing to the right edge. "There's a tiny notch. I'll get something to stick in there and pry it open."

"Should we be snooping? Your parents might catch us."

Amanda smirked. "Who cares? We're not ten. Besides, you can wait next to the top of the stairs and listen for the squeak. Then you'll know someone is coming up."

David remained near the attic's opening while Amanda quietly headed downstairs to the second floor and quickly went out of sight. He was amused they were sneaking around and still feared they would be caught. If so, Paul and Lorraine would not yell at them, but he did not want to see their disappointment, especially from Lorraine.

As Amanda came back into view, she held up a metal nail file and whispered, "Got it."

She snuck up the stairs to the attic, and then both knelt beside the open trunk.

In another whisper and with a wry smile, she asked, "Do you think we'll find Jimmy Hoffa?"

David said quietly, "Very funny. Just open it."

Amanda stuck the nail file in the notch and then angled it towards her. The plywood's right side popped up. She guided the file between the plywood and the trunk's side and pried it further open. Next, she grabbed the plywood and pulled it away, revealing a handgun with a short barrel.

David was stunned as he stared at the firearm. Even though he did not know much about guns, he believed he was looking at a snub-nose .38 Smith & Wesson, the same type of weapon that could have been used to kill Big Bobby. He then shuttered over the thought this was the Morelli family's way of letting him know Amanda had committed the murder. He shifted his eyes to the left and noticed Amanda looked horrified, which did not appear to be an act.

"Is this …"

Amanda gave a slight nod while fixated on the gun. "Dad's? … Yeah."

David tried to imagine an innocent explanation. "Maybe, maybe he bought another one."

Amanda grimaced and shook her head. "See the little nick in the butt? … It's the same one." She slowly moved her right hand into the trunk and grabbed the gun. After removing it, she opened the six-round cylinder, which was loaded except for two missing bullets. "Damn it," she said as she closed the cylinder and her eyes. Her right hand and the gun fell into her lap. "Damn it, he did it."

David did not know what to say and could only stare at the gun.

"And where did that other stuff come from?" Amanda asked with a pained expression.

What other stuff? David thought. The gun had mesmerized him so much he did not see anything else. He peeked into the trunk and was stunned again. Next to where the gun had been, he saw several small stacks of $100 bills wrapped in cellophane and, to the left of them, a newspaper was folded in half and also wrapped in cellophane.

David estimated he was looking at about $200,000, assuming all the bills were hundreds, and they looked strange. Benjamin Franklin's head and the numbers were smaller, and the bills lacked any modern security features. He retrieved one stack for a closer examination of the top bill. To the right of Franklin and near the bottom, he noticed "SERIES 1990," but the bill looked brand new. He leaned over and saw other hundreds from the 1980s and in the same condition.

David then noticed the newspaper was the March 4, 1972, edition of the *Miami Herald*. He scanned the headlines, which read, "Askew: Stop Rhetoric on Busing," "Jobless Rate Dips by .2 Pct," and "Airliner Smashes House; 18 Killed."

"Did your parents know anyone who died in a plane crash?" he asked.

Amanda opened her eyes and looked confused. David pointed at the newspaper. She glanced at it and shook her head.

"Then why do they have it?"

"I don't know." She ran both hands through her hair while the gun rested on her lap. "I can't believe this, the gun, the money. Where the hell did the cash come from?" She stared at the floor with her hands still on her head.

David also had difficulty processing everything he had just seen. His eyes darted from the gun to the money and to the newspaper. He then focused again on the money. He recalled Paul and Lorraine had paid him in cash, but except for a quick glance on one occasion, he had never seen it. Irene never mentioned older money. Perhaps she did not notice or simply did not bother to tell him.

Amanda moved her hands to her lap. She grabbed the gun with her right and put it in her waistband behind her back.

"Should you be doing that?" David asked.

"The safety's on." She reached into the trunk and grabbed the newspaper with one hand and a stack of bills with the other. She also tucked the money in the waistband behind her. "Time to get some answers."

David followed Amanda down the stairs to the second floor and then the next set to the first.

Right after the squeak, Paul called out, "Did you find it?"

"We found some old blankets," Amanda said coldly as she reached the bottom step. She turned the corner and headed to the dining room.

David was behind her and noticed Paul setting down a cup of coffee. He also heard water running and dishes clanking in the kitchen.

Without looking at them, Paul chuckled. "That's not it. It's in the other trunk."

Just as David and Amanda reached the table, she tossed the newspaper onto it. "We found this," she said.

Paul glanced at it and then looked up. With a grin, he said, "Oh yeah. That's a souvenir from the first time we all went to Florida."

"Uh-huh," Amanda replied with her hands on her hips. "The newspaper was issued before I was born, and we took our first trip together when I was ten. Try again."

Paul shrugged. "So, I got it wrong. It's nothing. Don't worry about it."

David again noticed the noises coming from the kitchen.

"Got a lame excuse for this?" Amanda asked as she reach around, grabbed the stack of hundreds and dropped it on the table. "There's plenty more in the attic, and all of it was under the false bottom."

Paul shrugged again and held out his hands. "What's the big deal? We keep some emergency cash in the house."

"Oh sure," Amanda said as she waved her right arm in the air. "What about this?" She reached around again and retrieved the handgun. "It's yours." She gently set it on the table.

"Okay," Paul said with another shrug. "I lied about getting rid of the gun. Your mother and me didn't want you to worry about it anymore."

"The police could've found it when they searched the house," David said.

"Yeah, but the cops were too stupid. So, it's not a big deal."

"Oh really, Dad!" Amanda exclaimed as she slapped her hand onto the table. "You did it! You killed Big Bobby, didn't you!"

Paul appeared to be defensive and held out his hands again. "I swear I had nothing to do with it, honest!"

"Oh sure!" Amanda said as she threw back her head. "He was shot twice in the head with a .38, and your gun was fired twice. I know because you forgot to load two more rounds."

"I swear it wasn't me, Pumpkin," Paul said louder.

"Yeah, right! You've always had a fascination with the mafia, and you decided to carry out your own hit. Stop lying! You did it, didn't you!"

Lorraine came out of the kitchen, and her eyes popped when she saw the gun, the money, and the newspaper on the table.

Amanda glared at her mother. "What?"

"Please leave him alone. He didn't do it," Lorraine calmly insisted.

Amanda held up her hands and rolled her eyes. "Oh sure! It was the Sugar Plum Fairy. No wait, it was Mickey Mouse. No, wait … it … was Dad!"

Paul insisted, "I swear. I had nothing to do with it."

Amanda scoffed. "Of course, then it was Mom," she said sarcastically.

David turned his attention to Lorraine, who had a half-smile and looked embarrassed. The wheels in his head began to spin rapidly, and he concluded Lorraine could have murdered Simpson. She was short enough to have been the shooter and knew how to properly use firearms due to the family outings at the cabin in the woods. Amanda had probably mentioned to her the routines of her old law firm, including no one working in the office late in the evening. He also guessed Lorraine had been aware of Big Bobby's proclivity for sexual harassment. However, she was scatterbrained, and the murder required a certain level of planning and sophistication.

Amanda was apparently too upset to notice her mother's odd expression. "Come on, Dad, out with it!"

"Please leave your father alone," Lorraine said. "I did it."

"What!" Amanda said. "It can't be you!"

Lorraine slowly nodded. "Yes, it was. It's not like it was the first time I killed someone."

"Honey," Paul said as he turned his head toward her. "You didn't kill the other guy."

"Yes, I did. I was involved."

David glanced at Amanda, whose mouth had fallen open. He then shifted his gaze to Paul.

The big man briefly held out his hands. "Hey, what can I say?"

"Well," David said. "Perhaps we should know the full story."

Paul gave a dismissive wave of his right hand. "You already know too much. Don't worry about the rest."

"Really? No, not this time!" Amanda demanded as she again slammed her right hand on the table. "Out with it!"

The big man sighed. "Honey, Amanda, David, please have a seat. Maybe we'd better explain everything."

As Lorraine sat down, she asked, "Okay, where should we start?"

"1972," Paul said.

CHAPTER 35

The same evening

LORRAINE STARED INTO space, as if her mind traveled back in time. "Okay … It all started about two years before you were born, Amanda. Daniel was a toddler and a real joy, and I had my circle of friends. One day, I was at the beauty parlor, you know, gabbing with Debra and the other girls. I said I was happy, had a great husband and a wonderful little boy. Even so, I wanted a little bit of excitement, something your father and I could talk about years later. It was … a little remark." Lorraine shrugged. "In my head, I was thinking of something silly, like driving to Boston for clam chowder and nothing else, but Debra had another idea. When she got home, she talked to Pete, and back then, it was an open secret he was a wise guy."

Amanda's mouth dropped open, and David was startled.

"Wait a minute, Mom. Pete was in the mafia?"

Lorraine giggled. "That's right."

"Dad, did you know about this?"

"Oh sure. Everyone knew. Let your mother tell the story. Go ahead," he said as he patted her arm.

"Where was I?"

Paul squeezed her hand. "Debra went home and talked to Pete."

"Oh yeah," Lorraine said as her eyes brightened. "Pete got himself in trouble with the mob and needed to make amends really quick. He had never killed anyone. Even so, his boss ordered him to travel to Miami to whack this guy named Bernie something. Maybe it was Bobby something. I can't remember his name. Paul?"

He shrugged. "Beats me. Bernie sounds about right."

"Okay, let's just say his name was Bernie, and he was a really bad person. Pete's boss, I think his name was ..." Lorraine tilted her head. "Frankie? Yeah, that's him. Frankie thought it'd look better if Pete traveled to Miami with Debra, like a married couple on vacation. That way, they'd draw less suspicion. However, there was one tiny, little problem. Pete was supposed to fly down to Miami, so he could get there really fast, and Debra was afraid to fly." Lorraine gave a light chuckle. "Imagine that. Debra became a travel agent, and she can't fly. That's okay, she's been such a good friend and –"

"Honey, please get back to the story," Paul said. "Debra can't fly and that's where you come in."

Lorraine smiled. "Yeah, right. Pete and Debra told me what was going on, and they asked me to pose as Pete's wife. I'd go down to Miami, have some fun, and not get involved with the whacking."

Amanda groaned. "Do you have to refer to it as whacking?"

Her mother's eyebrows raised. "That's what they called it. I've been around and heard things, and I've also seen *Goodfellas*." She glanced at Paul. "Now that's a great movie, right?"

"Yes, it is," David said. "But let's stick to the story. Frankie asked you to go to Miami with Pete, and then what happened?"

"Paul and I talked it over, and it sounded like fun. I got a free trip, and Frankie would throw a few bucks my way. We flew down to Miami, and we stayed in the same hotel as … uh …"

"Bernie," Paul said.

Lorraine nodded. "Right, Bernie. Pete went to see Uncle Tony to get the gun." She giggled again. "You know, he wasn't really Pete's uncle. On the way, Pete got in a car accident and ended up in traction at the hospital. I called Frankie, that's Pete's boss, and he was really mad. He wanted Bernie gone before he flew back to New York." Lorraine casted her eyes toward a window in the living room. "All of a sudden, Pete's boss stopped talking, I mean yelling, and started thinking …" She re-directed her attention to David and Amanda.

David was fully engrossed in the story and hung on Lorraine's every word.

"Frankie asked me to take care of it, and at first, I said no." Lorraine smirked. "I mean, the worst thing I ever did was smoke a cigarette in the girl's bathroom in high school. Boy, did that make me sick!" She looked at Paul. "I told you about the cigarette, right?"

"I remember. Please continue."

"Frankie wanted me to whack Bernie and told me some awful stories about him. He finally convinced me to do it. He also said Bernie was a womanizer, chased anything in a skirt, and my wedding ring wouldn't stop him. Frankie said I could use that to my advantage to get close and alone with him."

"So, then you shot Bernie?" David asked.

"Just wait," Lorraine said with a little smile. "It wasn't so simple. I first got the gun and silencer from Uncle Tony. Back then, I had a great figure, even after I gave birth to Daniel. So, to entice Bernie, I bought a new tight and sexy dress."

"Great Mom, just great," Amanda uttered as she rubbed her forehead with her elbows on the table.

"I found Bernie at the hotel bar and chatted him up. Boy, he had horrible manners. It was hard to put up with him. Before I tried to kill him, I didn't want him to put up a fight. I wanted to get Bernie really drunk, and you know, we started having drinks. I got a little tipsy, but I made sure Bernie drank more than me. A couple of times, I spilled my drink, so I didn't have to finish it, and he thought it was funny. After some time at the bar, I told Bernie we should get a bottle of wine and head up to his hotel room." Lorraine's eyes flashed. "Oh, that reminds me. Does anyone want another glass of wine?"

"Seriously?" Amanda said as she rubbed her forehead again. "Just continue with the story."

"Okay. Bernie grabbed a bottle, and after we got to his hotel room, I got more drinks into him. I hoped he'd pass out, and then I could shoot him if I got up the nerve. Even though Bernie got really smashed, he never passed out. He stepped onto the balcony and saw some girls by the pool. He yelled and waved at them, and I heard the girls yelling back, 'Come on down.'" Lorraine released a light chuckle.

David was like a school kid who had no patience. He leaned forward and asked, "What happened next?"

"Now I see an opportunity," Lorraine said as she stared into space. "Bernie's hotel room was on the seventh floor. I thought he could jump off the balcony and land in the pool. Since he was really drunk, he probably would've drowned, and I didn't think the girls could've saved him."

Lorraine turned her head toward Amanda and David.

"The girls yelled to Bernie again, and he took a couple of steps into the room and gave me a funny look, like he wanted permission to go downstairs. He took another step toward the door, when I stopped him and said, 'Take the easy way down. Jump off the balcony.' Bernie laughs and says, 'Yeah, ya think so?' I told him, 'Sure, you can do it.' Bernie laughed again and went out to the balcony. He climbed over the railing, pushed out as far as he could, and jumped. Then I heard the most horrible sound." Lorraine grimaced and shook her head.

David could not believe she stopped talking at the most dramatic moment. "Well, what happened?"

Lorraine took a deep breath. "I didn't see it, but it was easy to figure out. Bernie barely missed the pool, and his head slammed onto the cement next to it. I ran to the balcony and looked down. Blood was pouring out of him." She quivered. "It was really awful, and the girls were screaming and crying."

David pictured the scene in his mind and found it revolting.

Lorraine's eyes opened wide. "I panicked for a second and then came up with a plan. I hid the gun in the toilet tank and went downstairs as fast as I could. I got there before the police and the ambulance. Bernie's head was smashed in, and he died right there."

Amanda grimaced and looked away from her mother, as if she were trying to wipe out the horrible images in her mind.

"Yeah. It was really bad. They didn't bother to rush him to the hospital."

David asked, "Did you talk to the police?"

She smiled. "Oh sure. I told them I was Bernie's wife, and we'd been drinking. I said I was in the bathroom when he jumped. I was really nervous, and I guess that's why the police didn't believe me." Lorraine patted her hands on her lap. "So, I told them another story. I said I was married to Pete, and he had cheated on me. He was in the hospital after a car accident, and I wanted to get back at him and have some fun at the same time. That's why I hooked up with Bernie. I also asked the police to keep it quiet, and this time, they bought it." Lorraine giggled. "When I got back to New York, the wise guys were really happy. I got rid of Bernie and made it look like an accident. Pete's boss ..."

"Frankie," Paul said.

"Yeah, Frankie paid me a lot more than he had promised, and I used the money to buy the travel agency." Lorraine cocked her head. "You know, I had saved Pete's life. Years later, I learned if Pete hadn't gone through with it, he would've been whacked. If Pete had done the hit and left a trail back to New York, the same thing would've happened."

Lorraine's story overwhelmed David. He wanted to ask a question, but the words could not leave his mouth.

Instead, Amanda asked, "Mom, are you sure this all happened the way you say it did?"

Lorraine smiled. "Sure, I'm sure."

"Wait a minute," Paul said as he held up his right index finger. "I just remembered why we saved that newspaper. It has an article about Bernie's death." He grabbed the folded copy of the *Miami Herald* wrapped in cellophane and flipped it over. "See, right there," he said as he pointed. "It's at the bottom." He then chuckled. "Oh look, we got the name wrong. The dead guy was Carmine, not Bernie. Carmine Cicero."

Lorraine smirked. "Oh, yeah. How about that!"

"Can I see the newspaper, please?" David asked.

Paul handed it to him.

David and Amanda read the article, which discussed drunk Carmine jumping off the balcony and landing next to the swimming pool. It also stated Carmine had been staying at the hotel with an unnamed woman. David finally realized Lorraine's story was accurate yet still found it difficult to accept.

Amanda at first appeared resigned and then horrified. "So, it's true. My mom was a hit man for the Gambinos."

Lorraine waved her left hand. "I was never a hit man, and I never joined the mob. I told them I couldn't do it again, and it wasn't the Gambinos. Pete was a Genovese."

David was flabbergasted, and his future in-laws' blasé attitude made the evening more surreal. Although he believed he would regret hearing any more details about their lives, curiosity got the better of him. "Lorraine, did you say you bought the travel agency with mob money?"

"Uh-huh, and I was their travel agent. Most of the time, the wise guys sent their wives and girlfriends to book trips, and sometimes they showed up." She flashed a wide smile and added, "I once booked a trip for The Chin."

"The what?!" Amanda exclaimed and then dropped both elbows onto the dining room table and put her head in her hands.

"Vincent 'The Chin' Gigante," David stated. "He was the head of the Genovese crime family. He tried to avoid criminal prosecution for years by acting crazy, babbling incoherently, and walking the streets in his bathrobe."

Without picking up her head, Amanda said, "I know. I know who he is. It's just hard to believe Mom knew all these gangsters."

Lorraine gave a mischievous grin. "It was fine. All the vacations I booked were legitimate, and it was fun. Some wise guys booked the same hotel in Miami and asked for the murder room." She giggled. "That's what they called Bernie's room. I mean Carmine's room. We had plenty of regular people as clients too, even a couple of cops."

"Hey, David," Paul said. "Maybe that explains why the police thought I had mob connections. The guys sometimes came to the house on the weekends to book their trips with Lorraine. The police or the FBI probably tailed one or two of them to here."

Lorraine smiled. "Oh sure. I was home after school and on the weekends. Sometimes, they came here. You remember, don't you?"

Amanda picked up her head. "Do I really need to do this? … Fine. I don't remember. Whenever anyone came over, you shooed away Daniel and me into our rooms to do our homework, watch TV, or play in the backyard."

"Did you really kill Big Bobby?" David asked.

Lorraine looked into his eyes. "Oh yes."

Amanda flashed a pained expression. "Geez, Mom! You destroyed the firm!"

Lorraine smirked and slightly shook her head. "Oh, no. The firm was dying anyway, and people found new jobs. It all worked out. Right, Dear?"

Paul nodded.

Amanda's eyes got wide again. "Really? Did you see Old Man Thorton during the trial?" She pointed to an invisible person. "Did you see what you did to him?"

Her mother gave a dismissive wave. "Oh, he's fine."

"I don't think so! Dad, did you know about this?"

"Not until after it happened. That night, I thought she was out with Debra. When your mother came home, she told me what she did. She showed me her disguise and handed me my .38."

"Mom, why'd you do it?" Amanda cried out.

"He was a really bad person and deserved it. I knew you'd been telling your father about what was happening at work. You were always Daddy's little girl. Your father told me some, and I figured out the rest. I needed to do something to help you."

David held up his right hand with his palm facing out. "Hold on a second. You're saying you planned Big Bobby's murder? Look, I hope you don't take it the wrong way, but –"

"I know what you're thinking, and I'm not that scatterbrained."

Paul patted Lorraine on the hand. "Honey, that's not exactly what happened." He turned his head toward Amanda and David. "Your mother had plenty of help. After she got home, I needed to get rid of the disguise, and I guessed Debra had been part of it. I called Pete and Debra, and they came over. It took some cajoling, but the girls eventually explained how it all went down. Right?"

"Oh sure. It was confession time."

"The girls always talked about anything and everything, including Amanda's work. One day, Lorraine joked they should kill Big Bobby, and ..." Paul waved his right arm in a circular motion.

"History repeated itself," David said.

"Right. The girls got serious, and Debra called Lenny."

"Who's Lenny?" Amanda asked.

"Don't worry about it," the big man said with a dismissive wave. "All you need to know is Lenny arranged for Lorraine and Debra to meet … out-of-state talent."

David asked, "You mean the tall blonde woman?"

Paul pointed at him. "Bingo, and I'm pretty sure her name isn't Bonnie Parker."

Lorraine giggled. "Of course, it isn't. I asked her what her real name was, and she wouldn't tell me. She was really sharp. The first time, Debra and I met her at a little café in a neighborhood where no one knew us. She told us what to do, laid out the whole thing really good. I listened carefully, and Debra took really good notes."

Amanda put her head back in her hands.

Lorraine seemed oblivious to Amanda's body language and continued. "First, I started having lunches with Amanda more often. Sometimes I brought Debra so that we could, uh …"

"I know," David said enthusiastically. "So, you could case the building and figure out how to get in and out without being seen."

Lorraine nodded. "Yeah. Bonnie told us to do it, and Debra was really good at noticing stuff."

Without picking up her head, Amanda groaned. "That's just great, Mom."

"Look, Honey," Paul said. "You wanted to know. A little while later, your mother, Debra, and Bonnie had another secret meeting, and Bonnie told them the next steps. While Lorraine and Debra continued to case the law office and the building, Bonnie posed as a messenger to get Big Bobby's attention. She told Simpson she'd be out of town for a couple of modeling assignments, and when she got back, they could get together. Bonnie called and texted Simpson to string him along."

"Just before the murder, Bonnie stepped out to call Lorraine," David said. "How'd you get in and out of the building without anyone noticing?"

Lorraine smiled. "That was easy. Bonnie told me to swipe a key card from one of Amanda's co-workers so I could use it later. She drove into the parking garage, and I was hiding in the trunk."

"Wait a minute," David said. "How'd you know about the security guard and the camera at the parking garage entrance? You don't drive."

Amanda picked up her head and held up her right index finger. "I've got this one. Debra drives, and that's how they scoped out the parking garage beforehand. I probably don't want to hear the rest, but go ahead, Mom."

David remembered the camera at the parking garage entrance had not captured an image of a tall blonde woman driving into the garage before the murder. It instead had recorded a tall brunette with sunglasses and no passengers. Thus, he concluded Bonnie had been wearing a wig.

Lorraine exhaled. "Okay. After we parked, I climbed out of the trunk, and I was wearing the old lady outfit. Bonnie told me I had to disguise myself because people had seen me in the building. I got up to one of the higher floors, the sixth ... or maybe the fifth." She shrugged. "I don't know. Bonnie took off, and I hid in a bathroom until I got the call to go upstairs."

"You did what?" Amanda said with wide eyes.

"I hid in a bathroom. I brought a sandwich and a couple of magazines. It was fine."

"Not really," Amanda mumbled under her breath.

"There was one other important thing," Paul added. "After your mother got into the building, she followed a to-do list, and she later showed it to me. It was in Debra's handwriting."

"After Bonnie called you, you went upstairs and shot Simpson," David said. "Why'd you use the pillow?"

Lorraine's face went blank. "What pillow?"

"The dark blue pillow," David said. "It was in front of Simpson's face at the time you shot him."

"I don't know. Does it matter?"

"Maybe not," David retorted. "How'd you get out of the building?"

"With the key card, I used the service elevator and went out the back way."

"So that was you in the video!" Amanda said.

"Oh yeah." Lorraine laughed a little. "I guess so. I walked about a block or two and then Bonnie picked me up and took me home."

"My turn," Paule gently said. "Your mother didn't know how to dispose of her disguise. Maybe Bonnie didn't tell her. After Pete and Debra came over, I told Pete to get rid of the evidence, and I reminded him he still owed Lorraine a big favor."

Lorraine held up two fingers. "Actually, Pete owed me two favors. Don't forget I hired Debra."

Amanda asked, "You mean when you hired Debra after she and Pete separated for a while?"

Paul touched Amanda's arm. "That's not what happened. Pete went to prison for five years, and Debra needed to support herself. After Pete got out, Debra kept working at the travel agency."

"Why'd Pete go to prison?"

"Never mind," Paul said and leaned back. "It happened a long time ago, and it's not important right now."

David took a deep breath. "What happened to the outfit, thrown into the East River with everything else incriminating?"

Paul smiled. "Good guess, but no. Pete has a boat, and he dumped everything a mile or two offshore."

"Why didn't you get rid of the gun?" David asked.

Paul chuckled. "Because it was my gun. No big deal. The cops were too stupid to find it."

Amanda mumbled to herself. Then in a louder and clearer voice, she said, "This is so unbelievable! Mom, you shouldn't have done it! I could've gone to prison for the rest of my life!"

Paul scoffed. "Not a chance. We had it all figured out."

"How?" David asked.

"First, we wanted to see if the case would go to trial. David, you're a very good attorney, and we hoped you would've convinced the DA Amanda didn't do it. When that didn't pan out, we decided Lorraine would confess on the witness stand, or she'd have a *Perry Mason* moment. You know, stand up in court and say she did it. Simple, right?"

"Not really," Amanda said. "We went to trial, and you and Mom said nothing. What was your plan? Roll the dice, and pray I wouldn't get convicted … or better yet, did you bribe the jury?"

Weak smiles appeared on Paul and Lorraine's faces. Paul then uttered, "Now that –"

Amanda's eyes popped. "What the hell? You bribed the jury!"

He put up his right hand. "You didn't let me finish. We thought about bribing a couple of jurors, but it wasn't necessary."

"How come?" David asked.

"A good buddy has a cousin who works at the courthouse. Before the trial, I asked this cousin to help us out and get us access to the jury."

"I imagine he didn't do this out of the goodness of his heart," David said.

Paul let out a light chuckle. "Not really. He did it for twenty grand in cash."

"And how much were you going to pay the jurors?"

"We only needed two or three to make sure there wasn't a guilty verdict. You know, in case one of them got cold feet. We thought about paying them, oh, fifty grand a piece."

David tried not to physically react, but Paul's willingness to throw around so much money after paying his legal bills surprised him.

"Why didn't you bribe anyone?" he asked.

The big man let out an equally big smile. "We didn't have to. You know how judges tell juries not to talk about the case before they start deliberations?"

David nodded. "Yeah, and many jurors ignore the instruction."

"That's right. My buddy's cousin told me from the very beginning, three jurors couldn't keep their big traps shut. They didn't care if Amanda shot Big Bobby or not because they thought he had it coming." Paul chuckled. "Gotta love New Yorkers, right? Remember how you worried about Juror Number 7? He was one of the three. I was surprised the rest elected him the jury foreman. I guess they wanted to get out of there in a hurry."

Amanda turned sideways in her chair and looked away.

David instead pressed on. "Paul, how early did you know what was happening with the jury?"

"We knew about the three loudmouths after the first day of testimony, and before the verdict, we pretty much knew where each juror stood. Seven thought he had it coming, and the other five had no idea who killed Big Bobby. So, there you go. Not guilty, easy as pie."

Amanda mumbled and turned toward the table. "It wasn't so easy, and it was my life!" She waived her right arm. "And where was all this money coming from? There's a bundle in the attic. You were prepared to spend 150,000 on bribing jurors, and you paid the court officer 20,000. You also paid David's legal bills, which had to be …" Her eyes glanced toward the ceiling. "A lot. You covered my living expenses after I was fired, and there was also the money for bail. How much did you pay the bail bondsman? Ten percent, which would have been 100,000?"

"No, we got a big discount. We only paid forty grand."

"Oh, what a bargain," Amanda said sarcastically. "Mom, how much did Bonnie Parker cost?"

Lorraine shrugged. "I don't know. Fifty or sixty thousand, something like that. I got the money out of one of the safe deposit boxes."

"Wait a minute," David interjected. "When you reported your cash assets for bail, you listed about $163,000 in a joint bank account. Did you burn through it?"

Paul gave a sly grin. "No. It's still there."

David rubbed the right side of his forehead. "Okay. Lorraine mentioned safe deposit boxes, as in plural, not just one. How many do you have?"

Paul shrugged. "Six or seven, and some are larger than others."

"All of them filled with cash?" David asked.

"Of course."

"Mom, Dad, where was all this money coming from?"

Neither parent answered.

Amanda slapped the table. "Out with it! Don't stop now!"

Lorraine glanced at Paul and then returned her attention to Amanda. "Fine, fine. I had a little side business. The travel agency also laundered money for the mob."

Amanda's mouth dropped open again. "What the hell? Does Daniel know about the money?"

Lorraine smiled. "Oh no, and please don't tell your brother."

"Were you ever planning on telling Daniel and me about all of this?"

"No, not really."

Paul chuckled. "What should we have told you? After we died, you and Daniel would get a big surprise. You'd find all the money, wonder where it came from, and enjoy it."

"Lorraine, I'm not trying to be mean or anything," David said, "but it seems hard to believe you cooked the books at the travel agency all those years."

She giggled. "I didn't. Morty took care of it."

Amanda shook her head. "Sure, why not? Our family's accountant was involved."

Paul chuckled. "Of course, he was. How else do you think he could afford his second home in Palm Beach County? Next time we visit him in Florida, come with us and see it. It's got a great front yard, a nice indoor pool, and –"

"We got it," David said. "Getting back to the money. How much is in the safe deposit boxes?"

"The funny thing is we never counted it," the big man replied.

"Take a guess," Amanda said sternly.

Paul scratched his head and was lost in thought for a couple of moments. "I don't know, maybe 2.6 or 2.7 million."

Once again, Amanda's elbows hit the dining room table, and her head landed in her hands. David was so overwhelmed he could only stare at a wall and hoped Paul and Lorraine had no more startling revelations. Despite something inside telling him to leave the house, he instead moved his field of vision from the wall to Amanda's parents.

With arms spread out and a wide smile on his face, Paul said, "Hey David, welcome to the family!"

ACKNOWLEDGEMENTS

H AVE YOU EVER read the acknowledgements in a novel and wondered why the author had thanked so many people? The story originated from his or her mind, and there was no way so many other people made contributions. Sometimes I had these thoughts but not anymore, not after working on my first published work of fiction. Many people made contributions, and they should be recognized.

William Greenleaf is a recently retired author and editor. Before giving up his business, Bill reviewed two earlier versions of my manuscript and provided many helpful insights and advice. He was essentially my private tutor for an advanced writing class. So, if you like many aspects of this novel, you can give Bill at least partial credit, maybe a little more. For anything you don't like, you can solely blame me.

I'd also like to thank Stephen King. Yes, that Stephen King. I've never met him or have communicated with him in any manner, although either one would be a great experience. He wrote *On Writing: A Memoir of the Craft*. Many websites recommend this book for anyone who wants to break into his line of work, and I must concur. *On Writing* also discusses the early days of King's writing career and his horrific accident in 1999. If you want to gain a better understanding of one of the greatest authors of our time, both aspects of his life and his views on the writing process, you should read this book.

Jerry Rishe, Kay Bruce, and Ronald Phillips read earlier versions of the manuscript and gave their comments, criticisms, and suggestions. Even though Phillips is the Senior Vice Chancellor of Pepperdine University, I still refer to him as Dean Phillips, as he was the dean of the law school when I attended. In addition to providing a great legal education, Dean Phillips and the rest of the faculty cared about the students, which I still appreciate. Some names in the novel are direct or indirect references to Pepperdine.

I must also mention the following individuals. Dee Ann Deaton gave editorial tips, while Marsha Embree reviewed later versions of the manuscript to check for typos and other mistakes. Peter Lee gave frequent words of encouragement, and I'm glad he finally found a better job. Author Brad Chisholm gave advice on the writing process and valuable suggestions for creating dialogue.

My daughter, Caitlyn, was a sounding board for several ideas and plot points. In fact, we spent too much time discussing the wedding dress mentioned later in the novel. Caitlyn, her two brothers, Michael and Andrew, and my wife, Carolyn, also gave their input as to the character names and personas. I also thank my family for allowing me to spend many uninterrupted hours on what they probably perceived as a quixotic endeavor.

Finally, I must acknowledge Claire Kim, good friend, attorney, and author, who provided many words of encouragement and conveyed her experiences with the writing process. Claire also deserves the biggest thanks of all because she inspired me to create this novel.